Alan McMonagle

ITHACA

PICADOR

First published 2017 by Picador
an imprint of Pan Macmillan
20 New Wharf Road, London N1 9RR
Associated companies throughout the world
www.panmacmillan.com

ISBN 978-1-5098-2985-9

Typeset by Ellipsis Digital Limited, Glasgow
Printed and bound by CPI Group (UK) Ltd, Croydon, CR0 4YY

Visit www.picador.com to read more about all our books
and to buy them. You will also find features, author interviews and
news of any author events, and you can sign up for e-newsletters
so that you're always first to hear about our new releases.

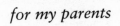

for my parents

And they all pretend they're orphans
And their memory's like a train
You can see it getting smaller as it pulls away
And the things you can't remember
Tell the things you can't forget that
History puts a saint in every dream
Well she said she'd stick around
Until the bandages came off
But these mamas' boys just don't know when to quit
And Matilda asks the sailors are those dreams
Or are those prayers
So just close your eyes, son
And this won't hurt a bit . . .

TOM WAITS, *Time*

JOYRIDERS

I am the cancer-ridden only son of a dangerous driver who has thoughts about turning herself into a man. The cancer is in my testicle. The left one. Every day it's getting worse. Black, tarry urine is coming out of me. My goolie is the size of a tennis ball. I won't even begin to describe the smell. A couple of weeks ago – just before school finished up for the summer – I was merely hobbling my whiffy way to an early grave. Now I am a swollen, leaky infestation liable to cark it at any moment. This was the story she had for them after Mattie Conlon put cop Lawless onto us.

Ma had borrowed Mattie's car without asking him. I think it was the fourth time in less than three weeks she'd borrowed it. Maybe the fifth. Let's go, she yelled out through the rolled-down passenger window when she spotted me on Station Hill, and without fully stopping she reached over and opened the passenger door.

Where are we off to this time? I asked her, as soon as I had jumped in and buckled up.

Don't ask unnecessary questions, she said, and sped away again.

She took the fast road out of town and joined the by-pass and we were soon at top-speed, giving chase to the hi-velocity jeeps and super-cars zipping their effortless way.

Are we off to the big city? I asked, straining for a glance at the large road signs flashing by, but received no answer. She didn't say a word as she drove, just kept her hands on the steering wheel, her eyes peeled on the way ahead, as though at any moment along the open road was suddenly going to materialize whatever it was she was searching for on these helter-skelter spins.

Mattie's car suited her driving style. And so did the two-lane road. She weaved her way in between slower-moving cars, took the shortest route around bends, a determined-to-leave-everything-behind look never leaving her face. She sped by suited men driving smooth cars. Some of them were talking into phones and during her overtaking manoeuvre Ma slowed a little and made a telephone out of her hand, caught the driver's attention by waving it as though she was having a fit while mouthing an enthusiastic *Call Me*. She sped by happy families tucked safely away inside cars large as buses, opened wide her mouth and inserted her make-me-puke finger. She sped by large lorries and waved out at the burly men driving them. One or two beeped back at her as though they were the best of friends. She sped by boy-racers, pouted her lips at them and blew kisses off the palm of her hand.

For a while we drove pretty much alongside the railway tracks. She slowed down some more and I thought she was waiting for the train to appear so that she could have something new to race against. Then she speeded up again and I thought we had missed the train and that she had decided to try and catch it. Soon the road swerved away from the tracks and I wondered what her next target might be. At some point she reached over and turned on the radio, fiddled with the knob. Through the static came a song I'd never heard and I clamped my hands over my ears when she started to sing along. After a few minutes she turned the thing off and she had both hands on the steering wheel again, was peering intently.

Like the times before, we drove until the petrol light came on. This time she swung off the main road and found another road and from there she turned onto another road, one that narrowed and narrowed, and the further we drove the narrower it became and either side of us tree branches reached out and bushes rubbed and scratched against Mattie's car. Soon one long tuft of grass appeared in the middle of the road and more and more tree branches reached and out-of-control bushes crowded the way until it seemed that nature had decided that this road was an unnecessary road and that it and any vehicles on it, and any passengers in those vehicles, ought to be squeezed out of existence.

You're going to get us lost, I said, when it seemed we could go no further.

Would I let something like that happen?

I'd say so, I replied.

Do you want to drive? she said to that, and there wasn't much talking for the remainder of this particular trip.

Somehow we found the way out of there, but not before all the petrol ran out. We had to temporarily abandon the car and walk two or three miles until we came upon a little shop in front of which stood the loneliest-looking petrol pump I had ever seen. Remember, you're as good as dead, Ma told me as she disappeared inside the shop. A few minutes later she was back to me with an eyebrow, a nod, and a plastic container that she filled from the pump.

It was near dark by the time we got back. For some reason the town lights had not come on – maybe there was a power cut or the ESB men were not happy and had decided to pull the plug – either way it didn't matter because a big moon was hovering, like a saviour lighting up the place, and I couldn't stop looking at it. Ma drove to our part of town and when we pulled up outside our house Lawless was parked along our road, patiently waiting. Straightaway he recognized Mattie's car and he stepped out of his squad car and made his way purposefully towards us.

Uh-oh, I said, we're in for it this time.

The words were hardly out of my mouth and Lawless was knuckling the driver-side window. Hey, kid, she said, looking my way. I've got the moon in my pocket. Don't ever forget that. Then she winked at me, rolled down her window, and switching on her famous smile, turned to face the newest trouble in her life.

FLUKEY

This was the summer after all the money disappeared. One minute it was here. The next it had vanished. All of it. Without trace. Annie the scryer had predicted it happening ages ago but nobody had listened to her. Now they were all interested in what she had to say. Couldn't wait to hear about the next disaster in store for us. A hurricane. Flood waters. Famine. It didn't matter. Now that all the money had vanished, everyone had their eyes and ears ready for all manner of doom.

Don't ask me why. Take a walk through the streets of our town and you would have seen all the disaster you wanted. Boarded-up windows, women crying into empty handbags, the Slug Doyle's protesting fist. There was a huge crack in the road going across Violin Bridge. Any minute now the unfinished shopping centre looked as though it was going to topple over. March into the bank and say, *stick 'em up, this is a robbery*, and you wouldn't be long finding out where things stood. *Go ahead, help yourself*, they'd tell you, handing over the keys to the vaults. *You won't find a bean in here*. I didn't care about any of that. After the latest high drama with Ma, I reckoned it was about time I took a good look for my da.

I had a feeling it might be Flukey Nolan. We both had

thin arms, shoulders not worth talking about, moles. Rosy cheeks and itty-bitty curls. Like me, Flukey had a habit of wandering about the place on his own. He was fond of the Swamp. And though I hadn't seen him in a while, he used to be around the house all the time. He and Ma were not shy together. The more I thought about it the more certain I became. If I had money and Patsy Fagan was taking bets on who is my da, I would have walked into his betting shop and put it all on Flukey Nolan. I couldn't wait to bump into him in the back lane and inform him of my discovery, let him know that from here on we would be living under the same roof, doing stuff together, thinking up schemes.

My first mistake was telling Ma. She had a good laugh for herself when I put it to her. If the sucked-in cheeks and rippling forehead lines were anything to go by, it was clear I couldn't have come out with a more ridiculous proposition.

Tell me something, Jason, what age are you now? she asked me when she took some time out from her laughing.

Nearly twelve, I said.

Nearly twelve. That's great, she said, now shaking her head as though she didn't believe me. Twelve years old and he wants to know who his da is.

I know who it is, I said. It's Flukey Nolan.

That set her off laughing again. Practically bent over in two she was. And the choking sounds out of her. Thought I might have to slap her hard on the back when she lost her breath.

Flukey is many things, she managed to say when at last she calmed down. But one thing he's not, is your da.

Are you sure about that? I said, giving her my narrow eyes, by now thinking that all the laughing and face-making had to be a decoy, that if I kept at her she might let slip something, provide a clue she couldn't take back. She didn't though. She hadn't another word to say on the matter. And when I did keep at her, the laughter wasn't long running out and she threw her arms into the air, warned me a fair amount of distance out of her way.

Our town was slap-bang in the middle of the country, miles from anywhere, and built inside a hole made out of bog, weeds, mulch, and the soggiest soil you might ever see. If that wasn't bad enough, we were surrounded by a dirty black drain that spent its time fooling everyone into thinking it was a river. There were two sides to our town. The rich side on the hill beyond the railway tracks and the side we lived on. The ghetto, Ma called it.

I went walking down the back lane. Of all the places in the ghetto, the back lane was the place to hang out. Anybody who was anybody on our road wanted to be seen out here, taking a stroll through the muck, hanging out by the ditch trees, making conversation about the Swamp in the wasteland beyond. It was a good place to find Flukey wandering.

Along came Harry Brewster and Fergal Flood. Harry's ears didn't work very well, and Fergal had only one good eye. So they went around together. Harry described what he saw. *Ah would you look, Fergal, Bliss Flynn has gone and cut her hair.* Fergal listened to all the gossip. *Get a load of this, Harry, the Slug Doyle says if they come knocking on his door one more time he's going for his axe.* It wasn't a bad system. On a good day, the pair of them were convinced they could run the entire country. But that usually kept until they were down town, perched on their stools, deep into their fifth or sixth stout inside McMorrow's dimly lit pub.

Along came Patrick Fox, squeezing out through his broken-down back gate, along with Rommel and Himmler, his mongrel dogs.

Hello Jason Lowry, he said, as we passed each other. Have you yet met anybody better than yourself?

I have in my arse, I told him, without breaking stride.

Do you hear that Rommel and Himmler? Patrick said after me, shaking his head at his mongrels as though it was the saddest thing he had ever heard. Young Jason has yet to meet someone better than himself.

Along came Lily Brennan, arrived all the way from Threepenny Terrace. Lily fancied herself as the star nose around here. Reckoned she knew what was going on before the sun came up and shined a light. Old Tom Redihan has started talking to the trees. That Joyce girl's mother ran away with her father's best friend. Fat Grehan is after getting married to the nanny. There was no doubt in her voice, she had the fast track on everyone. Along she came, the barrel shape on her waddling down the lane, at long last nearing the end of her daily nose about, a task that involved getting up at the crack of dawn and asking lots of questions she already knew the answers to. Look at you, she said to me every time we bumped into each other. You look just like your mother. That old wheezebag, I'd hear the Slug Doyle say, reckons she can hear the things people are thinking about. Today I was tempted to ask her what was Da thinking about. Then I thought: don't get into any of that with an old wheezebag.

Just when I thought I could continue my search in peace and quiet, along came Brains and No-brains McManus. They were four or five years older than me. Maybe more. Martin McManus was Brains. He could speak properly and often did before using his black, kick-hard boots. Mark McManus was No-brains. He wore an army jacket and matching brim hat that had a selection of tiny pistols and knives and swords dangling from it, the kinds of things you might get inside good Christmas crackers. A white band circled his hat with thick, blue marker-writing that said *I am a killer.* For as long as I'd known him he'd been wearing the hat. So far as I knew he hadn't killed anyone.

Look who it is, said No-brains after they had blocked my path and spent a ridiculous amount of time giving me their will-we-or-won't-we-mash-his-head-in look.

It's the boy from the hood, said Brains, flicking my pulled-up hoodie.

The most dangerous pipsqueak alive, said No-brains.

How is your ma? said Brains, the other one already starting to get excited.

The aliens have abducted her, I told him.

We'd like to see your ma, said No-brains, a stupid smirk lighting up his face.

Join the queue, I said to that.

9

I don't see a queue, said No-brains, and his brother gave him a look before passing it on to me.

Like I said. She's gone to the moon for the weekend.

It's not the weekend, you pillock, said No-brains. It's Tuesday morning.

Well, I'll be sure to tell her that when she gets back.

No-brains leaned in to me, pushed me over. For a second it was odds-on he was going to crack me one, open my nose most likely, at the very least I'd have a purple eye. Meantime, his brother had grabbed my legs and was yanking my tackies away from my feet. As soon as he had, he tossed them into the ditchwater.

You give your ma a message from me, said Brains, now jabbing my chest with his dirty finger. Tell her, I've got what she wants.

Tell her we've got plenty of what she wants, No-brains threw in for good measure, tapping the buckle of his belt, and Brains looked to his brother as if to say, *I should have strangled you when you were little.*

Their good work done, Brains gestured to his brother and the pair of them walked off. No-brains turned round to me and drew a slow finger across his neck. In case I thought I was getting off the hook, I supposed. He stumbled over a rock as he was doing it and his brim hat fell off. Brains kicked his backside when he bent down to pick it up. I picked myself up, wiped the dirt off and looked into the ditchwater. My tackies were already sinking more or less out of sight. I didn't care. Wiped more dirt off myself and kept going.

THE GIRL AT THE SWAMP

Through the ditch trees I could make out the Swamp. Drifts of steam floated above the surface scum. Nettles bunched around the cracked edges. Giant dock-leaves spread out and fluttered. There were midges and clammy webs. Flies dizzy with excitement. Long, reedy grasses pointed to the never-ending sky. Ladybirds crawled all over the place.

The girl was there. Sitting on my rock near the hidden pools. A wisp of a thing in dungarees, elbows on her knees, chin in her hands, looking out across the scumwater, towards the ridge banking up onto the railway tracks. Hey! I called in to her. That's my rock you're on. She didn't even look at me.

The council men were at the far side of the Swamp. Leaning against the wonky KEEP OUT sign. In their hard hats and high-vis jackets. Looking important. They'd been obsessed with the Swamp since the start of summer. Some-one noticed how it was rising even though it had hardly rained, and they wanted to find out why. One or two were wading around the edges of the Swamp, testing to see how deep it was. They waded around in wellingtons and dipped their rods and made notes in their little pads. They didn't like anyone being in here on account of the hidden pools and rising water. Your KEEP OUT sign is drowning, I was about to shout over at them, but they were already fed up slopping about in scummy water. This is thirsty work, I heard one of them say, and the rest of them weren't long agreeing. They packed up and left.

When I looked again the girl was in the water. It didn't look like she could swim, didn't look like she was trying too hard to stop herself from sinking. Hey! I yelled, breaking into a mad dash, and then tripping over some bindweed as I lurched for and then lunged over the edge of the Swamp. Stretching over the water's edge, I reached out both my arms and the daft loon tried to bat them out of her way. She had all but disappeared when I dipped my arms into the dirty water and managed to get a grip on her shoulders. I yanked her up, and dragged her kicking and spluttering onto the reedy grass. She was sopping wet, breathless, and red in the face. I could see her chest rising up and down, the dirty water dripping off her.

I looked around to see if anyone was knocking about. It was just the two of us. She was sitting up now, facing the Swamp, and had wrapped her arms around her bunched knees. I took off my hoodie and threw it round her.

At once she whipped it off. I picked it up and tried again, but she raised her arms along with a glare that warned me off. For a minute or two she sat staring into the water without saying a word. Then she looked me up and down and started laughing.

You're the second person who's laughed at me today.

Only the second?

Hey! I saved you from drowning.

What do you want from me? A medal? Eternal gratitude?

A simple thanks might be enough.

Oh, thank you, thank you, thank you. Now go away and leave me alone.

I'm not going anywhere.

Then do sit down, will you? You're blocking my view.

By now she had slid onto my rock. She was still staring out across the Swamp and not looking too bothered about being soaking wet.

Just so we're clear, I told the girl, standing fully in front of her. That's my rock you're on.

What are you going to do? Beat me up?

It won't come to that. Now scram.

Scram! Oh, you're funny.

Keep it up. You won't be laughing when your mouth is full of swamp again.

Ha! One minute you're pulling me out. The next you're kicking me back in. Now stop acting like a child. There's room for the two of us.

She slid over a little bit. She was about my age and I didn't want her thinking she was getting the upper hand on me. I could've pushed her off the rock, back into the Swamp. I could've walked away like a sap.

You can sit there for another twenty minutes. Then I'll be expecting an empty rock.

You're a tough fellow too, aren't you?

That's right, pigtails. I'm husky and tough and there will be blood if you don't get off my rock.

Oh, good! I like blood.

How long are you going to sit there for?

I don't know. Until doomsday. Maybe I'll wait for the train.

She looked out across the Swamp, towards the railway tracks. She had a blotchy bruise on the side of her neck. Freckles either side of her nose. The sun was out today and long, shadowy tree branches stretched out in front of us, mingling with the scum and mist over the Swamp.

Did you jump into the Swamp on purpose?

I think I'll let you figure that one out, genius boy.

What happened your neck?

Questions, questions. Everybody is always asking questions. Do they never tire, I ask myself? Now please. Do sit down. You're making me nervous.

For some reason I did as I was told. She was right, as it turned out. There was room on the rock for both of us. She seemed happy enough with the arrangement and I decided I'd let her stay for a little while, not kick her out of there. She kept gazing at the tracks, as though the arrival of this train she was expecting was going to be a momentous occasion. It made me think of the way Ma liked to perch for hours on end on the step outside our front door, smoking her roll-ups and sipping from her glass. What she was expecting was anybody's guess.

The train is late, I said.

Doesn't matter. Where I'm going I may not need the train.

Where's that, then?

I was thinking Egypt in the time of the pharaohs.

Never been there.

Oh, you should go. They know so much, the Egyptians. Invented paper, you know. And writing.

The Egyptians?

Last week I was at the Colosseum in Rome. You would not believe the crowds. Lots of blood too, once the gladiators arrived, you'd have liked it. Before that I trekked across the Russian Steppes. Don't go there. It's freezing. That's why I'm off to Egypt. I could do with some sun and sand. Where are you off to?

Nowhere.

That's no good. You'll need to find yourself somewhere to go. A destination.

You should talk to my ma. She's always looking to go someplace. Except she prefers to take Mattie Conlon's car rather than the train. I'm not going anywhere until I find Flukey Nolan.

Flukey Nolan?

That's right. He's my da.

Never heard of him.

I might ask the scryer.

The scryer?

Yep. She knows things. She's a good person to ask.

Never heard of her either. Do you think I am growing knockers?

Huh?

I'm going to be a celebrity when I'm big. I need to grow

knockers as soon as possible. And not just your average size. You know, they need to stand out in a crowd. So?

So, what?

Do you think they're growing?

No.

Have you got any cigarettes?

No.

Booze?

No.

What have you got? Not much if your feet are anything to go by.

I shrugged my shoulders. Took a look towards the back lane trees. Saw Old Tom Redihan standing beside them, nodding away. The girl was talking again.

My father has been crying for a year. He does it resting his elbows on the kitchen table and holding his face in clenched fists. After a while he slams his fists onto the table and yells at the top of his voice.

Does your ma not say anything? You know, when he is slamming and shouting?

Mother's gone.

To the Russian Steppes?

Ha! You *are* funny. If only you didn't ask so many useless questions.

If you're going to be a celebrity when you're big, what are you doing jumping into the Swamp?

This time it was her turn to shrug. Shrug and stare off into the distance as though I was no longer present. I tried thinking of something else to say, something that wasn't a question.

I'm going down town to look for my da. Do you want to come?

Not really.

I might go up the hill later. You can see for miles. Do you want to come up there?

No thanks.

It's really good when it gets dark and the lights come on.

I'll stay here.

But . . .

But what?

If I leave, you might . . . you know . . . take another running jump.

Well, if I do, I'll be sure to holler for my new hero.

If I leave, promise me you won't jump in.

Maybe.

Promise.

OK, OK. I promise. I promise with all my beating blood not to jump. There. Satisfied?

I decided not to say anything else. Just wait for the girl to start talking about the sand in Egypt or the Steppes in Russia or some other faraway place I'd never heard of. But she didn't say another word. And when I looked at her again I could tell she was far, far away. Gazing off into the distances of the voyage she was on. Chin in hands. Elbows on knees. I slid off the rock, looked at her one more time and picked my way out of there. I'd nearly made it back to the ditch trees when I heard her calling out.

Hey, you! Boy!

Listen to her! Boy, she was calling me. Who did she think she was calling me boy? All three feet nothing of her. With her uppity voice. Like a numpty, I turned round.

Are you sure I'm not growing knockers?

I shook my head vaguely, scratched my way quickly through the trees, crossed the ditch and already I was thinking: I need to put a lot of distance between myself and this loon. Like about three weeks' worth of Ma's driving.

MCMORROW'S DIMLY LIT PUB

Once upon a time, long before I knew I would be out and about on a useless search for him, I had a drink with Flukey in McMorrow's dimly lit pub. Step this way, Flukey had said to me after spotting me on the down-town street. He'd even held the door open for me.

It was my first time in the pub, a dark dungeon of a room with a beery smell and no windows. Flukey quickly made himself comfortable at one end of the counter, stared into the glass put in front of him. The black abyss, he called it. Harry Brewster and Fergal Flood were at the other end, busy running the country. Shirley Halligan was behind the counter pulling drink. Meantime, Barry the bank clerk was sitting at the low table by the wall, in his stripey suit and pink shirt and long shoes, the kind that went on long after feet end, and the wondering head on him because his mobile phone wasn't working.

I sat into a stool beside Flukey, tried to catch his misty eyes, and when I did he put a bottle of Fanta in front of me. We sat side by side for the next few minutes without saying a word to each other. Beside us, the steady mumble out of Harry and Fergal. Behind the bar, Shirley looking silently up at the portable television. And all the time from the low table by the wall, a procession of tutting and swearing coming out of Barry the bank clerk.

You know why I love this place? Flukey eventually said to me, leaning over in a low-down voice. There is no coverage for mobile phones. Then he started chuckling away to himself and it did not look like he was going to stop. I have a theory, he said to me when he finally calmed down again. Do you want to hear what it is? I'm going to tell it to you whether you do or don't. Of course I wanted to hear it, couldn't wait to hear Flukey's theory, but Flukey didn't seem to be in any rush, had lifted up his black glass, was taking what must have been the slowest drink in the history of drinking. There is no escape, he said when he had at long last finished swallowing and set down his glass again, and left it at that. Then he climbed down off his stool and shuffled over to try and convince Barry the bank clerk he had an idea that would make the pair of them the richest men in the world.

There was no sign of Barry the bank clerk today. He'd long given up on McMorrow's after his unhappy mobile phone experience, not that he had much need for the thing these days. There was no sign of Flukey either, but as far as pub-time went it was still early, and I sat into the same stool I'd sat in that time before.

Harry and Fergal were propping up the centre of the counter. Another lad, so old he must have owed the graveyard a few hundred years, was sitting at the far end, sipping from a glass with one ice cube in it. Times must have been tough for him. Another lad was wandering around the pub in short, staggered shuffles. His drink-arm shaking so much that beer was spilling out of his glass. His jittery eyes searching the dark, empty spaces of the barroom as though there was someone lurking. A woman sat by herself at one of the low tables by the wall. An unlit cigarette was dangling from her red lips as though she was at any minute expecting a prince charming to come along and light it for her. Then again, it was possible she wasn't even aware that a cigarette was resting between her lips. Her skin was so white, paler than white, flesh the sun never shone on. The lad with the shaking drink-arm approached her. I thought he was going to say something to her, maybe point out the unlit cigarette, offer her a light, and then whisk her away from her troubles in the chariot he had waiting outside. Pumpkin bus, more like. But he didn't say or do any of that. He just stood there, half-leaning into her, half-leaning away, the drink-arm on him shaking like it had workings of its own, the beer in the glass he was holding swishing to and fro like the early signs of a storm at sea.

A card game was going on at the other table. I didn't recognize any of the players, hadn't seen their faces before, and if the way they were concentrating on the cards was anything to go by, now was not a good time to start finding out.

I made myself comfortable in the high stool. Took out from my pocket an imaginary euro coin, set it spinning on the counter. Nobody paid any attention. I slapped the coin down in front of me. Shirley looked over.

I suppose you want a double whiskey.

No thanks, Shirley. Gave up the whiskey years ago. I'll have a bottle of Fanta, please. And a packet of peanuts. Have one yourself while you're at it. It's on me.

Shirley gave me the long and stern look she saved for her favourite customers. She reached for a bottle of Fanta, cracked it open, tossed a coaster in front of me, set down a glass and began to pour.

Keep the change, I told her, pushing the invisible coin in front of me. She gave me the long look again. Pushed the coin back towards me.

Fanta is on the house this afternoon, she said, and threw down a packet of nuts.

Harry and Fergal were talking low. I had my ears with me, though, could hear them running the country, the shite-and-all mess left for them to tidy up. Today, Fat Grehan was to blame. Last week, it had been Martin Power and his sidekick, Leech McGrath. Before that, if I remember correctly, it had been a pair of emptyheads called Peadar Skelly and Frank Diamond. And before that again, it was a snake in the grass called Prunty and an auctioneer with a crooked smile went by the name of Freeman. Today, everything was down to Fat Grehan. Wrecked the place Fat Grehan had. The damage done was irreversible. Irreversible. That's the word Harry and Fergal were using. So good a job had Fat Grehan made of things, they were talking about it all over Europe. England and France were talking about it. And the Germans were raging. And if there was one set of people you didn't want to be raging, it was the Germans. Bad and all as those dirty, rotten English bastards had been for eight hundred million years or however long it was, it was going to seem like a wine and cheese-cracker picnic along the banks of sludge river by the time the Germans were through with us.

Mention of wine and cheese-cracker picnics quickly brought on talk of times past. Do you remember? Harry began, and that's all it took. Do you remember? Around here the three holiest words a man could speak. As though he could not bear to be in the time he was now living through. As though the future was a place too awful to contemplate. Do you remember when you had a harking for something all you had to do was ask? If it was a new car you were after, you picked up the phone, called the bank and waiting for you at the end of the line was chirpy Barry asking for your details so that he could swiftly send on the price of the new car. If you wanted to stop working and take a year-long cruise around the world. If you wanted to hire a supersonic limousine for your little girl's first communion day. If you wanted to build a second house in your back garden. Own a place in sunny Spain. Buy fields in Bulgaria. It didn't matter what you wanted the dosh for. All you had to do was pick up the phone and talk to chirpy Barry. At the end of the day you didn't even have to have a reason. If you just fancied having ten or twenty thousand weighing down your pocket, word was you could just walk into the bank and ask for it.

And it wasn't just people living in the country to begin with who'd known all this. They'd heard about it as far away as Russia and Bangladesh and parts of Africa. One lad came all the way from Peru to get a taste of what the country had to offer. But he went home again after drinking six pints of Guinness and receiving an incurable headache. Everybody else, though. They were all showing up at the bank, crowding into chirpy Barry's office and then dashing around the place like let-loose maniacs to spend what they had asked for.

Not any more.

Thanks to Fat Grehan, the town, the country, the entire world was going under, fast. Every man, woman, boy and child will soon be on the happy pills, Harry said, staring into the glass in front of him. One half of the country on uppers, he said, letting out a heavy sigh. And the other half on downers, Fergal said, letting out a not-so-heavy sigh.

Ha! I bet that lad from Peru was delighted he didn't stick around. Was going to say it to Harry and Fergal, but they had gripped their glasses in preparation for their daily toast and I didn't like to interrupt their holy moment. Here's to another sinking ship, they said, raising their near-empty glasses. To the sinking ship, they repeated as they clinked.

It was nearly fun listening to them. Their doom talk. Their end-is-near wisdom. I was all set to tell them about the girl I saved from drowning and then ask them if they had seen Flukey, when the door swung open and Ma walked in, plonked herself on a barstool and without looking up raised a finger for a drink.

What are you doing in here? she said when at last she spotted me.

This time I knew better than mentioning Flukey. Didn't want her laughing at me again, not in here in front of everyone.

Shirley put a glass of vodka in front of her. Straightaway she took it and drank it down, ordered another. Looked my way again.

What's the matter, pipsqueak? Cat got your tongue?

She raised her glass and took a look around the bar, as though she might find answers to her questions. Then, glass in hand, she slid down off her stool and moved towards me.

Look at him, she said, standing behind me now, her spare hand poking me in the back. With his glass of Fanta. Is he looking for someone, I wonder?

Without waiting for me or anyone else to say anything, she moved right up behind the stool I was on, wrapped both arms tightly around me and started swaying. Could feel her boozy breath on my neck, the stink of cheap perfume she liked to put on any time she was going out.

Leave off, Ma, I said, after trying uselessly to shrug her away.

My, my. Touchy, isn't he? she said, releasing her grip and standing back from me. Again, she looked around the barroom, gestured to the place with a sweep of her drinking arm.

Set up a round of drinks, Shirley. And don't forget the pipsqueak's Fanta.

But I didn't want any more orange. I pushed the unfinished glass away from me, jumped down from the stool and legged it out of there.

RICH HILL

When I couldn't find Flukey and wanted to steer well clear of Ma and give the rest of the place a miss, be by myself, I made my way up the hill. Past Mel Campbell's shop at the high end of our road. Over the railway bridge. Already the road was steep, getting steeper all the time. Soon the high walls appeared and the fancy gates. The leafy trees and reliable cars. The air tasted different up here. It tasted of safety and comfort. Of cut lawns and wind chimes and proper perfume and soap and barbecued ribs. Of clean clothes and new flowers and fresh fruit. It tasted of good luck.

I made my way to the house with the unfinished wall. It's where Fat Grehan lived, he'd moved up the hill a few years ago when he became an overnight millionaire. He hadn't been around since the start of summer. Word was he did a bunk to London. Packed up in the middle of the night and, just like that, high-tailed it out of town. I didn't care where he was. What I liked was that Fat Grehan's place didn't have a gate that came with a top-secret code. It didn't have a high wall either. Not yet. It was about halfway done and he'd all the rocks in the world piled up in his driveway, as though he fully intended to get someone to finish it for him. It was some collection of rocks, sand-like and glittery, each piece cut in a slightly different shape and size to the next piece, not the sort of stuff they used for the grey walls that separated the places on our road and on more or less every other road I knew about.

The house was an impossible maze of a place. All split levels and jutting-out ends. Big-view windows, floor-to-ceiling efforts just begging for thrown stones. A couple of sheds out back. And more of the place just as you thought it was going to end, the builders must have been very confused when they were putting it together. It must've taken an entire week to walk through, Grehan must've found himself lost in there all the time. Maybe that was the idea.

Getting in was easy. There was a loose window round the back. This is it, I thought. By the time I've gone through the place I'm going to be a millionaire, ready to take my place on the rich list given out free with the Sunday papers. I'm going to buy Ma a new car, a home with a tree in the garden, maybe we can go on a sunny holiday for the next five or ten years.

Except for a snow globe containing a miniature ship and a drawer full of steak knives, I couldn't find a thing. Hours I spent going through the place. No wallets or purses left lying around. No easy cash piled high in tidy bundles with a note that said *it's all yours, Jason, take it away with you*. I saw no sign of a secret chamber or hidden jewellery box. Not one priceless painting hanging on any of the four or five hundred walls I must have passed. I checked the mattresses in the bedrooms – Flukey had once told me mattresses were a great place for stuffing cash. I ripped them open with one of the steak knives. Reached in and pulled out feathers, foam and whatever useless tat had been used to stuff the things. Not a bean, not a penny, not the glint of a red cent. I tried tearing up a couple more, then gave up. There wasn't even anything in the kitchen to eat. Just that drawer full of useless knives. The entire search was a huge let down.

And they called Fat Grehan the rich man in our town. Where did that leave the rest of us?

I went back outside, stood in front of one of the big-view windows. Could more or less make out my reflection, the flimsy shoulders on me, the next-to-nothing size of me. Then I spotted some tins of paint. Every one of them marked Marrakech. With another one of the steak knives I prised open the lid of the first tin, poked my finger into the reddish goop. Then I noticed the brush. And I thought, why not do some painting? Leave a message for Fat Grehan and everyone else up here to wonder at. Tell them they can't be setting themselves up in swish palaces without having the decency to leave some valuables lying around for budding burglars. Grabbed the brush and opened the tin and walked back out to the road. Dipped the brush and took it, dripping, to the half-built wall. What to say? What to say? Something that will hold their attention. Something they will remember me by. I stood there for a minute, dripping brush in hand, pondering. Was about to give up. Then I remembered Flukey's theory from that time in the pub. *There is no escape.* That got me thinking about some of those things Ma had said when we were off spinning around in Mattie's car. *Don't ask unnecessary questions. Remember, kid, you're as good as dead.* Then I thought of what she'd said when cop Lawless had come knocking on the window of Mattie's car.

I'VE GOT THE MOON IN MY POCKET

I stepped back as soon as the last letter went up. Took a minute to appreciate my work. The deep red went well with the sand-coloured wall. The message was clear and large enough for all to see. Looked around to see if anyone was out and wanted to join me in my admiration. But there wasn't. The road was quiet. The high gates were closed. I had the hill all to myself.

I walked back up the driveway to see if there were any other colours. There weren't, but not to worry. Prised open another tin, and brush in hand, looked around to see where else I could decorate. All I could see were those big-view windows. Stepped over to one of them. Whipped the hoodie off me. *My, my,* I said to my reflection. *Look who it is. The boy with the puny arms and pipsqueak head. You look just like your Ma. Has anyone ever said that to you?*

Flicked the dripping brush at my reflection. Saw specks of red appear on my curly hair and sorry face. *Hey! What are you doing up here?* I asked the paint-spattered reflection. Let the brush drop out of my hand and picked up the full tin of paint. *Well? What's the matter, pipsqueak? Cat got your tongue?* And I flung the contents at the glass.

SPLAT! As quickly again I grabbed another tin, and was all set to let rip at the next window when the glinting rocks caught my eye. I ditched the paint, picked up the sturdiest rock I could handle, stood staring at another version of myself. *And tell me something, Jason, what age are you now? Nearly twelve, is it? Nearly twelve and you want to know who your da is. Ha! Ha! Ha! Don't make me laugh.* OK, Ma. Whatever you say, Ma, I hollered, letting rip and watching the rock all the way. CRASH! it went, and I saw myself shatter into a million pieces. Stepped up to the next window, couldn't wait to see what damage I could do to the next me. But by now all I could see was the crazy look on Ma when I'd mentioned Flukey, could feel her laughter spinning around and around inside my head, as though it had no place else to be. *Ha! Ha! Ha! Ha! Ha!* And what was so funny about having Flukey for a da? So what if he'd been a layabout and general good-for-nothing for the last couple of years. It was better than nothing, better than having to be around a raving nutjob from one end of the day to the next. Telling yarns about my goolies. Calling me pipsqueak in front of everyone. Anyway. It was her who had gotten together with Flukey on and off for the last God-knows-how-long. If she was laughing at me, she was laughing at herself.

Could feel the blood surging through me, helter-skelter and faster than Ma had ever driven that car she liked so much. Pulled up the sleeve of my hoodie, gripped the steak knife, and without taking my eyes off the reflection in front of me, drew the knife across my arm. The skin tore easily, blood oozed, then spurted brighter than the paint, ran in dripping lines, drops landed on the ground. What age are you now, she wanted to know. Black, tarry urine is coming out of me, she reckoned. Rotting goolies and lopsided with it. THIS IS WHAT'S COMING OUT OF ME, YOU CRAZYWOMAN! I roared, and cut again, and again, wider and deeper, and man, it felt good.

*

I could see the entire town, the cathedral, the school I went to, the drain of a river, the cracked bridge. I could see the Tower jutting out of the unfinished shopping centre, looking over the town like some sort of sentry keeping an eye out for trouble makers. I could see the two cemeteries, one on either side of the town, why we needed two of the things was anybody's guess. I could see the half-built houses on the edge of town, the mill that made pig feed and bull nuts, the railway station and the tracks stretching out of sight. I could see the by-pass, cars on it, on their way to God-knows-where. I wondered where Ma and me had turned off and where exactly was it we had ended up. You could see for miles. No matter which direction you chose. I squinted my eyes, picked a far-off place and plotted my course.

Now it was almost dark, the town lights were coming on, and I remembered what it was I liked most about up here. I gazed down at the glittering spectacle, all of it frazzled and distorted, a mirage of some unrecognisable place, and it was easy to forget it was the boghole place I lived in.

At some point the moon came up full and high, and I almost wished the ESB would switch off the lights like they had that other time so that the moon could show the twinkling stars and the dark streets what it could do. *I've got the moon in my pocket, kid.* That I'd like to see.

I held up the snow globe, shook it and watched the snow flitter about the tiny ship. That was the place for her, alright. Inside a glass ball.

This isn't so bad, I told myself. Should do this more often. Spend time up on Rich Hill with the high moon and silent stars. The air was calm and warm and, hey, I had a great idea, I should stay up here all night.

As best I could I stretched out on the rocks, held up the snow globe and stared at the tiny ship. Where are you off to, then? I asked the ship. Well, wherever it is, just remember: there is no escape. Felt myself relaxing a little more, let the snow globe drop out of my hand and next thing me and Flukey were hanging out together. I wasn't sure exactly but it was a forest somewhere, full of autumn trees, and we were throwing sticks and trying to knock chestnuts out of the trees, and of course nothing was happening with my feeble throws and Flukey had me point out the chestnut I was after, and I did, and his very next throw took the chestnut clean out of the tree, and it landed right at my feet and I was thrilled to bits and reached down to pick it up and I held it high for Flukey to see. Look Da, I was saying, look at the size of it, but Flukey had disappeared, and before I knew what was happening, I was cruising the bluest river

I had ever seen. The sun was making light dance off the gentle waves, making rainbows out of beams of air and, Jesus, I was saying, how did I get from the autumn forest to this light-filled place? *Look, the Pyramids*, a familiar voice called out. A girl's voice. Next thing, I was standing tiny in front of enormous sand triangles. *Look out*, the same voice called to me. Wait! I knew who it was. Next thing the Pyramids were collapsing and the blocks were tumbling, hurtling right for me. *Run!* the girl urged. *Run for your life!* And I was moving now, moving and wondering where Flukey was, I wanted him to run for his life with me, especially as we had some unfinished business in the chestnut tree forest. I felt a hand clasp my own hand and pull me out of there. *It's OK*, whispered the comforting voice, *I've got you now*. And I was glad someone was looking out for me.

I opened my eyes. The moon and all the stars had disappeared, early birds were twittering, the sky was taking on light.

I looked around and hauled myself to my feet. Rolled the sleeves down over my arms and headed out of Fat Grehan's driveway. I paused at the unfinished wall and glanced at my handiwork. Then I saluted my deep red lettering, pulled my hoodie tight and sauntered down off Rich Hill. As a souvenir of my time up there I brought the knife with me. The snow globe, too.

EARLY MORNING

How do you know Jesus was an Irishman? the Slug Doyle asked me. He was hovering over the ditchwater, mooching about with his rod. Like he often was at this hour, fishing about for something. Perch. A pair of boots. The treasure of a long-since sunken boat.

I don't know, Slug. How do you know?

He didn't leave home until he was thirty-three. He used to hang around with twelve other guys. He thought his mother was a virgin, and she thought he was God.

I don't think my mother is a virgin, Slug.

Well that's OK then, because no way are you the son of God.

What are you fishing for, Slug?

Mary.

The Virgin?

No, the witch that stole my heart.

I had no idea who the Slug was talking about. He cast his line a couple of more times and on this occasion he landed one of the tackies Brains McManus had yanked off my feet and chucked into the ditch. He raised his rod, let the sodden tackie bend it, then flicked his wrist and the tackie dropped back into the ditchwater. He shrugged his shoulders, reeled in and shuffled off to find another spot. As soon as he had, I leaned in and fetched my tackies out of there.

I saw Barrabas Diffley, the whistling postman, just about the most unpopular lad in the whole world around here these days because all he ever did was bring bad news. That's why he was out and about with his sack of letters at this hour. With pretty much everyone still in bed, he stood a better chance of getting through his day without receiving a sledgehammer fist down on top of his head or a steel-cap boot up his rear end. For the right price I had once offered to take the sack of letters off his hands, do his dirty work for him. But the right price hadn't been offered, no price had been, now that I think of it, and my pockets stayed empty while Barrabas went about his rounds risking a good clobbering.

I looked into the Swamp to see if the girl was there, quickly scanned the hidden pools to make sure the crazy loon hadn't gone chucking herself in again. Instead of the girl, I saw Annie the scryer. She was standing at the low end of the lane, staring into the ditchwater. The long silver streaks of her hair looked blue in the early sun. The skin on her face looked stretched. She's like a stick in the mud, I'd heard Ma say about her. Others said she was ready for the knackers' yard.

Annie wasn't her only name. She had other names – witch woman, the black-and-midnight-hag, mother of doom, angel of death – but I couldn't be bothered using any of those. I thought she might have some answers to my questions. Calling her angel of death was hardly going to encourage her. Let the others call her what they liked.

Hello Annie. Tell me, where am I going to be in ten years' time? I said when I got as far as her, thinking it might be a good way of getting around to what I really wanted to ask.

I waited for a reply, but none came.

OK. We'll leave it at five years. Where will I be in five years, Annie?

Still nothing.

OK so, Annie. Let's bring it back a bit further. This time next week, where will I be?

Still nothing.

Answer this one for me, then, Annie. Flukey Nolan is my da. True or false?

She gripped herself and started swaying. Over and back she went. Like a timid wave. Or a change of heart. It wasn't any kind of answer to my question. Still. It was better than no reaction, better than just standing there like a mute.

Tell you what, Annie, I said. Keep it to yourself for now. Tell me next time. OK?

And I made my way home.

CRAZYWOMAN

There was no doubt about it. I was living with a crazy-woman. To look at her you wouldn't have suspected a thing. She was slim and wore short-length skirts that made men whistle. She paraded about in fashion boots that went to her knees. She had bleached hair she kept in a tidy bob. I suppose she wasn't a bad-looking woman, and she always had a good story for the lads that came knocking for the money she owed.

The lad she owed for fixing the hole that appeared in the sitting room ceiling had come knocking. It was about the tenth time he'd been around, and that after several polite phone calls and a handful of reasonably worded pay-up letters. Hello, Barty, she'd said to him, after accidentally letting herself get caught at the front door. Hello indeed, Barty said, all set to offer his harsh let-me-have-my-money words. But, of course, she was already a step or two ahead of Barty and she was swaying from side to side, fiddling with a button on her shirt, letting it open a little bit, and before Barty had a chance to pretend he hadn't been distracted by the bits of flesh now visible, she was into her story about Mario Devine, our evil landlord, and how he had been bullying the last coppers out of her pocket to pay the rent while at the same time paying no attention to the broken radiator that was causing her suffering child to half-freeze to death every night. And next thing, not only was Barty letting her off the hook for the hole in the ceiling, but he was on hands and knees in the upstairs bedroom going at our broken radiator with his wriggly wrench. You are a hero of mine, Barty Brophy, she said to him three hours later and blew him a kiss as she was seeing him out the front door.

That wasn't even the start of it. Before that, Gavin McGoldrick wouldn't hand back the keys of the useless rust bucket that passed for our car after he'd patched it up for about the one hundred and fiftieth time. Oh, please, Gavin, she said, turning on her lips. Please, Gavin, it's an emergency. It's Jason. Jason? said Gavin. Yes, Jason, she said, nodding back in my direction. He's not well. In fact, it's serious. They found another lump. A lump, said Gavin. Yes, she said, a third one. You should see it. It's like he's growing another testicle. Already Gavin was nearly choking to death and you could tell he couldn't let us out of his garage fast enough. Please, he said, giving the oily keys a wipe with his cloth, take your car. Whatever you need, take it, he said, gesturing to the array of banjaxed cars scattered about his workshop. I'd say he'd even have gone so far as to lend her the high-octane sports car he'd been working on when we showed up to begin with. But she was only getting started now and she was soon filling Gavin's head with forceps and scalpels and punctured scrotums and the rivers of pus pouring out of me. My poor boy, she said, clutching herself. My one son. My only child. And all the time Gavin was shrinking further and further back inside his workshop, and for every backward step he took, she was swaggering forward, those hips doing their thing again, her big poor-me eyes working their irreversible magic.

Just imagine, she said to me on our way home again, as she drove straight through a red light. Just imagine if I was a man. I'd be dangerous, you know. I'd go places. Where would you go? I asked her, and she called me a numpty, said she didn't mean it literally. Tell you one thing, though, she went on, if I was a man I would raise my arm and own up to some of the stunts that have been pulled around here. If I was a man I wouldn't be long fixing the mess this dump of a place is in. What has being a man got to do with fixing it? I wanted to know, and she let go of the steering wheel, put her hands on her popular hips, looked my way and said, Don't you know anything? Then we mounted the footpath and nearly ran over Old Tom Redihan out on his daily walk.

Can you keep a big secret? she said to cop Lawless the night we returned from our spin in Mattie's car, as soon as Lawless was finished the stern speech he had been waiting to deliver. She'd listened wide-eyed and attentively to every word that left his lips, occasionally bringing her hand to her mouth or placing it elaborately on her chest and from there onto the sleeve of Lawless' uniform, every gesture she made and every surprised breath she took, further distracting Lawless from what it was he was trying to do. I wasn't sure what exactly she was doing myself or how she was doing it, but you could see the stern expression on Lawless start to dissolve, and soon not only was he returning Ma's smile but was starting to convince himself that maybe this tale of the stolen car wasn't such a big deal, and that maybe it should be hardened criminals answering tough questions in the middle of the night and not this innocent beauty giving me her big eyes.

By now he had the garda hat off and he was leaning right in through the rolled-down driver window, and I could tell by the way he glanced at me that he wished I could some-how vanish so that he could slip into the car and he and Ma could continue their cosy conversation side by side. That's when Ma made that comment about keeping a secret, and I thought she was going to make some crazy confession to Lawless about her love affair with Mattie's car or start in on some of that if-I-was-a-man talk. Instead, she reached over and brushed some invisible dust off the shoulder of his uniform. He looked to where her hand had brushed, and then into Ma's eyes, the loon was probably wishing he had dust everywhere. Then she gestured him even closer, nodded sadly towards me, and told him all about my sorry state.

DEATH

She was alive and well when I showed up back at the house after my night up on Rich Hill. Doing twirls around the kitchen, and singing along to the cranked-up stereo.

There you are, she said when she spotted me. For a minute there I thought you had run away. Hey! Are you hungry? I can make something.

No thanks.

Anything you want. Go on, tell me. How about a fry? I might have some sausages.

I'm a bit sleepy, Ma.

Are you sure? You've had plenty of porridge this week. We should mix things up a bit. Let me take a look at what we have.

She made a bee-line for the kitchen press. Threw open some doors. Started pulling down whatever was there. Tins of tomatoes. A jar of gherkins. Some Mars bars. The telephone started ringing and I answered it. Listened to the familiar voice.

It's the Credit Union, Ma, I said, covering the receiver. They want their money back.

Tell them they can sing for it. Tell them I'll have it for them in my next life. Tell them I'm busy cooking breakfast for my boy. Have you decided what you would like?

I might go for a lie down, Ma.

Lying down is for dead people. Look at you. You need to eat. Now tell me. Anything you want.

She was practically climbing inside the press. Mumbling her breakfast menu. Tossing out bags of rice. Packets of cream crackers. Cans of soup. Again the ringing telephone came to my rescue.

It's the Hungry Worm, Ma, I said when I answered it. They want you to come in.

Well tell them I can't. Tell them I've got the hiccups. Tell them I'm dead and I'm not coming back.

She can't, I said into the phone. She's got the hiccups. She's also dead and not coming back.

Good boy. Now, come on. We have eggs. Let me cook you an omelette.

She pulled a soggy box out of the press, opened it and at once turned up her nose.

Maybe we'll skip the eggs, she said, and took a good look around the kitchen as though she was convinced a second press, one with proper eggs and other food, was hiding on her. Her scan complete, she shook her head sadly, threw out her arms and yelled, What a dump! As fast again, she jerked her head towards the stereo, her face lighting up at what was coming out of it.

And off she went. *De-de doo-duh. De-de doo-duh.* Clicking her fingers. Her crazy head moving forward and back like a camel. And, turning towards me, hand on her heart, the high-pitched voice chipped in.

People say I'm the life of the party
'Cause I tell a joke or two
Although I might be laughing loud and hearty
Deep inside I'm blue

Hey! Who sings that song? she said next, and before I had a chance to let her know that sorry, I have no idea who sings it, and that sorry again, I have been up all night and am not in the mood for sing-song games, with either hand she had grabbed both my cheeks and was singing crazy again. *So take a good look at my face,* she squeaked like an out-of-tune canary, hunkering down and giving me her intense stare. *You'll see my smile is out of place.* Well, who is it? she said, relaxing her grip a bit, her big eyes imploring me to take a guess.

I don't know, I said.

Take a wild guess.

Madonna.

No! she howled.

Marilyn Monroe.

Now who have you been talking to that has you handing out answers like that?

Is she the answer?

No, but today I'll give you an extra egg for thinking it might be. Guess again.

Madonna.

You said that already.

Who do you want me to say?

Whoever you think.

Madonna.

If you say her name again I will stab you in the spleen with this fork. After that, I reeled off the first names to enter my head. No, no and no, she kept howling at me, and I shrugged my shoulders. I hadn't a clue who it was, but I had started guessing and she wasn't going to drop it until the correct answer left my lips. I'll give you a clue, I heard her say, and she was into another verse, sashaying across the kitchen, looking over her shoulder at me when it was time for the high bit. What the hand-on-heart and poor-me look had to do with it I couldn't say, either way it didn't matter because I still had no idea who she was supposed to be, was starting to wonder did she know herself. Then she swung around to face me, arms spread out before her, that don't-you-know-anything expression forming on her face. Quickly I shook my head, was all set to make a fast dash for my room, when yet again the ringing telephone came to the rescue. For once in her life Ma decided to answer it, and as soon as she heard the words spoken at the other end of the line she wasn't long forgetting her guessing game.

She paraded about the place some more, the phone clamped to her ear, someone babbling down the line, and it took Ma a few minutes to realize that someone was dead, someone she knew, and at last she was telling me who it was, but not before she had disappeared upstairs for a few minutes and then come back down, dabbing her red eyes with a hanky and yelling at me to get ready, that we had a dead man to say goodbye to, not that I could see the point in that, and I was cursing myself for not staying well away when I had the chance.

Flukey Nolan.

That's who it was.

Ma's ex-boy.

The man I had been looking for.

How can Flukey be dead? I wanted to know, but she wasn't listening to me, was too busy in front of the cracked mirror making sure she looked OK for the farewell party being thrown for the dead man, not that it was going to make any difference to Flukey how she looked, and already I was thinking how it was only last month the two of them were hanging out together, making plans, talking up some bright idea of Flukey's. And all the time I was looking at Ma and her powdered face, waiting for her to answer my question, waiting for her to tell me that this was just another one of her stories. Then one or two of Ma's friends showed up and I didn't get a chance to ask anything else.

And I was listening to them talking about what had happened. At the beginning of the week he did it. Jumped off Violin Bridge and into the drain of a river and by the time they managed to haul him out he was not a pretty sight. Word from the hospital was that he had died of bronchitis, a huge liver and the finishing touches of pneumonia. And even then the doctors had been scratching their chins and saying how baffled they were he'd stayed alive as long as he did. I was tempted to get word back to the doctors that not three full weeks ago he'd been eating a plate of Ma's cooking, but I thought that would only baffle them more, and so I said nothing. To be honest, I didn't know why the doctors had even bothered taking a look at him. Scrub Flukey from head to toe for a long time, give him a new set of teeth, a normal coloured nose, good breath, trim back the hairs growing out of his ears and then dress him up in a suit, tie, coat and top hat and chances are he still would not have been a pretty sight. And that was before he had ended up at the bottom of the river. Three nights and three days. That's how long they reckoned he'd been down there. Dead. All by himself. I was not looking forward to the dreams I would have about that.

Flukey.

That's what everybody called him. If you ask me, an arse-over-heels name for someone ending up as fish food at the bottom of sludge river, but that's the way it was around here these days.

Arse over heels.

Flukey of the top tips and big bets. Flukey of the latest get-rich-quick scheme. Flukey of the lend-me-a-tenner-today-and-I'll-give-you-back-a-twenty-next-week. Flukey of the trembling lips and curly nose. There would be no more tenners for Flukey, and no next week either.

He was broke.

That's what they were saying drove him to it.

Oh, boy.

I was broke. The crazywoman I lived with was broke. Everybody else was broke. Imagine the state of the river if we all went diving off Violin Bridge. The skin-and-bone fish quivering in the dirtwater would think they had won the lotto.

Take off that hoodie and put on some clothes, Ma was yelling at me when we were heading out the door. What did she think I was going to do? Show up to say goodbye to Flukey in my numbskulls? That would've looked good. Not that it made any difference as far as Flukey was concerned. Put on some clothes. She was a good one to be using words like that.

The men were all ogling her at Flukey's farewell party. Could see their leery eyes all over her as soon as she entered the room. Taking in her shape inside the black dress she was wearing. All the way from head to toe their eyes travelled, pausing at certain parts of her before continuing their way. And all the time the question on the tip of their practically-hanging-out-of-their-mouth tongues. What did Flukey have that we don't?

He was laid out in the front room of his shack of a house. I kept my distance, had no desire to get too close to the curly nose on him, wished they'd hammer down the lid on the coffin and be done with it. There wasn't a sound out of him. It was hard to get used to. Up until his running jump he was well able to make himself heard. Especially when he and Ma got together. *Oh, Jacinta, baby, that is so good. A little to the left, Jacinta. That's it, baby, that's the spot. No, wait, baby. A little to the right, Jacinta. Oh, yes, baby. Oh, yes, yes, yes, baby. Don't stop. Oh, wait, baby. A little to the left again. Oh, yes, baby. Oh, please, baby. Oh, yes. Oh, no.*

Don't stop. Hold on. To the left. To the right. Jesus, the loop-the-loop could never make up his mind.

The house was already filling up with the cream of the town's gobshites, each and every one of them determined to spend a lot of time saying what a great lad Flukey was, even though every last one of them would've happily walked out to the useless by-pass and gone round the town the long way if they thought it would've meant not having to pass him in the street.

After a little while, groups of men gathered around in little circles and spoke in low huddles because, by now, they had a few early whiskeys inside them and once the early whiskey was inside a man around here he had to be a part of a low huddle. I grabbed a seat in a corner of the front room, did my best to pretend I was somewhere else.

You should've heard the things they were saying about the dead man. He was full of brains. He had the soul of a poet. He knew everything there was to know about fish. He had a unique way of looking at things. He was a personal friend of trees. Why didn't any of you lot tell him all this when he was alive and well instead of crossing over to the other side of the street to avoid him? is what I wanted to know, but there was no time because already they were quickly into talk about how Flukey managed to do it.

Sure, how could a lad end up dead after throwing himself off that moany old bridge? one lad pointed out. It's no distance to the water. A bump on the head and a watery nose you might end up with. Nothing more. You thick eejit, someone else barked, it wasn't the throwing himself off the bridge that did the damage, nor for that matter was it the landing in the two feet of mucky water. It was the fact that he was more than half soused when he jumped and that he had decided to stay exactly where he was until someone took it upon themselves to notice that he had been lying there for the better part of seventy-two hours. And still that explanation wasn't good enough for the first lad. Well, I don't know what he wanted to go messing with that crock of a bridge for. If it was me that was feeling at the end of despair I would have gone some place else. Where would you have gone? they quickly asked. And of course he held off for a minute before offering another word, and of course some jackass couldn't wait, he had to know what was coming next and he urged the first lad to go on and spit it out and don't be keeping it a big secret, God knows there were enough of those already floating about the place. The first lad didn't need a second urging. I'd go to the Tower, he said. The Tower! the others repeated after him as though it was one of the wonders of the modern world and not the sort of place a fellow at the end of despair should be contemplating jumping off. The first fellow folded his arms. He was terribly satisfied with the effect of what he had just said and he was going to bask in his moment like a lad put out of doors for an afternoon of rare sunshine.

And that got them started on the Tower. And how it was good for nothing and all the money spent on it and it just there, an empty coffin of a building trying to reach all the way to the sky. A waste of money, about as useful as a lighthouse in a bog and no sign of the lad who thought it was a great idea to build it, and if anyone should be made take a running jump off the thing, it's that fat bastard Grehan, milking the place for all he's worth and then taking off when it all goes sour. And a few others weren't long weighing in with how Fat Grehan should be dealt with. String him up, said one. Pin him against the wall and riddle him. Castrate the fucker. They liked the sound of that idea. That's the thing for him, they said. Castration. And it all came back to the Tower and how its construction had been a bad spell cast on the town, a bad-luck charm. It's good for nothing, they said, and kept saying it. Good for nothing except jumping off, said the first lad. Castrate the fucker, said the other lad. I was listening to all this, it was hard not to, was even starting to enjoy some of it, but one or two of the women must have heard that castrate the fucker comment because they were upon the whiskey huddle like flies on dead dogs and they were shushing the men or else there would be castration galore required, and of course, knowing that, unlike themselves, the women often carried out their promises, the men did shush, and that was the end of all the jumping and castrating.

And anyway, they had said all they wanted to say about the bad-luck Tower and wanted to move on to more important topics. Weather. The fucker of a ref who blew up four minutes before he should have last Sunday. The knock-down price of a pint on offer in McMorrow's. The lack of perch in that same useless drain that spat out Flukey. And the big question on everyone's lips – what had happened to all the money? That summer it was the number one hot topic of conversation. It didn't matter what else might be happening. A psychopath could've charged through the streets gunning down women and children. The Swamp could've finally burst its banks and destroyed our neighbourhood once and for all. The entire town itself could've sank into the ground. Nobody would've batted an eyelid. Because there was only one thing worth talking about and that was where had all the money gone? I wished I was armed and dangerous. I could've pulled my gun. Annihilated the entire room.

When Ma wasn't looking I slipped out of there, took a walk through the kitchen, grabbed a triangular-shaped sandwich with a flimsy slice of ham flapping out of it and stepped outside. I went round the side of the house. The sun was doing its best to make an appearance, and a few teapots were shielding their heads and staring up at it like it was an apparition. I ditched the sandwich, picked up a nail I saw lying on the ground, and wandered further away from everyone.

Had rolled up a sleeve and was about to cut my arm when I heard the familiar voice.

What are you doing?

Nothing.

Crap, nothing. You're cutting up your arm. I can see the marks.

Listen to her that goes jumping into swamps, I said, quickly rolling down my sleeve.

Well then.

Well then, what?

I suppose we both have a secret to keep, don't we?

Yeah. Well that doesn't mean anything. And no more occupying my rock. OK? Tomorrow, I'll be expecting it back.

Oh dear. Here we go again.

I'm not going anywhere with you.

She brought her hand to her face and mimicked an almighty yawn. I saw one or two bruises on her arm. Was all set to ask about them but she beat me to it.

If that had been me, I wouldn't have got caught.

I wasn't caught.

Yes you were. By me.

You're not so special.

And you are?

I didn't say anything to that. Shrugged and looked away from her.

Now what will we do? she said next.

What do you mean?

You've started something between us. We need to carry on. So?

So, what?

Come up with something for us to do.

We could go through a few jackets.

No!

Steal a parked car?

Sorry, don't have time.

Break in to a few empty houses?

How boring.

Well then, you come up with something.

Let's spill some blood. Other than our own, I mean.

Huh?

Choose your weapon, she said, offering her empty hands to me and I looked from her outstretched hands to her face, reached out and made to take whatever she was holding in her left hand.

The .44 Magnum. Good choice, she said. That leaves me with the Colt .45.

Without another word she raised her gun, spun around and fired three shots into a lad with a beetroot-coloured face. She brought the gun to her mouth, blew smoke off the end of the barrel, spun round again, went down on one knee and quickly took out a circle of men containing Harry Brewster and Fergal Flood. Patrick Cox was next to go. Mr Saj, the Bangladeshi man who lived next door to us. Fock me! he said, clutching his chest as the bullets ripped through him. Then she started on the women. Lily the Nose. Bliss Flynn. Three or four friends of Ma. She reloaded, edged her way around the side of the house, sprang out and let rip at whoever was out the front. She crouched again, allowed herself fall into a roll, and when she settled, pumped countless bullets into a few more unlucky enough to be standing in her line of fire. Then she was on her feet again, standing still, one eye closed and taking aim at one or two passing cars. Then she made her way back to where I was standing, letting off one or two random shots for good measure.

The rest are all yours, call me when you need back-up, she said. Then she blew some lingering smoke off the end of the barrel and drifted back towards the house. Oh, I almost forgot to ask, she said, just before she disappeared inside. Do you still think he's your da?

I moved off myself, drifted further away from the house, towards the shed at the end of Flukey's garden. I saw a jacket hanging all by itself, the bulging pockets inviting my hands. I looked around, the coast was clear, and was all set to plunder when I heard voices inside the shed. I moved quietly around the side and through the window saw Mario Devine and Ma. They were having a sweet time of it, canoodling together and rubbing up close and twisting each other this way and that and Ma's black dress was hitched up around her waist and her loverboy's hands couldn't get hold of enough of her. I took one step back from the window, raised my gun arm, trigger finger poised, and was about to let them have it when Ma decided it was high time she did up her buttons, fastened a few clips back together, tidied some strands of hair and, before I could say as much as *bang, bang, you're dead*, before Flukey could sit up in his coffin and have a right good go at her for carrying on like that and he barely pronounced dead to the world, let alone cold in the ground surrounded by the worms, she was dressed and out of there, up the garden and back inside the house.

By the time I had stepped back into the room and reclaimed my chair, Ma was standing beside the coffin. She even managed to fire off in my direction one of her special glares. That's a good one, I thought, and turned to another low huddle of talking men. And suddenly Flukey was no longer a great fellow. For starters, his brains had evaporated. Nor was he sensitive like the trees. He didn't know the first thing about anything, let alone fish. Was about as unique as a soggy field. And as for his soul. Well, poet or not, there was only one place *that* was going.

Where is that then? I was all set to shout out, and out of nowhere, it seemed, Ma's voice was reaching me. Get the hell over here and say goodbye to Flukey, she was screeching, you'd swear I'd left my ears at home. She looked good, though, in her short, black dress and spikey heels, bet she'd love to hear me say that, and the whiskey huddles couldn't keep their eyes off her. Like I said. You would never have suspected a thing.

PICTURE THIS

It was much later in my room, long after they had screwed down the lid on Flukey's coffin and everyone had gnashed down all the sandwiches and drank all the whiskey and wobbled off to McMorrow's to stare longingly at Flukey's empty barstool, and Ma and her friends had parked themselves downstairs in the kitchen and started swapping Flukey stories long into the night, when it hit me that Ma was right: I was a fair size numpty thinking it might be Flukey.

Da. I knew he was still out there. Somewhere.

Lay there on my bed, closed my eyes and pictured the man I wanted him to be. A dapper man. Dressed in a suit with stripes. A high hat on his head. Shiny shoes on his feet. Gold cuff links. Matching finger ring. Snazzy watch. Cigarette dangling from his mouth. A man who moves with a mysterious air, the kind that turns heads and raises eyebrows, the kind that takes years to learn. Owner of a fast car and money to burn. A good way with words. Likes a steak or two. Knows how to land a sturdy fish. Oh boy. I could practically see him come walking through the front door of our tin-pan house, watch Ma sashay into his arms and give him her killer smile. I could see him tip his finger off the edge of his high hat and fire a look in my direction. *Well, kid, what are you waiting for? We've got places to be, things to do. Let's hit the road.*

Yeah. That was a good picture. I could take that one and keep it in my album.

THAT TIME OF THE MONTH

A couple of weeks later, we were well into the joys of July, and Ma was having a great time cursing her way through the list of everyone she owed. The shite-and-all bin man. The fuck's-sake oil company. The gob-prick of a mechanic. The plague of arse bandits that were the phone rental company, the television licence people and the ESB lads all rolled into one. There was Cunthook the fridge repair man. Bollox the boiler fixer. Shove-It-Up-Your-Cooch from the Credit Union, and the Bank of Wank-Me-With-A-Spoon. She owed our bull-nut selling landlord big time. Mel Campbell's shop at the top of the road, a place from which we had both been barred. I even had her down for thirteen euros after she robbed the few coins I was keeping in my jam jar. Not even in your next life, she howled any time I reminded her to pay me back, not even when I turn myself into a man.

I wouldn't mind but, unlike me, she had a job. She was a waitress in the Hungry Worm café. Selling buns. Taking orders for death-by-chocolate cakes. Traipsing through the dusty storeroom in search of a misplaced apple tart. Icing messages onto birthday cakes. You name it, she did it. Don't ask me why she bothered. It was only a part-time job, two or three days a week, and even then she only showed up if she felt like it. She'd even been fired from time to time. Still. It was better than nothing. Better than having to stay at home all the time. Better than having to board up your shop windows. Better than having to empty out your big house, and high-tail it under cover of darkness. It was better than feeling you've come to the end of despair and have to go jumping off Violin Bridge.

On my last count she'd been fired eleven times. A couple of times for not showing up when she was supposed to. A couple of times for screaming at customers she had taken a dislike to. A couple of times for screaming at the other wait-ress. A couple of times for screaming at me when I called in to see if she'd throw a sticky bun my way, a jam tart, or a rocky road. Very often she screamed at Mattie Conlon, owner of the café and, by now, sorest set of ears in our town. Her idea of a waitress was someone who did a lot of screaming, and if Mattie Conlon didn't want his customers taking off to another café he had no choice but to give Ma the occasional heave-ho.

My favourite was the time she was fired over a message she iced onto Imelda Grehan's birthday cake. Imelda was going to be ten and her mother was in, wanting the biggest, most colourful, spectacular cake this town had ever seen, and she was telling Ma exactly what the cake had to look like, and not to be skimping on the icing like had happened with another cake she had recently ordered. I think she even produced a picture cut out of a magazine and slapped it down in front of Ma, there, that's what my little girl needs, and she was jotting down the you-are-the-best-daughter-in-the-whole-world-ever birthday message she wanted iced all over the cake. But somehow Ma misheard the precise wording, and when two days later the finished cake was delivered into the room full of screaming children and set down on the table in front of the birthday girl, Imelda Grehan was opening the cake box to a message that now read *Happy Birthday, daughter, I wish I'd given you away*. Oh boy, did Ma get it from Mattie Conlon over that. GET OUT! GET OUT! he roared at her. Sling your hook and don't come back. But back she did come, swinging her hips, fluttering her eyelashes, her voice softened to little more than a purr, and surprise, surprise, all was forgiven. Just like when Lawless persuaded Mattie no harm had been done after her latest spin in his car.

You had to hand it to her. You really did.

All I wanted to know was what it was about Mattie's car that attracted her attention so much. Ma, I said to her when she was back at the house, free and innocent of the latest stunt she had pulled. Ma, why are you always taking Mattie's car? She just looked at me, twisted into paper sticks the batch of pay-up letters Barrabas Diffley had just sent sailing through the letterbox and lobbed them into the fireplace.

She was due in right now but surprise, surprise, she wasn't stirring. Maybe she was still brooding over Flukey. Maybe she was contemplating another spin in Mattie's car. Maybe she just thought to herself, to hell with it, I don't feel like flogging buns today. Whatever her reasons, she was done with her I-owe list and was now out on the doorstep, dragging on her roll-up, sipping from her glass, that empty expression on her face that made it seem she was looking at nothing and everything at the same time. They need you, Ma, I said when the call came through. They want you to come in. But on this occasion she had nothing to say. She had no hiccups. She wasn't dead and not coming back. I put down the phone and tried not to listen to Mattie's voice babbling out through it. Then I heard a car pull up outside our house. Aha, I thought to myself. It's that time of the month again.

SUPER MARIO

At about a quarter past nine in the morning on the middle Friday of the month, Mario Devine showed up at our door. Mario was the star salesman for the feed mill at the edge of town and owner of our house, and when he wasn't collecting his rent he got to drive all over the county offering farmers bags of bull nuts at knockdown prices. Ma said he couldn't flog bread in a famine, but as soon as he appeared she was all smiles and plates of food and cups and saucers. You would think we had royalty wiping its feet on our step.

Howya, Jacinta, the lug said, pulling her to him and putting his boggy hands on as much of her backside as he could. Over her shoulder he winked at me. Then it was up the stairs with the pair of them and I sat on the bottom step and counted twenty or thirty ooohs, a few dozen aahs, and one almighty spasm. It wasn't quite the show herself and Flukey put on, but it wasn't a million miles away from it either.

Next came Mario's sweet talk. You're a foxy woman, Jacinta Lowry, he told her. You're a foxy woman and I wish I'd met you before I was married. If Ma had anything to say to that, I didn't hear, and anyway, it didn't matter because this was now the Mario show and he was pouring his thoughts down her throat like sugary medicine, his voice sounding like one of those lads on the six o'clock news ready to swear on their mother's and daughter's life that everything is going to be alright and they knowing full-well that nothing could be further from the truth.

You know what you and me are going to do, Mario was telling her. We're going to take a trip together. That's right, just you and me. And you know where we are going to go? We're going to go to . . . you know, I'm not going to say another word. I'm going to keep it a secret for now. You can guess if you want, and maybe I'll give you a clue. And so Ma offered a few guesses and Mario laughed and gave her a couple of hints and they went over and back like that for a little while and I wasn't long getting bored with all of it, was even starting to doze off where I was sitting and when I tuned in again all I could hear was Paris this and Paris that. No, there is nothing wrong with your ears, Mario was saying as though for my benefit. We are going to Paris. We're going to book into a nice little hotel near the river and we're going to have a Champagne time of it. There! What do you think of that? And know this, he said, getting all serious, and I could picture the sombre head on the lug and he putting his hand on his heart as though promising the best ever bag of bull nuts, it's not every woman I invite on a trip to Paris. Now! What do you think of that?

Boy, was he laying it on thick. And to go by the coos and aahs out of her, Ma was starting to get interested in what was coming out of Mario's mouth. I was too. And I was getting to thinking: this is some show Mario is putting on, this lad is fast getting my attention. And so there was no budging me yet, because Mario was still in Paris – *Gay Paree* he was now calling it – and the river Seine, and the Louvre, and the Notre Dame Cathedral and the palace at Versailles, and the Bastille which was stormed, and the guillotine which lopped off everybody's head when things went crazy over there years ago, Ma made sure to let out a suitable gasp at that. He was telling her all about the little cafés and bars and the markets and the flower stalls along the river and all the famous people who lived in Paris. He told her they would buy some French bread and cheese and a bottle of wine at a little market he had discovered on his last trip and they would stroll down to the river and sit along the banks and sip the wine and nibble the cheese, and while they were at it they might even nibble each other and, Jesus, she was giggling at that, eating up every word he said. Boy, was he good. And that wasn't all. Hold on to your *Champs-Elysées*, he said next, whatever that meant, I'm only getting started, and the lug was talking moonlight and riverboats and strawberries and cream and more flowers and more French bread, the most delicious bread in the world, he was saying. And we can go to the Luxembourg Gardens and walk under the famous arch and get a lift to the top of the Eiffel Tower. Do that Mario, get a lift to the top of the tower and take a running jump for yourself. And after all of that there was still time for more French bread and wine. Jesus, the lug must have won a ticket for free bread all over France the way he was talking about the stuff. It's a promise, he said. I'm going to put in for some time off and we are out of here. Then the lug must've started pretending he was a Frenchman and he was singing some crazy French-sounding song and she was loving every minute of it, was actually laughing now, something I hadn't heard her do since I made that crack about Flukey being my da. It was pretty good listening to all that Paris talk. And before I knew it he had me convinced this trip was really going to happen, made me wish I was going with them.

You had to hand it to him. He really knew how to lay it on. It was enough to get Ma more than cooing, and soon they were shaking up the place again, sending tremors through the bedsprings, and I was thinking, that riverside Paris hotel won't know what's hit it when this pair shows up.

Couldn't be listening to any more of it. Stepped into the bathroom, grabbed one of the razors Ma used on her legs. Sat down on the tiled floor and made fast work of breaking out the blade. Rolled up the sleeve of my hoodie, sucked in my breath, and sliced down my arm. It was an untidy slice, jagged and deeper than the cuts I'd made on the hill, and I gasped with delight as soon as the blood spurted out and ran in messy swirls, dripped in red blobs onto the bathroom floor. I stared at where I'd cut, saw the blood gather in little bubbles, held my arm to my mouth, tasted grit and rust. Closed my eyes and cut again, and then again and again, each cut rushing giddy waves through me, taking me further and further away, until at last I was floating beneath that clear sky and blue sea, my boat gently bobbing and caressing the friendly water, and the sounds of dripping oars and lapping tide, and the high sun lighting the way before me.

And the girl's voice was coming through again. *Keep going. Don't stop.* And so I dipped my oar and pulled, and with every stroke could feel myself getting closer to that distant place of light.

A high-pitched gasp from next door took me out of that happy scene, and for a few minutes I half-listened to them, next door, to their giggles and lovey-dove talk. Then I wiped the floor, cleared the runny streaks off my arm, reached for the box of plasters and rolled back down my sleeve.

About twenty minutes later, when she temporarily re-appeared to grab the plates of food she had prepared, Ma was in great form. Here's a euro, she said, flipping a coin in my direction. Go get an ice cream.

IF BRAINS WERE CHOCOLATE . . .

Was only too happy to get out of there. No point hanging around, not with Ma clinging onto Mario like there was no tomorrow. He was too talkie-talkie for my liking and I had little desire to be around a bull-nut seller, let alone someone who couldn't flog bread in a famine. Still, though. Here he was. Landed on our doorstep. Spring in his step. Sharing his Paris tales. Suppose I wouldn't've minded having a talk about Paris with him, share some ideas of my own. Play my cards right and, hey, who knows, this time next month I could be floating along the river Seine, chewing on some of that bread he kept banging on about. Wouldn't that be grand?

Indeed it would, Jason. Indeed it would.

Dropped the coin in my pocket, alongside the razor-blade. Grabbed my bag and legged it out the back door. Cut through the scutch and bindweed that passed for our back garden. Not for us the daffodils and tulips that dominated Old Tom Redihan's colourful plot next door. Or the tidy vegetable ridges belonging to Mr Fock Me from Bangladesh on the other side. No. Only the best scutch grass and bind-weed would do us. Nettles so tall and billowy they could be used as umbrellas. Tropical mushrooms sprouting everywhere. Swampy sounds underfoot. Every few steps I checked my pockets to make sure the coin was still there. We'll have to tighten our belts now that the country's back to the shite-and-all mess it's always been. That's what I was hearing on the down-town streets these days. Every euro counted.

They were all out today. Talking Harry Brewster and pointing Fergal Flood. Patrick Fox and barking Rommel and Himmler. At the low end the drunks were drinking early. Old Tom Redihan was standing in front of the ditch and I thought, Lily the Nose is right. He has started talking to the trees. And just as I brought her up, along she came, smiling sly and wagging her waxy finger.

Look at those eejits Harry Brewster and Fergal Flood. Closhin' together all the time. Convinced they have all the answers. If brains were chocolate, between them they wouldn't fill a Smartie. And look at that teapot Tom Redihan talking to trees. You'd think a man of his age would know better. And as for that other one. Who in their right mind names their dogs after a pair of butchering Germans? If brains were elastic, that fellow wouldn't stretch a sparrow's garter.

I didn't have a clue what she was chirping on about, wasn't even listening to her. I was trying to see round that barrel shape and get a glimpse of the Swamp to see if the girl had shown up. Lily wasn't giving up so easily, though.

How is that mother of yours?

You could tell by the way she asked it she had already composed inside that witchy head of hers the one and only answer she wanted to hear. I was only too happy to oblige her.

She's in great form, Lily. Why, just as we speak she has that amazing bull-nut seller Mario Devine chained to the bed and she's giving him ten of the best with her sturdy whip. You should hear the yelps out of him, Lily. I wouldn't stray up there if I were you. She's in a no-mercy mood.

That was enough to send her waddling, and at last I had a clear view of the Swamp. There was no sign of the scryer but the Slug was out. His wart-and-speckled hands casting his line along with bitter words at the witch who had stolen his heart. Some council men had shown up. They were wading through the shallow end of the Swamp, taking measurements, making notes. I wasn't interested in any of that. I looked across the Swamp, over towards my rock, the blood inside me galloping a little when I saw her sitting there.

SWEET TALKING

Oh, look. It's the tough guy. Been cutting yourself lately?

No. Been jumping into any swamps?

No.

Yeah, well, just so you know, that's still my rock you're on.

I'm so pleased. Now sit down, you're blocking my view.

Without another word I did as I was told. Plonked myself down on the rock beside her. Was glad my friends were no longer around. Now that the country was a sinking ship, the one or two I'd half-had had moved as far across the world as their parents could drag them. If they could see me now. They'd have a good laugh. Look at him! Sharing a rock with a girl.

Going anywhere today? I asked her.

I'm thinking ancient Greece.

I've heard of it.

Of course you have. Ancient Greece is where civilization began.

It hasn't reached our boghole town.

The Greeks gave us Achilles and the wooden horse. They even gave us sewers.

That I can believe.

Or was that the Romans?

How was Egypt?

Oh, it was fine. The pharaohs were sleeping, so I didn't get a chance to talk to them.

Can't say I know any of them myself.

What do you know?

Now you sound like my ma.

I saw the Sphinx. Took a cruise along the Nile. Stopped at the Aswan Dam.

The Aswan Dam?

That's right. Have you ever taken a river cruise along the Nile? No? Well, you should. Next to the Mississippi, I can't think of a better place to cruise. Well, maybe the Amazon. Have you got a favourite river?

I have a least favourite river.

The girl didn't say anything to that. Instead, she leaned a little forward on the rock, chin in her hands, elbows on knees, and stared out across the Swamp.

Do you ever stare in another direction?

This is the way. What other direction is there?

I took a look around. Over my shoulder, the soggy patches between here and the ditches trees. Straight ahead, the stretch of swamp, its scummy surface glistening in the bright light, the giddy flies having the time of their lives, here and there bits of timber and beer cans peeking out, bobbing in the brown water. To my right, the rushes grow-ing high, swishing gently, concealing the hidden pools. I looked at the girl again, followed her line of vision.

Flukey liked to hang out here. Well. Before he went

jumping off bridges he did. We used to drink together in the pub. You should have heard him laugh.

What's your favourite method?

Favourite method of what?

If I was going to try and end it all again, I would choose to walk the plank. Disappear beneath the waves. Spend eternity with the sea.

Like a mermaid.

That's right. Maybe.

Are you?

Am I what?

Going to . . . try again?

I'm going to be a celebrity. Remember? Hey! Are you afraid of ghosts?

I don't know. Are you?

No. They're afraid of me.

We sat side by side in silence, she giving the place her full stare, me wondering to myself what exactly I was supposed to say next. Before I had a chance, she was speaking again.

You know, you should think about doing something to impress me. It will be too late once I am a celebrity.

You want me to impress you?

That's right.

What do you want me to do?

Oh, I'm sure a tough guy like you can think of something. If you do, I'll let you put your thing in me.

Huh?

That's all I'll end up to you. Someone to put your thing

into. Might as well get it over with. But you really should try to impress me first. Something small will do.

She brought her hand to the side of her neck, touched a couple of fingers off the bruise. It was darker than it was before, black-blue, yellow around the edges. Saw another one on her arm.

What celebrity are you going to be like?

What do you mean?

My ma likes to pretend she's a famous singer. She does these crazy little singing acts. She's always trying to get me to listen and guess who it is. I never get it right.

You should listen. One day you'll be glad you did.

I'll be glad on the day she gives my head a rest.

What's your favourite song?

Don't have one.

Of course you do. You just don't know it yet. As soon as you do, you can put in a request to have it played for me on the radio. Then it will be our song.

Our song?

That's right. Anyway. When the time comes I'm not going to be like anyone. I'm going to be me. My own person. You won't believe how famous I'm going to be. Play your cards right and you can be one of my minders.

Your what?

Though you're going to have to start growing. And very soon. And that hoodie will have to go. Here. Take my hair slide. It's going to be worth something someday. Go on. Take it.

I don't want a hair slide.

Are you sure? It will be valuable one day.

What? A pipsqueak's hair slide!

Well, when I'm famous, don't say I didn't offer it to you. Oh look! You've got something on your feet today. That's good.

What? These useless things?

Don't underestimate shoes. They'll take you places.

What places?

Whatever place you choose.

I choose pretty much any place if it gets me out of this boghole town.

Well then, the world is all yours.

Could hardly keep up with what she was saying. Wasn't even sure that I liked all of it. Put your thing in me. That's all I'll end up to you. I picked up a couple of pebbles, flung them into the Swamp. The world is all yours. That bit I did like.

As soon as they're through smashing all the bed springs my ma is going to Paris with Mario Devine.

Who?

Mario Devine.

Never heard of him.

Swing by our house and you'll hear plenty of him. He's a salesman. Big hands. Talks a lot. Lives up on the hill. When he's not at our house, that is.

Oh him. Yes, I know him. I fired three warning shots into his skull at the funeral.

If you did, you'll have my ma to contend with. And

believe me when I say it, that is one thing you do not want in your life.

I suppose he's your new da.

Who? Mario? I hope not. Don't think I want to be the son of a bull-nut seller. Like the sound of this Paris trip, though. Wouldn't mind getting a seat on that.

Ask him can you go.

He's too busy with my ma.

Suit yourself.

She stopped talking and stared out into the distance. I didn't know what to make of her. A feather of a thing beside me on the rock. If a notion took me I could've blown her away. Scattered her into the summer air. Here she was, though, talking to me. Being my friend. That was good enough for me.

Is your da still crying?

Oh yes. He's crying and banging his fists on the table and howling like a crazy dog. How many boyfriends has your ma?

Don't know.

I should send my father to see your ma.

I told you. She's too busy with Mario. You should hear the pair of them. Then comes his sweet talk.

What? He doesn't do the sweet talk first?

No.

I think I need to send my father over to your ma.

For the next few minutes we sat there without saying a word. She closed her eyes, bunched up her knees and wrapped her arms around them. It was a good opportunity to leg it out of there, but some other part of me made me want to stay. She was talking in riddles, my head was swimming listening to her, but it was better than the usual stuff I heard around here.

How are the pyramids?

I'm in ancient Greece, silly.

So?

There are no pyramids. Just the Parthenon. And the Acropolis. And the Temple of Zeus.

How's the temple?

I'm not sure if I want to go inside. I think I'll wait outside, admire it for a few minutes before I rejoin the cruise.

How do you know all this stuff?

Internet. The library. Beats the stuff we do at school.

Don't mention that place. My ma used to tell me stories when I was very little – like this daft stuff you're going on about. Some of it was good. Then she got interested in other things. Ma, I said to her one time, why don't you tell me those crazy stories any more.

And what did she say?

That's what school is for.

Ha! If she only knew. I'm seriously thinking of giving it up – school, I mean. I won't need it. Not where I'm headed. Are you sure I'm not growing knockers?

She was sticking out her chest, making sure I had the maximum opportunity to see whatever parts of her I was supposed to be on the lookout for.

I'm sure, I said.

Is that why you don't want to put your thing in me? Because I have no knockers?

I have to go now. Here, you can have this. It's got a tiny ship inside.

I reached in my bag and took out the snow globe, set it down on the rock beside her.

What am I supposed to do with this? I heard her call out, as I picked my way out of there. I turned round and shrugged my shoulders. Turned again and continued out of there. Was almost at the ditch trees when I heard the splash.

GAB GAB GAB GAB GAB

Down town the headbangers were on patrol. Up and down Main Street they marched, in pairs, in clusters, in single file, each one of them with a harsher face than the one before, each one of them daring me to give them the eye so that they'd have an excuse to cut loose. They could have belted me into the middle of next week for all I cared.

Pulled my hoodie tight, kept my eyes on the path in front of me, made my way further up the street. I stopped outside Masterson's jewellery shop. Stared at some watches, thought about grabbing a diamond ring in a velvet-lined box. Masterson was onto me though and I shuffled off again. Passed a building bricked-up where its windows should have been, couldn't remember what it had been before. A fashion shop. A high-class restaurant. A cocktail bar. Who knew? Passed Danté's chipper, Dunnes Stores Better Value Beats Them All, paused at where I was sure Murtagh's newsagents used to be, was greeted by a sheet of paper taped to the blacked-out window and a scrawl of handwriting that said SHOP CLOSED UNTIL FURTHER NOTICE. A couple of more headbangers appeared out of Cutthroat Alley and I turned to the window of Lally's Fashion. The naked dummies were standing in the window, and a couple of women had stopped in front of them as though they were remembering the first time they clapped eyes on the dressed dummies, gasped and turned to each other with a look on their faces that said *all I ever wanted was a fur coat*. I stopped outside Beauty by Helen and read Helen's special offer of the week, an all-inclusive face mapping, eyebrow shaping, back exfoliation, skin brightening, full body massage and something called a Brazilian that guaranteed to leave only a landing strip – whatever that meant. More empty spaces, idle offices, unfinished apartments, the paint flaking away, gaps in the windowless walls, whistles of wind trying to escape out of them and into the street. No wonder Harry and Fergal had to spend time fixing the country in McMorrow's. The entire place was up in a heap.

Pacing up and down the street got me thinking about what the girl had said about Mario. Wouldn't hurt to swing by his house. Have a talk with him about a couple of things. Man-to-man style. Without any gasping women getting in the way. I could ask him about this Paris trip. When is he planning on going and is there room for one more? Oh, and while we're at it Mario, you wouldn't happen to be my da, would you? Wasn't such a crazy idea now that I was starting to think about it.

I stopped outside the Hungry Worm, and what with Ma busy busy with her fancy man, figured it was safe to step inside today, have a think about what I would say to Mario. Pushed open the door. In I stepped.

Inside the Hungry Worm I was famous. Three gabbing women – stick thin and glistening as though they had just stepped out of a bath of liquid gold – were going on about my handiwork on Rich Hill. The three of them spoke using their throats, and such an effort for them was it to squeeze out these sounds that every word uttered sounded like it was going to be their last. Didn't recognize numbers one or two, with their batwing ears and chins you could fly an aeroplane off. But I knew who number three was.

Mario Devine's wife.

Of course they had no interest in the hooded pipsqueak sitting in to the table next to them, all set to eavesdrop on their conversation, which now involved each of them taking a turn to ask a question and then making a face as though they had just bitten into a lemon. *Who would do such a thing? What should we do? Tell the local newspaper?* Listen to them, would you! The yoga heads on them.

Tell the local newspaper! Ha! That was a good one. Imagine the headline. *Rich Hill residents express concern over defaced wall.* They could even print a photograph of the wall with my painted words, right alongside one of the three ghouls determined to find out who it was. The questions were still coming. Why do people do such things? Why do they feel the need to go about vandalizing private property? Have these young brats nothing better to do with their time? A question or two later and I was the most dangerous man who had ever lived. We are no longer safe in our homes, Mrs Mario declared. Who is this thoughtless perpetrator? Not a word of appreciation about my arty graffiti, my interesting choice of words.

So that's what I was. A perpetrator. I couldn't wait to let

Ma know. Hey! Guess what, Ma? I am a perpetrator. Good boy, she'd say. You have made me so proud.

Like hell she would.

I looked around me. Suddenly big in my boots. Feeling tough. Everything on the menu was going cheap today, and by the time the waitress was hovering, I really didn't know what to choose first.

What would you like? she asked me.

Right now, I could really go for a fast car and a million dollars' worth of cash, I said to her.

Sorry, cars are off today.

I'll leave it at the cash so.

Sorry, all the money is gone.

OK then, make it a plate of French fancies, and some doughnuts, please.

We don't have French fancies.

What kind of buns do you have?

Rock buns.

You can keep those. Just give me a doughnut.

I'm sorry, we're all out of doughnuts.

Tell you what, you choose.

My pleasure, she said, and about-turned.

The gabbing women were fairly going for it now. Washing machines. Golf holidays. Spray tans. Their ideal skin colours pouring out of them. Ah. Nothing wrong with them a cold swim in the Swamp wouldn't sort out.

Then I noticed the baba. Wasn't sure if it belonged to Mrs Mario or one of her click clack sidekicks. I stood out of my seat and stepped over to the buggy, stared down at the sleeping lizard of a thing.

Hello, baba, and what's your name? You look just like your ma, has anyone ever said that to you? They have? You look like your da, too. But I bet you get that all the time. I think I know your da. Mario. That's his name, isn't it? Super Mario he should be called. They say that around here he's the main man when it comes to selling bull nuts. My ma says otherwise. Do you know my ma? Super Mario knows her . . .

And there I was chatting away to my new friend the baba, when I was interrupted by Mrs Mario dragging the buggy and baba away from me. And I turned to the women and a look on their collective faces that said no way are we and the neighbourhood we live in going to stand for this kind of behaviour.

Ladies, I said, spreading out my arms either side of me. You don't need to look any further. It was me. I'm the one you're after.

I beg your pardon? Mrs Mario said, pulling her buggy even closer to her.

Oh, there's no need to beg. Now listen to me. The perpetrator. It's me. Jason Lowry. I just thought you might want to know.

To make sure I was getting through to them, I rolled up the sleeves of my hoodie and with both hands pointed to myself. I saw their eyes go from my face to my arms and before they could get a proper look I had the sleeves rolled back down again. By now they were looking very confused,

as though they couldn't believe they were now face-to-face
with danger, were sharing café space with a perpetrator.
Tried thinking of ways to lessen their confusion. Didn't
matter. The three of them didn't want to know a thing
about me. They were quickly finishing their cups of sugar-
free milk-free gluten-free preservative-free herb juice or
whatever it was they had ordered. One of them was at the
till paying, while another one was already out the door and
Mrs Mario was packing up her baba's soothers and wipes,
and she was putting her purse away and pulling her buggy
out of there, backing her way hurriedly into the street. I
sprang to hold the door for her, make it easier for her to get
out. Which she managed, and without a word of gratitude
for me. In a rush and ungrateful. Not a good combination,
that. Not good at all. And so fast was she out of there, she
left after her the baba's rattler. And I was out the door
myself, shaking the rattler after her, but she was gone, out
of sight, nowhere to be seen. Not to worry. I could drop it
off at her house when I called on Mario.

GRAFFITI ARTISTS

Mario lived on the other side of the hill. Not quite along the stretch of fancy houses. But close enough that he had a reasonably high wall, a couple of trees and of course a buzzer gate. Close enough that if he wanted to he could claim membership of the plush neighbourhood. I pressed the buzzer on his gate and waited for an answer.

Don't make any rash accusations. Making a rash accusation had been the ruination of many a man, I'd heard them say up the back lane. Just try to get a proper look at him. See if we had anything in common. Eyes. Attitude. Blood type. And remember: try to find out more about this Paris trip. If it was a trip for two only. If I could tag along.

There was no answer. I tried several more goes on the buzzer. Kept my finger on the keypad. Then let my pounding little fists go at Mario's gate. Banged my head off the gate until I was reeling. Still no answer. I bet the lug was still talking Paris with Ma. Maybe he'd been held up selling bull nuts to an awkward farmer. Maybe that yoga wife of his had found out what he was up to and was now busy bouncing his head into the middle of next week. I hunkered down, peered through the gap at the bottom of the gate, strained for a decent peek. That's enough of that, I said after a decent squint and I stood up again and started looking at the wall.

I was still looking at it when I saw her. Half-skipping, half-floating, almost, through the open gate of one of the plush houses. The same raggy dungarees. The tattered tackies. My first thought was: she couldn't live there. No way. No one dressed the way she dressed could live on Rich Hill. My second thought: what was she up to?

Hey! I called after her, hurrying toward the bend she had disappeared round. For a minute I thought she'd slipped away from me. Like an eel. Or one of those mermaids she was keen to end up as. But look! There she was. Standing in front of Grehan's unfinished wall. Admiring my handiwork.

I did that, I said as soon as I reached her, scarcely able to contain my excitement. She looked at me and repeated the words I'd painted.

I've got the moon in my pocket.

Good, isn't it?

What the hell is that supposed to mean?

My ma said it.

Whoopideedoo. Where did you get the paint?

Inside. There's loads of it. Brushes, too.

Well.

Well, what?

Well, go fetch. I haven't got all day.

I didn't need to be told twice. I dashed up the driveway, praying that the tins were still where I had left them, that the gabby plush-buckets from the Hungry Worm hadn't gotten to them first. They hadn't.

Is that the only colour there is? she asked me when I set down the three tins.

Yep. It's Marrakech. Goes very well with the sandy walls.

Listen to you. You'll be telling me next Picasso is your da.

Who?

Nevermind. Now. Choose a wall.

Without giving it a second thought I pointed back towards Mario Devine's place. Already she was skipping ahead of me, swinging a tin of paint.

Open the lid, please, she said as soon as we were standing in front of Mario's gate.

She yanked the brushes out of my back pocket and dipped one of them into the dark-red paint, took the dripping brush and started to paint something. I wasn't able to see until she finished and stood back like I had done the first time. I stood beside her and we both looked.

POOR PEOPLE WITH MONEY LIVE HERE

What does that mean?

Oh, I'm sure a bright boy like you will figure it out. Come on, I'm only getting started.

She wasn't lying. For the next I had no idea how long, she was busy slapping lines on the walls in front of Mario's house. Quickly she ran out of room and she was skipping on to the walls and gates of the next house. Then she asked me to go find a ladder, and I did find one by one of Fat Grehan's sheds, and she used it to scale Mario's wall and I lobbed unopened tins over the wall after her and then followed suit, and we had the lids off and she was slapping paint on the walls of the house itself and so quickly I hardly had a chance to stand back and read what was going up.

Here, she said, throwing a second brush at me. Don't just stand there. Have a go yourself.

OK, I said, and took a turn at the next wall she was moving in on. She was so fast with her lines. Was worried I wouldn't be able to keep up. No need. As soon as I approached the wall, an idea for what to slap on came to me. Then another. And another. And for the next while we took turns slapping on our lines.

DON'T GO TO WORK,
IT'S A TRAP

MARIO DEVINE WOULDN'T
SELL
BULL NUTS IN A FAMINE

FREEDOM IS AT THE BOTTOM
OF THE TENTH GLASS

MY MA CAN SHOW
YOU
A GOOD TIME

YOUR FUTURE
IS BEHIND YOU

THESE DAYS SHE LIKES
CUNTHOOKS AND GOB-PRICKS

DON'T LOOK
UNDER YOUR CAR

WANK ME WITH A
SPOON

SHE WILL LIKE YOU TOO IF
YOU PROMISE HER PARIS

TO SAIL IS NECESSARY,
TO LIVE IS NOT

STAY INSIDE TODAY OR ELSE

SHOVE IT UP YOUR
COOCH

CALL HER

THE CANCER IN MY TESTICLES IS SPREADING

By the time that last one went up we were both standing back, scarcely able to read each other's lines, so hard were we laughing. It seemed each line was better and funnier than the one before.

Wait. I just thought of another one, I said, still laughing, and quickly slapped up one last message for Mario, all the way across his buzzer gate.

PS: ANY CHANCE OF A SEAT ON THE TRIP TO *Gay Paree?*

Sign your artist name here, the girl said when we had stopped laughing. She was handing me a sharp-edged stone and pointing to the bottom of the wall where she had already scratched tiny lettering I could scarcely make out. I took the stone and did as I was told.

Good. Now, follow me, she said next and she was up and over the front wall of Mario's place, and on to the next gate and, turning to me with a grin and wink, she slapped up in great big zigzag letters:

PUT YOUR THING IN ME

I'm finished now, I said, and in spite of the imploring face on the girl for some kind of response from me, I threw down my brush and made my way back to Fat Grehan's driveway.

Hey! she called after me. We're not finished.

My arms are tired, I called back, heading up the driveway and then plonking myself down on one of the rocks. A few minutes later the girl arrived. We had used up four or five tins of paint and now I watched as she put everything back, including the ladder. Then she picked out a rock and plonked herself down beside me. Nobody had seen or heard us.

That was fun, she said when she was comfortable beside me. It's a pity there was just the one colour.

I like it.

So you keep saying, Picasso.

Your lines are good. I don't know what they all mean. But they're good.

Yours are good too. Shove it up your cooch. I like that one.

It's a line my ma uses. To sail is necessary, to live is not. What does that mean?

Whatever you want it to mean.

I like the sailing part. Sailing sounds like a good way to pass the time.

Sailors belong to no one. Not even to themselves.

I wish I knew who I belonged to.

What does that matter?

It matters because I'm living with a crazywoman. Been anywhere since I last saw you?

Oh yes. I've spent time in the lost jungle cities. I've been to a desert where it hasn't rained for four hundred years. I've taken a train that travels through the clouds.

Sounds great.

There's this place I want to go to above all others.

Where?

Ithaca.

Ithaca?

You say it very well. It's somewhere in the Mediterranean. Next to impossible to find. I've been searching and searching and I still cannot find it.

Is it part of ancient Greece?

That's right. The famous hero lived there. After the war he spent twenty years trying to find it.

What, he spent twenty years looking for where he lived?

That's right.

He sounds like a numpty.

He was a hero.

Heroes can be numpties, can't they?

You really ask the oddest questions.

Tell that to the numpty who takes twenty years to find his way home.

Twenty years is nothing. Time flies, you know.

What happened your arm?

They've been running a brush along walls all afternoon – in case you hadn't noticed.

That's not what I meant. And that bruise on your neck. It's getting worse. Where did you get it?

I can't remember.

Where is your ma?

She's out of town.

Doing what?

Oh, saving lives. I don't know. Now, please. Stop the questions.

I turned away from her. Looked out in front of me, at the town below, the Tower reaching for the sky, the cemetery where they put Flukey in the ground. She was talking again.

I wonder whose house it is. They're in for some land.

It's Mario Devine's.

Mario your-new-da Devine?

I've left a message for him – about going to Paris.

I saw that. Look. You can see my house from here.

Where?

She raised her arm and pointed towards a faraway cluster of houses, not far from the turn for the by-pass. Wondered about her da. What he did. What he looked like. Was he really as crazy as she made him out to be? Was about to ask her but she was busy reaching down in front of her to pick up something.

Show me your hand, she said.

What?

I want to check something.

Like the usual numpty I was, I offered my hand and she took it in her own, stared at it, turned it over, stared some more.

Hmmm.

Hmmm, what?

Nothing.

You can't just stare at my hand and make uppity sounds.

Can't I?

Show me *your* hand.

No.

Why not?

You'll just end up comparing and it's bad luck to compare hands. Let's make a blood pact instead.

What?

Without another word, she gripped the splinter of wood she'd picked up and punctured the palm of my hand. Then she did the same to her own hand.

Now we join, she said, holding up her hand and getting me to do the same. We locked fingers. Touched palms. Swapped blood.

Now we are inseparable, she said, glowing. Now you'll have to put your thing in me. I'll let you. Anywhere you want. I'll let you put it in my mouth if you want. You'll like it.

I pulled my hand away, looked at the cut in the middle of my palm, the smudgy blood.

You know, she said next, looking out at the view. All this painting has made me thirsty.

We could go to McMorrow's.

Have you any money?

I have two euros.

You have two euros.

Yep.

You really know how to sweep a girl off her feet, don't you?

Is that a yes?

Maybe. Oh, look! There's my father's car. Flip! He's home early. I have to go now.

She was already on her feet and heading quickly out of Fat Grehan's driveway.

Hey! I called after her and she turned around. See you in McMorrow's?

She shrugged her shoulders and kept going. It wasn't the big Yes I was hoping for, but it wasn't a No either.

HAPPY HOUR

Harry and Fergal were deep in conversation, practically touching heads, looking like a pair badly in need of those happy pills they were on about last time. Times were still tough for the lad at the end of the counter sipping from a glass with the one ice cube. At her low table by the wall, the pale-faced woman was smoking her unlit cigarette. The card game was still in progress. Shirley was staring at the high-up TV.

I climbed into a high stool at the bar. I took out the first of my euro coins, set it spinning on the counter, slapped it down in front of me.

Look who it is, Shirley said, without even turning to me.

The one and only.

Back for more punishment, then.

You'll get a crick in your neck staring up like that, Shirley.

Don't be smart. It doesn't suit you.

You were in a much better mood the last time I was in.

I'm a woman, kid. My mood changes a million times every second. What'll it be?

The usual.

Shirley grabbed a bottle, uncapped it, set it down in front of me along with a bag of nuts.

Fanta and a packet peanuts. That comes to – one euro.

I slid the coin across, took the drink and tossed it back in one long gulp. The peanuts didn't last long either.

Same again, I said, pushing the empty bottle out of my way. And another bag of peanuts.

That'll be – one euro, Shirley said.

Can you put it on my tab, Shirley? I left the rest of my money at home.

No tabs during Happy Hour, kid.

How long does Happy Hour last?

Until you run out of money.

Harry looked over and started laughing. He told Fergal what he'd heard and there were two of them at it. The lad with the one ice cube couldn't care less. Over my shoulder, the card players were slapping down coins on the table. The woman with the white face was in a world of her own. Was reaching in my pocket for the second euro when I heard Harry's voice.

Set up a drink for him, Shirley. It's on me.

I settled back into my stool. Harry winked at me. Shirley was in front of me, with an uncapped bottle of Fanta.

I suppose you think you can fly as well, she said, setting the drink down on the counter.

Of course I can, I told her. I have a magic carpet parked outside.

Shirley slid over the Fanta. Harry and Fergal raised their glasses in my direction.

Here's to the sinking ship, I said, and the pair of them were chuckling again.

And tell us, what brings you in here today, young Jason?

As my ma says, if I tell you that, Harry, I'll have to kill you.

You're a funny man, Jason.

I am, Harry. Tell me, how do you know Jesus was an Irishman?

They probably knew, but they let me finish anyway and had a laugh for themselves. We toasted the sinking ship again and I looked up at the TV, at scenes of what looked like one big happy street party going on somewhere. Then I asked Shirley for the time and she made a big show of letting me see the watch on her wrist.

Expecting company? she asked me.

Maybe.

Like that, is it?

A girl. I'm waiting for a girl.

A girl. Well, then. Tell me more. What's she like, this girl?

Short hair. Freckles. Green eyes – I think.

You think! You'll have to look closer.

Yeah. Crooked nose on her, too, but I don't mind. Lets on she knows more than she does. We hang out together up the hill.

Ohhhhh . . . I look forward to her arrival.

No sign of her, though. The loon was probably back up on the hill messing with tins of paint. Not to worry. It was still early. I finished my drink, took another look about the sorry light, was thinking of asking could I join the card game when Shirley put another Fanta in front of me. Happy

Happy Hour, she sang out, then the door swung open and in walked pretty much the entire town.

Women.

In no time the place was full of women. They arrived in all shapes and sizes, a steady parade of them, all perfume and make-up and handbags, and I didn't know where to look. Some arrived together, chattering over each other like a haggard of sparrows. Some came in pairs, and so quiet they set themselves down without anyone noticing. Some came alone.

Virgin Gemma walked in. She was a long, bony thing with lots of sharp points on her face. Everyone called her Virgin Gemma because she spent most of her time avoiding men. You would need the driveshaft of a continental lorry to get through her knickers, I'd heard the Slug Doyle say. Wasn't fully sure what he meant, but it sounded good and I'd made a point of remembering it. Steel Knickers was another name they had for her. She reminded me of a stork.

Scary Mona Quinn showed up. She always carried a stick which she used to tap the ground in front of her – as though she was blind. But there wasn't a thing wrong with her eyes. Any time somebody accidentally got too close to her she raised the stick to clobber them and never missed.

There were lots more. Julie Oaks whose bum could touch her ankles. Fionnuala Quirke who had a missing little finger on her left hand. Nora McGuinness who wore hardly any clothes no matter what weather we were having. Big Beatrice Glynn who once arrived into our house and tried to convince Ma and me she was our cousin even though she never knew my name. And a few others I didn't want to look at because I would only put myself in a worse mood.

Don't ask me where they all crawled out of. Or what was suddenly so special about McMorrow's that made it the important place for them to congregate inside. I had no answers to questions like these. And a look on Harry and Fergal that let the place know when it came to women there were only two things they wanted – distance and silence. They might as well have been asking for a trip to Jupiter.

Then Ma showed up. Wearing a black singlet with glittery writing that said *Lazy Days* and a denim skirt not much longer than the belt hitching it around her waist. The others were delighted to see her and she passed down the length of the bar, pausing ever so briefly when she caught my eye and blew me one of those kisses I thought she saved only for the boy-racers. A wonder she hadn't stayed at home listening to Mario Devine's sweet talk. No sooner was that thought in and out of my head than Mario walked in. He kept to himself at the door-end of the counter, though, giving Ma and the crew she was now with the occasional eye.

Listen to the stuff they started gabbing about. First up was the weather. The sun had been shining for more than a week and everyone was falling over themselves to make a comment about it. Wasn't it a lovely day, the women said to each other, and got nodding as though they had just come out with the most remarkable observation. They didn't leave it at that, though. It had to be a lovely day *for* something. Wasn't it a lovely day *for* the garden. Wasn't it a lovely day *for* a picnic. Wasn't it a lovely day *for* walking by the river. Wasn't it a lovely day *for* the seaside, search me how they intended getting there.

Once they had made their emotions known about the weather, they tried to have several conversations at the one time. Popular topics were *Style* magazine's ultimate guide to looking glamorous, places to see before they died, the incredible number of morons in the country, lotto numbers, hair, toddlers not going to the toilet properly, wrinkles, lip plumping, shedding pounds, Indian food, mobile phones, Mrs Redihan's garden, salsa dancing, the unopened shopping centre, the state of the Swamp, bad breath, coriander, rotting houses, men and life plans.

Then they had a conversation about car accidents. And all the things that caused the accidents. Holy Nora! I thought the day would never end. Forgetting to put on the handbrake. Opening the car door when a cyclist was going by. Pressing the accelerator instead of the brake. Putting in the wrong petrol. Driving into walls after leaning across to answer a mobile phone. They listed out damage done. Broken wing mirrors. Cracked windscreens. Twisted wipers. Falling-off registration plates. Flooding engines. Smoking engines. Slipping clutches. Banjaxed starters. Worn brakepads. Torn handbrakes. On and on it went. They must have mentioned every car part there was. They sounded like real experts. One of them – Julie Oaks I think it was – said she almost knocked down the same person three times in the one day. Was it your ex-husband? Mona Quinn asked, and they all had a good laugh.

Then it was shoes. Smoking Gemma! I never knew there were so many kinds of shoes. Wedge heels. Gladiator sandals. Thigh boots. Flip flops. Ballet pumps. Peep-toe cutouts. Glittery platforms. Ladybird wellingtons. And more. Then they started on about feet. And how feet contained secrets. And transmitted these secrets to other parts of the body. Did you know that no two feet are the same size? I didn't. Julie Oaks even said her left foot was three inches longer than her right foot. Then, as I knew she would, Ma showed them one of her feet – the one with the big toe growing in a completely different direction to the others. The rest of them had never seen anything like it. You can get that fixed, said Nora McGuinness. That got them started on operations. And the miracles doctors could perform these days. And all the things wrong with them that needed miracles. And there and then they made a list of the one thing they didn't like about themselves. The one thing they would change. Nobody mentioned the things I would have. Virgin Gemma said she wished she had Julie's teeth. Julie said she wished she had Nora's waistline. Nora said she wished she had Gemma's legs. Big Beatrice said she wished she had Mona's attitude and made a little speech about the useless cocktail of pills she was on. There was an awful lot of wishing and swapping going on. Next thing Mona said she wished she had a little boy. Then Ma started to make her wish, but stopped, and everything went quiet. I have saggy boobs, said Julie Oaks into the silence and they all started laughing again.

That got them started on men, and they were filling their

glasses with vodka and orange juice and picking bits of sausages off plates Shirley had sent out from behind the bar. But by now, I had stopped listening. As far as I was concerned, there was only one thing wrong and it was wrong with the lot of them – they were crazier than the birds.

When I looked again, Mario was on the move through the bar. He passed by me and then the gabbing women and headed down the back towards the toilet. Aha, I thought, climbing down off my stool, this is my chance to corner him for that face-to-face talk, and I started after him.

Look who it is, the women said as I made my way past them on my way through to the toilet. The one and only. Quickly, one or two made room for me where they were gathered. Arms were waving me over, then pawing at me. Ma put on her sly smile and I knew it was useless trying to keep away from them.

Look at his lovely curls, said Fionnuala, whipping the hood off me. And she ran her hand through my hair, her missing-finger hand.

I think it's his eyes, said Julie. They are so blue.

He is going to break many, many hearts with those eyes, said Big Beatrice.

It's his little cherub cheeks. They are so adorable, said Mona, and she started pulling at my jaws as though I was some sort of pet. Then Fionnuala Quirke said I looked like an angel.

An angel!

For crying out loud.

He's a sensitive boy, Ma said, putting on her best sympathy voice, I'd never heard her use words like those before and her head nodding in agreement with everything that had been said. Had a feeling she was angling for something and it was annoying me because I couldn't figure out what it was. For now, though, one thing was certain. Every woman in this room, they all thought I was the most precious thing on two legs. Every one of them wanted to be my ma.

Had just managed to wrangle myself away from them when Mario reappeared. He walked past the women and me, all the way to the far end of the bar and stood leaning against it, the leery head on him facing this way, as though all he had to do was click his fingers and Ma and all the rest of the women and every other woman in the town would drop everything and start a stampede in his direction.

And still no sign of the girl. Maybe she had an aversion to dimly lit pubs. Maybe her moods were like Shirley's and she had changed her mind a million times. Maybe she was stuck at home with her crying da and his fists banging on the table. Wait a minute! WAIT A MINUTE! Maybe he was howling like a crazy dog and busy taking everything out on the girl. Three or four hours I'd been stuck here listening to a gaggle of women talk their Happy Hour heads off while the girl's da was laying into her like there was no tomorrow. Now a big hush was going out all around me, Shirley was reaching and turning up the TV volume, and a loud call was let out, IT'S TIME FOR TONY.

Next thing, Shirley had turned up the TV volume even

more, and Ma and the rest of her crew were bunching in around me to catch a glimpse of Tony and the rest of the Sopranos and I had to listen to nonsense talk about their all-time favourite television show even though I'd say most of them had seen every episode when it was first shown, and here we go again, I was thinking, as the familiar music came on and Ma, who else, started to sing along.

It was time, alright. Time I was out of here. I had to get to the girl. Make sure she was still in one piece. Mario would have to wait.

Wasn't going anywhere fast just yet, though. Hey! Tough guy. Catch! Ma yelled at me, her voice like glue in my ears and she lobbed a shrivelled-up sausage that bounced off my shoulder and onto the grimy floor.

That Tony Soprano! said Virgin Gemma, and the rest of them weren't long chipping in.

I hope he gets it this time around, said Julie Oaks. I'm fed up with him getting off scot-free all the time.

Tony is the crime boss. He's never going to get it.

His mother had the right idea. She should have had him taken care of when she had the chance.

May his testicles shrivel up like leaves, said Mona Quinn, and that got a good laugh. May his chopper cause him severe pain before falling off, said Helena Larkin, reaching out her hands and squeezing hard. May he contract a debilitating dose of syphilis, said Una Groarke. Syphilis wouldn't be good enough for him, said Dearbhla Halpin. And what would, Dearbhla? A virulent case of the clap? The Black Death?

I know, said Emily Casey, who had been quiet up till then. Gonorrhoea.

Gonorrhoea! I thought only women could get that.

Not at all, said Loretta Waldron. Men can get gonorrhoea too. And the more the merrier.

That cracked it open. Patricia Gibbons saw Emily Casey's gonorrhoea with an abrasive assault of herpes. Wilma French saw the herpes and raised it with an irreversible case of genital warts. Sonia Breen saw the warts and trumped with a slow-burning attack of chlamydia. Joan Cahill must have been sitting on something very special because she saw the syphilis, the gonorrhoea, the herpes, the virulent case of the clap and raised the lot with an everlasting dose of the trembling shits. And after that they had to stop they were laughing so much.

And still no sign of the girl. Where was she? What was happening to her? So much for all her talk up on Rich Hill. So much for being inseparable. And then I remembered something else she'd said.

If I was going to end it all again.

Fock me!

And in an instant I knew where she was.

By now, Shirley had switched off the TV and turned on the music and they were all yelling at Shirley to turn up the volume and, uh-oh, the song coming on sounded familiar and, yes, it was the song Ma had been singing into my face at the crack of dawn the morning we heard about Flukey. A choir of screeching women erupted, singing their trollied little heads off, and so bad was it I had to cradle my face in my hands as I tried to squeeze through the jungle of limbs and flesh blocking my path out of there. And they were all pointing at me and pulling and tugging and, Jesus Christ, what did I have to do to get out of there?

Women. The lot of them out of their seats. Gyrating about the room. Howling along to the music. Falling into each other's arms. Tumbling over chairs. Slipping on puddles of spilt drink. Harry and Fergal didn't know which way to look. Mario was lapping up every minute of it. Then they were pointing at me again, and then reaching out and pulling me this way and that and making me dance with them, and there were so many arms tugging at me I couldn't do a thing to stop them.

Look at him, Ma squealed. A regular disco king. And Harry and Fergal looked, and Shirley looked, and the card players were looking at me and all that was in my ears was one long corridor of non-stop laughter. Next thing, Ma had kicked off her heels and was sliding across the room towards me. Sensing that something special was about to happen, the women made space and Ma glided up the floor, reaching out her arm and beckoning me to her with a curling finger. *So take a good look at my face. You'll see my smile looks out of place.* Closer and closer to me she glided, the booming music and non-stop laughter in my head, and suddenly the walls were closing in on me and the barroom was far too small.

Get the hell away from me, you witch! I roared into her face, and at last I was out of there. Into a mad dash down the street and panting hard.

PEOPLE LIKE CLOUDS

Getting late now, light fading. Clear sky and the air so calm. And I was running. Fast as I could. All the way down the street and onto Violin Bridge. Stared out over the bridge wall, down into the dark river below. Nothing. There wasn't a sound coming out of it. No glug-glug-glug out of the water. No sounds of hungry fish chomping on the latest loon to go flinging herself.

Then I thought: the Swamp. She's in the Swamp.

And I was moving again, faster and faster, trying my best not to picture her plunging off the rock and sinking deep. Past Mel Campbell's shop and ducked into the high end of the lane, already straining for a glimpse of her anywhere through the ditch trees.

Please let her be on the rock. Let her be gazing across the Swamp. Off on one of her adventures. The best one yet. Let this be the scene I find when I reached the Swamp.

And still not fully dark. Moved down the lane as fast as I could. The scorched breath wheezing out of me. My useless feet refusing to go any faster. Watched for jutting-out tree-roots ready to trip me up, branches curled for grabbing loons on their crazy way. Wished I'd stepped into Mel Campbell's shop and got her something. An ice cream. One with a flake. All that painting was thirsty work, I'd tell her, here, have an ice cream. Could almost see the sunny look in her face, the words forming in her mouth. *At last. A good idea out of you. Now I am impressed.*

Brains and No-brains McManus had other ideas. There they were. The ripped denims on them. The kick-hard boots. Their grinning heads spread wide across the lane. Blocking my way. Almost wished I had their knack for appearing out of nowhere.

And ice cream! The pair of them were sharing an ice cream.

Look who it is, said No-brains.

The boy from the hood, said Brains.

The most dangerous man alive, said No-brains.

And he's in a hurry, said Brains.

And they went over and back like this for a couple of minutes. Would I like some ice cream? they wondered. Maybe some for my ma? My girlfriend? Except of course they didn't really like the sound of sharing because neither one of them had had an ice cream in ages. And the pair of them stood there grinning at me, blocking my way when I tried to get by.

Let me past, I said, the blood gathering inside me. My breath hot in their faces.

What's the rush, pipsqueak? Are you late for something?

Please, let me by, I said, the heart clapping inside me now, the blood roaring.

Ha! Listen to the polite head on him.

I NEED TO GET BY! I screamed. LET ME BY, MORONS!

Didn't need to scream for too long after that. No-brains tumbled me to the ground and pinned me down. Brains stood there taking gobfuls of ice cream while his brother's arms flailed away at me.

Come on, said No-brains, have a go. But his brother wasn't in a fisticuffs mood. He dug his tongue well into the ice cream, licked for all he was worth, let the stuff smear all over his face. After another gobful or two, Brains looked gleefully at his brother, then smashed the cone to the ground. At once, No-brains threw his arms in the air, but the brother was already walking off.

No-brains was not happy. Straddling me, he picked up the useless ice cream, held it close to my face, so close I could see the dirt and weevils and earwigs and other things it had already attracted.

My brother isn't the sharing kind, is he? No-brains said, raising the filthy ice cream. But lucky for you, I am. Now, come on, open wide. He had the cone in one hand and with the other was jawing my mouth open. Come on, open wide, he said, angling the cone, and then mashing it into my mouth, nose, eyes, hair, wherever he could. Then he rubbed his sticky hands on my clothes, stood off me again and headed off after his brother.

For a few minutes I lay there in the dirt. Wiped ice cream away from my eyes, gazed up at some dark clouds. They were skidding by and the early stars were breaking through. I watched a jumbo-jet ski across the atmosphere until it disappeared, wondered where it was headed at this late hour, wished myself aboard. I felt a line of ice cream run down the side of my face and wiped it clear. Poked a finger into a white blob that had landed in the dirt, closed my eyes and sucked good. I thought of the girl, the look on her face when she saw the ice cream head on me. Reached my hand inside my pocket, wrapped my fingers around Ma's razor-blade and, keeping my eyes closed, squeezed until I was wincing with relief.

When I opened my eyes all the clouds were gone, was looking up at an empty sky. And I thought: People. Around here some of them are like clouds. Once they clear out of sight, it's a beautiful day.

Fully dark now. Temperatures coming down.

There was no sign of her at the Swamp. No sign of anyone having taken a running jump into the hidden pools. Well. That was something at least, and I breathed easy.

I saw the scryer hovering over the ditchwater, holding herself. Made my way as far as her.

Annie, let me have tomorrow's lotto numbers please.

Not a peep out of her.

OK then, let me have five numbers please. Five is plenty, Annie, whenever you're ready.

Still nothing. I was starting to wonder if she could see into the future after all. At this stage I wasn't even con-vinced she could speak.

Four numbers, Annie. It's my final offer. Otherwise, I'm

going to have to force you to speak. And, believe me when I say it, it will hurt me more than it will hurt you.

She didn't say a thing. And she wasn't about to fall for my rough talk.

Don't suppose you have an answer to my usual question either? No? I thought not. Your gift is wasted on you, Annie, I said, resting my hand on her shoulder. And I continued down the lane.

The drunks were gathered around their cans. Cracking them open, glugging good and staring at the black sky. Booze always brought out the pop star in some of them and they were croaking out their three-word-songs.

I loved her. I loved her. I loved her.
So I did. So I did. So I did.
She left me. She left me. She left me.
So she did. So she did. So she did.

Ah, would you look who it is, one of them said as I approached, a long stick of a thing in a raggy suit. He didn't have a clue who I was.

He looks as though he has the world on his shoulders, chuckled another, a gargoyle with mulch for teeth and a furry nose.

There's a story from the past preventing him getting on with his life.

He's lost all his money, declared a squint-eyed thing with hollowed-out jaws.

Maybe he's in love, said Raggy Suit.

He's in the last of the last days so, the gargoyle said, and the comment was greeted with a collective roar.

Let me buy you a drink and you can tell us all about it, Raggy Suit said, reaching out a can to me. But I was in no mood for a can. I was eyeing up the starlit Swamp, still casting about for a glimpse of the girl, wishing I hadn't bumped into Brains and No-brains McManus, all the time thinking to myself, next time, next time. Next time I'd have something for her.

As though they could see into my thoughts, the drunks let another collective cheer out of them, and I looked at the beaten-down state of them and half-smiled, glad to have received their support. I left them to their songs and headed home.

*

Through the crack in the door I could see her. Bouncing up and down on Mario's sturdy knees. Her knockers swinging good-o. Her face a picture of steely intent. Up and down, she went. A little to the left, a little to the right. Oh, yes, baby. Oh, please, baby. And all the time those boggy hands of Mario steering her hips around and around. I couldn't look for more than a few seconds or I'd get dizzy.

Are you back already! she screeched when I marched in, and a face on Mario somewhere between Holy Fuck and Thank Christ.

How much does she owe you, Mario? I said, and a spiky heel I needed to duck away from, or else, came whizzing across the room.

MORE COCKROACH THAN WITCH

I was lying in my bed. Had no idea what time it was. After midnight, I'd say. Well after. Another calm night. Quiet too. Wondered if Mario was still knocking about.

Raised my arms and looked at them. Thought about the girl. The bruise on her neck. Hoped she was OK.

Thought about Ma. Her singing friends. That crazy Happy Hour. That spinning shoe.

Had even started thinking about that Paris trip, when I heard them in the next room. Fock me! He *was* still knocking around. Listen to him. The cobblestone talk out of him. The Moulin Rouge and the Left Bank Café. Before he had a chance to mention bread, I was whipping the blanket off me.

Downstairs I switched on the TV. The picture was pink, like it had been since the start of summer. News was coming on. It's Saturday, the 18th of July, and here is the late news, the newswoman purred. She looked pretty good in pink whoever she was and I turned up the sound in time to hear a story about a jumbo jet on its way to France missing somewhere over the Atlantic since the start of June. The search team was still looking for wreckage and bodies – in the middle of a raging storm. Good luck with that, I said, and turned the thing off again.

Could still hear them upstairs. Urgent and noisy with it. Turned the TV on again. Cranked up the volume. Watched a chef showing a kitchen full of learner-cooks how to do it properly. He had a funny way of going about it. Fuck me, he said, as soon as one of the others put on a saucepan of potatoes. Soon the learner-cook was in tears. Fuck me, the chef said again, as soon as he saw the tears and the learner-cook ran out of the kitchen. Fuck me, he said again, flicking his apron and going wrinkly all over. If it was me, I wouldn't have run away. I'd have grabbed the saucepan and clattered Mr Fuck Me down on top of his wrinkly head. Imagine if he ever landed inside our kitchen. *Oh my, that is very delicious, the most delicious thing I have ever tasted,* he'd tell Ma, licking the fingers he had just poked into one of her simmering pots. Like hell he would. *Fuck fuck fuck fuck me*, he'd say to her when he saw what she was up to, and give her several clips across the ears.

Turned it off again.

Listen to them!

Fock me!

Switched on again just in time for the late film. Something with a lad in jeans and a t-shirt, who had just struck up a conversation with a girl spinning a baton in the middle of the road. I've got some things I want to say, he said to the girl and, though she didn't let on too much, you could tell she was interested in what those things might be. Was interested myself. He was a cool customer, standing there in his jeans and tight t-shirt, the sort that had detected a big picture for himself, even if all he did for now was empty rubbish bins. If he did have anything to say, he was keeping it to himself. He was just standing there, flicking his hair, like someone without a care in the world. Next thing he had shot the girl's da, torched the house she lived in, and they were on the run together, shooting everything in sight.

So much for not having a care in the world.

I liked the girl. She reminded me of the girl at the Swamp – a slightly older version. Another wisp of a thing. Freckles either side of her nose. Shorter hair, though, and a softer voice. Maybe they were related, sisters who had never met. She didn't seem to mind her life on the run with a killer, didn't care that they had no place to go except drive through vast territories where there were no towns, no people, nothing to see save for telephone poles and the sun going down at the end of the day. They stopped when they needed to find some petrol for their car, get something to eat, one night they did a little close-up dance beneath the dark sky. They were so alone, and whenever either of them spoke you could tell that deep down they both knew it. Knew that there was only one way their story was going to end. Of course the ad break had to ruin the mood. Still though. Got to see what the movie was called. *Badlands*. That's what it was. I liked that name. Liked it a lot.

Left Freckles and T-shirt to it, and wobbled like one of the back-lane drunks into the kitchen, stumbled into a chair, rested my head on the table. What was I like? Hadn't even tasted Ma's vodka and here I was staggering about the place. Rubbed my eyes and then stared at the bockety wall clock. The second hand took one step forward. Then it changed its mind and went back to where it was. Forward it went again, then back to where it started from. And again. Gave my eyes another rub, but it made no difference. The second hand was going nowhere. The clock stayed at the same time. Then I knew the girl was wrong. Time didn't fly. It didn't go anywhere. It made me wonder how I came to be here, sitting at this rickety table, staring at a no-go clock. Then I was worried that time had stopped and that I'd be forever stuck inside the boghole town I lived in.

Opened the back door and stood outside. Thought of the Swamp out there and felt scryer Annie's eyes boring through me. Heard some laughter. A man's. Whoopee! The bull-nut seller had just made another sale. Thought if I hung around down here long enough Mario would show his face. Could have that talk with him. Man-to-man style. Could find out how he was fixed for having another kid in his life. Didn't sound like he was in a rush, though. Stepped into the back yard. Gazed up into the dark sky. That was the place for her. My mother the witch. Put her aboard a broomstick and let her take off. That's it, Ma. Fly away. You'd be doing us both a favour.

Although now that I had a chance to think about it, she was more cockroach than witch.

Indestructible.

Reached for the razorblade. Gripped it tight. Held up my arm and let the starry night shine on it. Let the blade edge dance cold and ticklish along the cuts I'd made. Thought of the girl again. Wished her beside me now. Tried to come up with some words I could throw her way if she was. Impressive lines. Stuff to make her admire me. Hey, girl! Let's spill some blood. What do you say? No? Not tonight? Another time, then. What's that, girl? You want me to say something else? Something cool. Something hip. Something you'll remember me by. OK, then. I like who I am when I'm with you. That's the best I can do for now.

Inside again, I heard the pitter patter of feet, the toilet flushing. More sounds arrived. A giddy moth. Worried floorboards. Clinking in the darkness. Upstairs, I heard Ma coughing as if she was having a fit. Maybe her fast life was finally catching up with her, her kidneys had gone into revolt, or some other inside part of her. Maybe she was thinking of all the money she owed. Maybe, like me, she was thinking about faraway places. I hauled myself upstairs, and fell into bed.

Some time after – seconds, minutes, a half an hour – I thought I heard someone come into the room. Ma, I supposed, who else could it be? She sat at the end of the bed. And for once I was almost hoping she might start into a song and have me guessing names. Or get stuck into one of those stories she used to tell me when I was very little. One I hadn't heard before, about some mystery man she had known sometime in the past, someone she suddenly had lots to tell me about. But she didn't start into a song or any kind of story. She just sat there in the darkness, saying nothing.

FLOATING KIDNEYS, RENAL MALFUNCTION, GALLSTONES IN MY PANCREAS AND DANGLING RUGBY BALLS

Early morning, the phone was ringing and lo and behold there was something wrong with my pancreas. It had enlarged, was full of stones, the juices leaking out of it were playing havoc with my bowels. I needed intensive care and expert medicine. More than money could buy. And my kidneys. They were more or less kaput. One of them was floating. The other had been invaded by parasites. It was all down to the drinking water. Any day now E-coli was the likely possibility.

That's right. E-coli! I could hear Ma yell, really revving up now. A deadly thing. Has wiped out much of Africa. AFRICA you hear me! Then there was a little more about my symptoms. My skin was blue and blotchy. The black, tarry urine was now a yellow-green sap. The smell continued to defy description. Meantime, just like I could have predicted, the cancer in my left goolie had spread to the right one. My poor boy, she whimpered into the phone. It's like he has two rugby balls dangling out of him. You should see him try to walk.

She was pacing about the sitting room, one hand pressing the phone to her ear, her free arm wrapped around herself the way Annie the scryer did, shivering. And she was twisting and turning, and flicking her bobbed hair, and moving the receiver from one hand to the next. It was a great show. So convincing was she, I could feel the various body parts inside me squirming as soon as they were mentioned.

What do you mean this has nothing to do with you? I heard her say next. She removed the phone from her ear, held it out in front of her and gave it a look that could've turned round a big ship. Well, I have to say I disagree with you, she said next. This has everything to do with you. It has everything to do with you and the lord and master telling you to call me up first thing with your bully-boy tactics. What's that? Don't make me throw up. I need every penny to save my boy. Do you understand me? You don't! Well, I have to say I find your attitude very disappointing. Let me ask you another question, then. Have you ever had renal malfunction?

She was rolling her eyes as the words left her mouth, squeezing her free hand into a little fist.

Yes! They'll end up hard as rocks if we're not careful. And this can lead to renal malfunction. Then he'll need dialysis. And a transplant. And I think it's safe to say that you and the bully-boy you work for won't be the ones rushing in to the emergency room with a set of dripping kidneys to hand over. Now if you don't mind. My poor boy has just pissed himself for the one hundredth time this week.

*

You better sit down, I told her after she'd hung up. Sit down on the sofa and I'll turn on the television.

She ignored my invitation. She was wandering aimlessly about the sitting room, all tossed hair and streaky-make-up eyes, she looked like someone who had been sleeping in the back lane ditch.

What did the caller want? I asked.

I don't remember.

They didn't sound like the sort who will take no for an answer.

Didn't they?

You told them what to do, I said.

What would you do without me? she said, waving me out of her way and making her way in to the kitchen.

Is Mario still here? I called in to her.

What? Is who where?

Are you going to work today?

I haven't decided yet. Please stop asking questions.

She padded back into the sitting room, a rollie in one hand, a drink in the other. This time she cleared some empty cans off the sofa and sat down.

I was thinking, Ma.

Uh-oh.

When you're on the phone you should say there is something wrong with you. Not me.

You think so.

It would save you a lot of pretending.

What the hell is that supposed to mean?

I was just thinking.

Well, here are three words of advice for you: don't think so much.

That's four words.

That's good advice.

Before I had a chance to say another word there was a knock at the door. And before she had a chance to tell me otherwise, I made a dash for it, and when I swung it open there was cop Lawless standing on the step. It's for you, I yelled, hurried on and plonked myself at the top of the stairs.

Cop Lawless. The large lump of him all over our doorstep. The stern head. The garda hat. And he wasn't going anywhere until Ma came to the door and listened to what he had to say. I was interested myself and could soon hear Lawless rehashing my latest trip up Rich Hill, and the small matter of a number of walls and gates being defaced and residents coming home from work to find upsetting slogans painted all over their property.

Slogans! Ma gasped, doing her best to give Lawless the reaction he was chasing from her.

That's right, Lawless said, at last taking off his garda hat, delighted with himself to have a chance to say some more.

What sort of slogans?

Well, that's just it, Jacinta, it's OK if I call you Jacinta? Thanks. Well, the slogans mention, among other things, a certain woman and things she's interested in, things I'd rather not say out loud – if you get my drift – and there's a phone number up there and . . .

. . . And did you call it? Ma interrupted, reaching for the sleeve of his uniform.

Well, I did, you know, just to see, and, well . . .

. . . Yes, said Ma, returning her hand to her face, scarcely able to stand the suspense.

And nothing. It rang out.

Oh. As a matter of interest, why are you telling me all this?

Well, I thought you should know.

And what are these things this woman is supposed to be interested in?

Well, I can't recall the precise wording. But it's . . . just . . . you know, childish stuff.

And he was fumbling away and getting his lines mangled and Ma was standing there enjoying his discomfort, and when I tuned in again, Ma was not making it go easy for him.

Let me get this straight. He defaced a wall.

That's right.

A wall!

That's right.

What sort of a wall?

A granite wall.

A granite wall! Nice walls, I hear. Granite walls. And how did he deface this granite wall?

He must have found some paint.

Paint?

Yep. Marrakech.

Marrakech? What's that?

The colour.

Marrakech is a colour?

It's a dark-red colour.

Why not just say dark red, then?

I suppose so.

And you're sure it was him? Out of all the brats and wasters and general scumbags knocking about the place with nothing to do, he's the one.

That's just it. He admitted to it – in the Hungry Worm.

Say that again, please.

He announced it to one of the residents, and more or less in front of Mattie Conlon and the other waitress.

What!

That's more or less it.

He said it was him.

That's right.

The little pri—! Hang on. You don't think someone could be trying to frame him?

And why would someone do that?

Yes, I see your point. Well. What should we do with the little toe-rag?

Well, for starters, he ought to apologize to the residents. Then, perhaps he can clean off what he did. And maybe on this occasion we can issue him with a severe warning. It's not as if he's a menace, now, is it?

A warning! Ma said to all that, as though she was scarcely believing what she was hearing. Surely, we can do better than that.

Well, I don't think . . .

We should put him in stocks in the Market Square. Make a proper example of the little pup.

Well, eh . . .

I know. We could use the Tower. About time that useless monstrosity was put to some good. Take him to the Tower. Yes. Let's do that. Then we'll go for a coffee and plan some torture.

That's funny, Jacinta . . .

Funny! Do I look like I'm joking?

Well, no, I suppose you don't.

By now I was silently applauding every word and gesture out of Ma, was doing my best not to laugh every time she opened her mouth. I knew she knew I was listening.

What about hauling him before Deeley the judge? I hear he's a real bastard.

Ah, I don't think that will be necessary.

Ah, come on. Please tell me you don't at least have a dirty dungeon we can chuck him into. Into the dirty dungeon with him and throw away the key. I, for one, would be glad to see the back of him.

Lawless didn't know what to say to that and she flashed a glance up the stairs at me and winked.

Let's just make sure it doesn't happen again. What say you we leave it at that on this occasion, Jacinta?

That's it. He's getting off with a soft warning and some cleaning?

I think so.

What did you say that colour was?

Marrakech.

Marrakech?

That's right.

I must look out for it. Well, if there's nothing else, I have to get dressed.

But of course there was something else and now I was hearing about my visit to the Hungry Worm and the fright-of-her-life bat-ear Devine had for herself when she saw me yakking away to her baba. Next thing, cop Lawless was relaying the highlights of my talk with the baba, the strange questions I had, my peculiar interest in all things Mario – a wonder Lawless didn't produce the baba as a witness there and then, the way he was going on. And then it was back up to Rich Hill and more graffiti talk, with special mention of the message I'd left for Mario and the trip to *Gay Paree*.

Harassing! I heard Ma howling at Lawless when I tuned back in.

Well, now, I probably wouldn't go quite that far myself, Lawless was saying, but, you know, at the same time, the little fellow had them worried. Not that that means any-thing, Lawless was fast to add, and sure he wouldn't be the first lad to be seen chatting away to a baba. So don't worry, Lawless went on, she doesn't want to take it any further. So long as he doesn't show up pestering her again. Between you and me, I think she felt sorry for the lad.

I'd say Ma wasn't listening to any of it, especially to that bit about feeling sorry for me, could even hear her chuck-ling at Lawless, and then Lawless was having a giggle about something too, he was trying not to, but between Ma swish-ing away for him and the way she was reacting herself, who could blame him? And listen to the pair of them! Next thing they were both cracking up, they thought the whole business was hilarious, were regarding me and my idea for tagging along on the trip to *Gay Paree* as some source of amusement, like circus-clown entertainment.

Is there anything else, Garda Lawless? Ma asked him when the giggling simmered down, knowing full-well he was dying to stick around, the dressing gown practically falling off her. By now, Lawless cared little about defaced walls, Rich Hill could fall off the end of the world if it meant he could come sniffing the breeze that was threatening to once and for all open the belt on Ma's dressing gown.

Eventually he put his hat back on, about-turned and was on his way, but not before he made sure to let Ma know he was there for her if she needed anything, and he meant *anything*, and not to be shy about calling him up, at any time, he'd be only too happy to drop everything he was doing and dash to her assistance. And I could see the winking eyes on him, oh yes, he thought he was next in line for something very special. Well, think again, Lawless.

Ma closed the door and stepped back inside, shaking her empty glass as though wondering what had happened to the tall drink in it a few minutes ago. And I was thinking to myself, that's some show you just put on, Ma. If ever I get around to annihilating everybody in this town and am hauled in front of the bastard judge Deeley and anybody else who wants to find out exactly what was going on inside my mind, I am going to get them to direct all their questions to you, Ma. Ask her, I'll say, pointing you out, she'll put on a fine spectacle. The only part I didn't like was bat-ear Devine saying she felt sorry for me. I didn't need any sympathy. Not from her. Not from anyone.

What an arse! I heard Ma say to the closed door, and she made some crack about the bandy legs on cop Lawless stepping up to our door, accusing her boy of vandalism and harassment.

Ah, there you are still, she said, looking up the stairs at me. Good boy. You know what I think I am going to do today?

No.

I think I'm going to smash the place up. You know. Cut loose a little. Take out my frustrations. By the way, before I start, what exactly had you in mind messing about at Devine's house?

She stood at the bottom of the stairs, looking up, leaning against the door, her fingers drumming the hallway wall, waiting for an answer out of me. I could tell she would wait until doomsday if she had to.

I wanted to see Mario, I said.

Oh, it's Mario, is it? And what did you want to see him for?

I wanted to ask him something.

Oh yes. And what would that be? You better not be thinking what I think you're thinking.

I said nothing to that and she stood there, her hand still drumming, trying to figure out a way inside my thoughts.

Anything's possible, isn't it? I said next.

Mario Devine! Eh, let me have a little think. No. It is not

possible. And what's all this about graffiti? You better not
be saying awful things about me on these Marrakech walls.

It was just a bit of fun.

A bit of fun. Yes. I like fun, too.

I didn't mean anything by it.

Of course you didn't.

She started to ask another question, but for some reason
she lost interest as soon as she began.

And for a minute, quiet and uncertain, she stood there
at the bottom of the stairs, still as stones. It was hard to
know if she wanted more of a response out of me or if she
was going to forget about the whole thing. I was about to
offer up some more about what I'd been up to, anything
to break this eerie quiet between us, when she was on
the move again, swaying from side to side, giving me
and the place in general her don't-you-know-anything look,
letting all about her know she had a couple of hundred
lumps she wanted to knock out of everything including
maybe me, and she must have been itching to get started
because by the time I hauled myself fully downstairs she
was already smashing up the place.

What's wrong, Ma? I asked, following her into the
kitchen, and she marched to the window, lifted up the potted
plant and flung it. I had to duck out of the way, but luckily
her throw arm wasn't very strong and the pot bounced off
the wall and landed harmlessly on the floor, some clay spilling out of it the only damage done. She thought better of
having another go. Instead, she picked up the eternity candle
she'd bought ages ago to bring some calm into the house and

flung it in the same direction. This time she fared out better. The eternity candle smashed and pieces of glass and bits of candle sprayed everywhere. She wasn't finished yet. She yanked out a drawer of odd knives and forks and let it drop to the ground. She hopped a couple of cooking pots off the kitchen wall. Cups, glasses, plates and bowls quickly followed. Then she marched back into the sitting room where she picked up one of the candlesticks from the mantelpiece and swiped at framed photographs of herself as a young girl, and one of her holding me as a baba. The mantelpiece clock was sent tumbling to the ground. Her tobacco pouch. A box of matches. The second candlestick. When there was nothing left on the mantelpiece she scanned the rest of the sitting room, and hurled the candlestick at the television. Then she picked up one of the photographs – the one of her holding me as a baba – pulled the frame apart, and tore the photograph in two. She looked around her again, but she was losing energy now, and after an out-of-breath couple of minutes she let the torn-up photograph drop to the ground. It was some show.

OK, she said, putting out her arm to lean against a wall, panting. You are now receiving a warning: go near Devine's house again and I am going to have you thrown into a septic tank. Are we understanding each other? I nodded. She had to wait to get her breath back before she could get this complete mouthful out, but I could tell she wasn't that interested in hearing a thing out of me. Listen to this, pipsqueak, she said, and it seemed another person had stepped into Ma's skin, a demon of a person at that, whose voice I barely recognized, and whatever it was this voice had to say, it was going to get said only once, and if I so much as dreamt about presenting myself in front of Mrs Mario Devine ever again I'd better get ready to spend the rest of my life without arms and legs and a whole bunch of inside parts. I will dropkick you into the Swamp, she said. I will hop your head off the roadside kerb, she said. I will stab you in the spleen with this, she said, picking up a shard of glass. Have you got that? she screamed at me. A nod of your daft noggin will do. Well?

I nodded my daft noggin.

Good boy, she said, and kneeling down in front of me, with both hands she gripped either side of my face and squeezed for all she was worth. Then she grabbed her vodka bottle and tobacco pouch, stormed out of the room, and stomped upstairs and slammed the bedroom door after her. That suited me fine. It was just me and the shard of glass.

THE NEXT HAPPY DAY

Ma kept a hurley stick in the press beside the cooker. A photograph of Marlon Brando and two bottles of wine, one empty, one full. I was thinking about the first time I'd seen the photograph, how I'd made a fast grab for it and then went running to her. Is this Da? I said and, oh boy, did that set her off. You should have seen her. Bent over in half, out of breath, red in the face, and all the time this hysterical laughter coming out of her, the pointing finger on her going from me to the photograph I was still clutching. Two hours later she was still laughing. I didn't know a person had so much laughter inside them. I felt like a fool asking the question, made sure I gave Marlon Brando my dagger look and from that point on set myself the task of not asking Ma questions about photographs of men kept in kitchen presses. What's with the bottles of wine? I asked her when she was normal again. The empty one, I drank two hours after giving birth to you, she told me. The full one, I'm saving for the next happy day in my life.

The next happy day in my life.

That might be her birthday. She was going to be thirty in a few weeks. Or thirty-one. I wasn't fully sure, and the mood she was in right now I knew better than to ask. I wrote a fast list of things I thought she could do with. A lead cake. Some sods of turf with candles. Cleaning products and a six-pack of Dettol. Happy Birthday, Ma, I'd tell her, handing over the bucket and mop, may the best of your past be the worst of your future. Like hell I put down those things. My noggin wasn't that daft.

Ask the girl. Her know-it-all head would come up with something. She'd point me to the shapeliest high-fashion dress, the rarest pearl necklace, the most sought-after perfume, the best-tasting chocolates this side of those Russian Steppes. Wait a minute. Her ma was gone. What would she know about it? Ah. No use getting into a flap about it just now. I still had time to think of something.

First things first, though. I took one look about the place and knew there was one thing that could be done.

Tidy up.

After her smash-up it was the least I could do. Get back in her good books. Make myself useful. Essential even. Let her know that chucking me into a septic tank was the last thing she should be at.

As best I could, I bent the candlesticks back into shape and gathered up the soil that had spilled from the flower pot. Had a go at gluing the eternity candle back together. Even tried to patch up the torn photograph, put it back inside the damaged frame. It was while at this that I noticed the pile of cans and bottles that had been steadily accumulating and I grabbed a bin bag and cleared them all out of sight. I picked rollie-ends off the carpet floor, matches out of holes in the sofa, scratched away at burn marks. Between the folds in the sofa I pulled out socks, dirty tissues, some copper coins, a banana skin, an ashtray, part of an old atlas and a pair of underpants that definitely did not belong to me or Ma.

Asia and Africa were missing from the atlas, and more or less all of North and South America, which didn't leave much else of the world to choose from. But there was a good portion of Europe still intact, including two fair-size pages of the Mediterranean Sea with Greece and so many islands that no wonder the girl couldn't find the one she was looking for.

Once my work in the sitting room was done I hauled myself as far as the upstairs bathroom. A pyramid of knickers and bras greeted me. Glittery singlets and short skirts and other skimpy things with see-through sections, whether the holes had appeared over time or were there to begin with was hard to tell. I gathered the colourful pile and crammed them all into a clothes basket that had seen better days. Then I grabbed a towel and went at the sink and bath. From around the rim and plugholes collected several wigs' worth of hair. Toothpaste stains and eyeliner and blobs of makeup. Put the lids back on perfumes, moisturizers, creams, and lots of other stuff that kept her looking the way she did. Threw out dirty shampoo bottles, emptied mouldy glasses. With a page of newspaper cleaned the mirror until it was clearer than air.

After the bathroom I took myself back downstairs and spent some time with the kitchen sink. Washed dishes, cups, plates, spoons, forks and pots. Swept the floor, polished tiles, scrubbed the grimy cooker. I had to get down on my knees, crawl into corners, gather all the broken glass, cup handles, bits of smashed plates. Then I opened up the food presses. Inside was heaving with activity. A gang of ants having a great time feasting on a ripped-open sugar bag. Three or four wasps pigging out deep inside a lidless jam jar. Teabags sprouting fur. I pulled out shrivelled-up cabbage leaves, mouldy apples, a soggy box of eggs. Spotted an intact Mars bar and pocketed it to keep it out of harm's way. I grabbed a spatula and thought about massacring a troop of dancing daddy-long-legs. With my fist squashing into goo a handful of blue-arse flies. But I let them all buzz and dance about the place, somehow managed to shoo them into the back yard.

In the yard I spotted a rat and chased it round the walls. With a rusty nail thought about skewering the worms and scalping snails, pressing between thumb and finger the slimy flesh that remained. But I could think of better ways to use the nail and slipped it in my pocket alongside the Mars bar. When I wasn't looking, a squadron of black beetles decided the coast was clear and made a break for a crack in the mossy wall, but the coast was anything but clear and soon they were skittering here, there and everywhere, their ranks a scattering chaos fearful of being levelled into a tarry mess. I lifted up loose rocks and thought long and hard about using them on woodlice thinking they could hide forever from the world. I could've bludgeoned a quarry of earwigs, made dust out of a nest of caterpillars. An army of ants scurried helplessly for the ragged hills in the wild garden.

And, at last, I cornered the rat and with the spatula raised high, loomed over the skin-and-bone rodent, all set to bash it into a beetroot-coloured pulp. Before cutting loose I glanced at the wild garden and thought: the council men faffing about the Swamp are right. This is thirsty work. And when I looked again the rat had disappeared.

By the time I was done and rested, Ma had reappeared. She made straight for the fridge, took a look for more booze, made herself comfortable on the patchy sofa.

Look, Ma, I said, with my arms making a sweep of the room.

Look at what.

Notice anything different.

No.

Ah, I'd say you do. Go on. Take a guess. First thing that comes to you.

We've won the lotto.

No.

You've changed your hairstyle.

Not that either.

Well, whatever it is, break it to me gently.

I've tidied up, Ma. The place is spotless.

Oh, you've tidied up, she said, nodding vaguely. Good boy.

I did the living room.

Oh, my.

The kitchen is as good as new.

Isn't that something.

And I cleared the yard.

What would I do without you?

By now she had spread herself on the sofa, was reaching for her glass and tobacco pouch.

Here, let me get those for you, I said, lunging to her assistance. And I can turn on the TV. There might be an afternoon movie for you. An episode of Tony Soprano. That's it, make yourself comfortable.

She stayed on the sofa, staring at the pink TV. From time to time I refilled her glass, made sure her tobacco was close by, checked the fridge for ice. There was no sign of Tony Soprano, but soon one of those old gangster films came on. A lad with frightening eyes and a wide ugly mouth was giving someone his marching orders. Get out of town by tomorrow, he snarled, pointing his tommy gun, his wide ugly mouth getting wider and uglier. Otherwise you'll be leaving in a pine box. Next thing, all hell was breaking loose on the mobster streets, machine-gun fire lighting up the dark-of-night screen, sirens blaring. She wasn't in the least bit interested. A pig could've come flying through the window. A bouncing bomb could've landed on top of the house. I could've poured petrol over the television, the sofa, the person spread across it. I could've flicked a lit match, cut loose with a blow torch. She wouldn't so much as bat an eyelid.

A penny for your thoughts, I said to her, fed up now with all this silence.

Ha! Don't make me laugh.

OK, then. What about a euro?

It'll cost you more than that.

You want to know what I was thinking?

Not right now.

I'll tell you anyway, I said next, opening the ragged atlas and getting set to join her on the sofa. I was thinking me and you should go on a holiday.

Oh yes.

The Russian Steppes. That's where I was thinking.

Think some more.

Or the Colosseum in Rome.

I wonder what we'll do there.

And I hear Greece is a great spot. There's loads going on in Greece.

Oh yes. Loads.

My friend has been there. Did I tell you about my friend? We've been hanging out together.

You have a friend? That's interesting.

She tells me things. She knows lots of stuff.

Oh. It's a *she*. This *is* interesting.

We hang out together. Talk about where we might go.

Talking is good.

Her ma is gone, but her da is still around.

Is he now?

He's been crying for a long time. He doesn't sound like he's camped out under a happy star.

My heart is bleeding for him.

We were thinking. He could call around to see you.

What did you just say?

Her ma is gone and her da is crying and taking his fist

out on everything. He sounds like he needs to call around to see you.

I think you better stop talking now. Have you stopped? This might encourage you.

And with those words she was up on her feet and stepping into the kitchen where she rummaged for what it was she wanted before she marched back into the sitting room and, with a tremendous thud, brought the hurley stick down on top of the television. At once the picture changed from pink to green. She didn't seem to mind, though. She dropped the hurley and returned to the sofa.

So? Have you stopped? Oh, good. And now I would like you to make yourself scarce. Think you can manage that? There's no need to answer. A nod will do. That's it. OK. Goodbye now, see you later. Much later.

She hadn't another word to say, and somewhere inside the slow glare she was offering the room, I caught a scene from my near future. A mad woman flinging glass across the room, leaping off the sofa and with her weapon of choice – spatula, brush handle, hurley stick – one more time ripping through the sitting room, scalping and battering and lashing out at everything in her line of vision before turning her wrath on her one son, her only child, and with one almighty swipe knocking his head into the nearest septic tank. And I was looking at her and all I wanted to say was, *can I get you something, Ma? Anything you say. Just name it.* But it was obvious she was fed up with all my questions and wanted me out of there. I wasn't getting another word out of her, not even a let me have a think about that, Jason, let me think about what I want and I'll get back to you. No sir. All I was getting was make yourself scarce for a good while.

Whatever you say, Ma. Whatever you say.

A PLATE OF SPUDS SKINS AND ALL

So there are three men waiting to be executed. A Frenchman. An Italian. And Murphy. In turn, the captain of the
execution squad visits the condemned men in their cells to
offer them a last meal. So what would you like? he says
to the Frenchman. I would like *chicken cordon bleu* the
Frenchman says, flicking an index finger off the tip of his
proud moustache, and a few minutes later he is served
his meal which he gnashes down like there is no tomorrow.
Then he is taken out and shot. What would you like? the
captain says to the Italian. *Pasta primavera*, implores
the Italian, with a theatrical though fatalistic sweep of his
arms, and a few minutes later he is served his meal which
he forks inside him as though his life depends on it. Then
he is taken out and shot. What would you like? the captain
says to Murphy. I'd like a plate of spuds, skins and all,
Murphy says, licking his chapped lips and rubbing together
his huge, boggy hands. A few minutes later the captain
returns empty-handed, and with regret informs Murphy
that his request cannot be granted at this time because
potatoes are out of season. Not to worry, Murphy says,
making himself comfortable on his bunk, I can wait.

Was that a joke, Slug?

Of course it was a joke. What the hell did you think it was?

I don't think I get it.

What! What do you mean you don't get it?

What's Murphy waiting for? Apart from a spud and a bullet.

Ah, for feck's sake. Why are you even asking that? You know what your problem is, little man?

No.

You're thick as well as clever. Now go away, I'm trying to catch something here and I can tell you're bringing me bad luck.

The Slug stopped talking, turned away from me and cast his line into the Swamp. I watched his wizened old face and brittle arms, and for a second wondered what he would've been up to as a boy. Then I watched four or five council men try to straighten the KEEP OUT sign. On a dock leaf below me, two ladybirds approached each other. A frog stuck its head out of the scumwater, took a look around with its beady eyes and ducked below again. Didn't blame him. I could still hear the Slug muttering unhappily to himself as I made my way out of there. And he thought I had problems.

I headed up the back lane, thinking about that useless joke, thinking about Ma's reaction when I mentioned the girl's da. Thinking about the next happy day in her life and what I could get for her birthday. Some kind of skirt. Fancy eye make-up. A bunch of flowers from the garden next door. I thought of calling over to see Gavin McGoldrick, ask him did he have a sports car going cheap. I could see the look on Gavin's face when I showed up. Don't worry, Gavin. The tarry urine is no more. The swelling has gone down, the smell belongs in the past. Now like never before Ma could use a fast car, Gavin, show what me you've got.

I was kicking stones ahead of me when I heard the ticking spokes and ringing bell. Then the familiar voice.

How's Medusa? Barrabas Diffley, the cycling postman, asked me. He was lurking about the bushes stretching over the end of the back gardens. His big arms ferreting about inside his sack of letters. His bicycle now on the dirt track, the back wheel spinning.

Who are you calling Medusa? I said.

I've heard you call her worse yourself.

Well, I've got to live with her. You don't.

You make a useful point, Jason, he said, smiling away like someone who had never broken sweat in his life.

You know what I'm going to do, Barrabas? One of these days I'm going to chop off her head and use it as a weapon of mass destruction.

He still had the happy face on him, but now he wasn't sure if he should be laughing.

One look at her is all it takes, Barrabas. You'll turn to stone. Head to toe, arms, legs, waist and all, every inch of you rooted to the one place for all time. Eternity! Think of it, Barrabas. You'll be about to drop one of your letters through the letterbox and bam!

He was dying to try out a little laughter, but something made him think better of it.

What sort of a mood is she in? he asked me.

Right now or in general?

Right now.

Well, if I was to put it in weather terms, Barrabas, I would start off by calling her the liveliest cyclone this side of the Russian Steppes.

Ah, Jaysus. Don't say that to me.

Like I say, Barrabas. Try living under the same roof as her for five minutes.

I hear you, Jason, I hear you.

What have you got for her?

I'll give you one guess.

In that case I wouldn't risk it.

Would you mind?

I took the letters off him. Barrabas breathed a sigh of relief. Then looked up and down as though he couldn't remember which way he had been travelling.

Hey, are you likely to see the Slug? he asked me, waving another letter.

Are you afraid of him as well?

No, but he's after taping up his letterbox. I can't get a thing through it.

I nodded in the direction of the Swamp, to where the Slug was casting his line. Barrabas sighed heavily.

Ah, maybe I'll call it a day, he said, closing up his sack of letters. I didn't blame him. He grabbed his bike and away with him.

DEATH BY ICE CREAM

Oh, look, the girl said as soon as she spotted me coming through the door of the Hungry Worm. It's the tough guy.

What are you doing in here? I said, leaning into the empty chair at the window-table she was sitting at.

I could say the same thing to you.

My ma wanted me out of her way. Whooeee. Was she mad.

Well, then. I suppose you better take a seat.

I pulled out the chair and sat in opposite her. We were the only customers. By the counter, the other waitress was trying to bring some dead flowers back to life. There was no sign of Mattie.

Are you alright? I asked her, doing my best to check her face and neck for any fresh bruises without making it too obvious.

Of course I'm alright. Why wouldn't I be?

You didn't show up in McMorrow's. And I . . .

. . . and, let me guess, you thought something terrible had happened to me. Were you terribly worried about me? Did you come looking for me? I bet you did. My hero! Now we really are inseparable.

I wouldn't go that far.

Are you having anything? she asked, reaching her hand across the table. Anything you want. It's on me.

What have you got?

A smoothie.

I might go for a rocky road. Or some ice cream.

You can do better than that. Order something. Pretend you're a condemned man and it's your last meal.

Huh?

Did you know, before he was executed, Ted Bundy had steak, eggs, hash browns and a cup of coffee?

Who's Ted Bundy?

Oh, please! He was a killer. He was loose in America twenty or thirty years ago. He did awful things.

You know a lot about him.

It's amazing what you can find on the internet. Did you know a notorious baby thief had celery, olives, chicken and chips, peas, cherries and a slice of cake? For his last meal, I mean. And a bomber in America asked for two pints of chocolate-chip ice cream. A German killer didn't want anything to eat. He just drank half a bottle of red wine.

This is starting to sound like a joke I heard.

Another lad who was executed with a lethal injection for stabbing his neighbour thirteen times and stealing fifteen dollars, paid for his last meal.

What! He paid for his meal before they killed him?

Another lad asked for a lump of dirt and was denied.

The next time my ma asks me what I would like to eat that's what I'm going to say. I'll have a lump of dirt, please.

Hey! I almost forgot. Cop Lawless is on to us. He knows what we did up on the hill.

That's no big deal.

You should've seen my ma.

Have you asked her about my father yet?

No, I lied, not wanting an earful when I told her how her suggestion had gone down.

What's keeping you?

Nothing.

Are you afraid?

No.

I'd say you are.

I said I'm not.

If I told you to jump off a high building, would you do it?

No.

If I told you to climb up onto the tracks and throw yourself in the front of the train, would you do it?

No.

What would you do?

I've done some things.

Oh really. Like what?

I didn't know what to say to that. Couldn't think of anything, not with her wide eyes all over me, putting pressure on me for a sensational response. By the counter, the other waitress was drowning the dead flowers. I reached in my bag and took out the photograph of Brando.

What have you there?

A photograph Ma keeps in a press.

Who is it?

Marlon Brando. He's a big time movie star. Have you heard of him?

Yes, I have. Women love him. Men respect him. Oh, and he's dead.

First time I saw the photo I thought it was my da.

You thought Marlon Brando was your father!

It was ages ago. I kind of look like him.

Don't be daft.

I have his teeth.

Right.

And his lips and eyebrows. When I frown I look just like him. Watch me.

Now I know you're joking.

I mightn't be.

What did your mother say? Let me guess.

She laughed.

I wonder why. Want to know how he died?

Please don't say he was executed.

He ate too much ice cream.

Let me guess. You found that out on the internet.

You catch on fast when you want to.

She grabbed her smoothie and started to suck on the straw. By the counter, the waitress had given up on the flowers and was now slumped forward on a table beside the counter, her sleeping head in her spread-out arms. I looked back to the girl and the smoothie she was making fast work of.

So, tough guy, she said, nodding in the direction of the

sleepy waitress and letting go her straw. It's just the two of us. You know what we could do?

No.

I think you do.

What? Gobble down a bucket full of rocky roads?

Ha! You're a fruitcake, you know that. I was thinking we could slip into the toilet for a few minutes and you could put your thing in me.

No thanks.

Why not? she asked.

I don't want to.

You know, it's not much fun hanging out with you.

Well, no one said you had to. Why don't you head off to the Russian Steppes? Or hang out with some of those Ancient Greece heroes you keep banging on about?

Who's your favourite?

Favourite?

I like Perseus. And Hercules. And Achilles. I like Hector too. Even though they were enemies. Who do you like?

I . . . I like . . .

And I love the horse. You know it, right? The wooden horse? Of Troy? I love that story. The warriors hide inside and capture the city. They were clever and so brave. They were real heroes. They made sacrifices. Though I was sad after what happened to Hector.

What happened Hector?

Don't you know anything?

That's what my ma says.

Achilles gutted Hector with his sword. Of them all, I

think Prometheus is my favourite. Do you know Prometheus? He stole fire from the gods and gave it to mankind. Then they punished him by chaining him to a rock forever.

I know a few I'd like to see chained.

The gods sent an eagle to eat the liver of Prometheus. Every day.

How many livers did he have?

It grew back, silly. Then the eagle ate it again. Finally he was rescued by Hercules – the greatest hero of them all.

There's a fair haul of heroes knocking about in this story. Did you ever find that other place you were looking for?

Ithaca? Not yet. I'm too busy trying to avoid Cyclops and not look the Gorgons in the eye. The sea is angry too. I've lost count of the number of times I've almost been washed overboard. I need to find something to appease the gods. Otherwise they won't be happy until I become part of the water.

Sounds scary.

Well. It's better than listening to my father. The shouting is worse than ever. His fist is moving beyond the table. The other day he put it through the bathroom window. Yesterday, it was the mirror. This morning, I ducked out of the way in the nick of time.

So I'm right! That's how you get the bruises.

I have to get him out of the house before it gets out of hand. That's where you come in.

You mean my ma.

He has to see her.

When?

Oh, I think I'll let you figure that one out. OK. I'm bored now. See you around. Maybe.

Without waiting for another word out of me she slid out of her chair, stepped up to the counter, lifted the lid on a tray of rocky roads and picked one up. Here, she said, spinning around and lobbing the thing at me. I hear you like these. She flipped a coin over her shoulder and I watched it land on the table alongside the resting arms of the dozing waitress. Then she was out through the door, out of sight, and it was just me and the rocky road. I sat there by myself for a little while more, nibbling on the crispy chocolate. Then I took myself to the library.

BRANDO

The girl was right. Everybody loved Brando. At the library, I put his name into search and in less than half a second the internet gave me two million, nine hundred and eighty thousand websites about him.

In the movies he was a tough-talker, a rabble-rouser, and a wild man who rode around on a motorbike asking everybody what they had. Then he was in charge of a mutiny aboard a ship in the high seas. A soldier in the war. A cowboy. A Mexican revolutionary organizing rebellions. Then he was the top man in a family of gangsters. Just like Tony Soprano. Then he was Superman's da. In one movie he was a lad who used to be a contender for the boxing title, now working on the docks with his brother and a bunch of hoodlums. Surprise, surprise, there's a girl he's keen on and it's tearing him apart because the hoodlums he's involved with have flung the girl's brother headfirst off a rooftop. Turns out the hoodlums have told him to lose the boxing fight and he has to settle for a one-way ticket to Palooka-ville.

There was lots more. Brando's da was a travelling sales-man, always on the road, and his ma liked to act, but preferred heading to the nearest liquor bar and staying there from one end of the day to the next. Brando would go out looking for her and drag her home. Best of all, he would perform little one-man shows to keep her from heading out in the first place.

He didn't care that he became world famous. He drove a fast car down Sunset Boulevard with a fake arrow stuck in his head. He ducked around movie sets firing his water pistol at the other actors. He had a pet raccoon called Russell he used to bring to parties. Brando could swim, too, and when he made enough money he bought himself an island that was next to impossible to find.

He had lots of clever things to say. If I wasn't an actor, I would have been a conman and ended up in jail. That was something he said. And he was expelled from school for riding a motorbike through the halls. And he could speak French.

Oh boy.

No wonder Ma kept a photograph of him.

He liked ice cream and cinnamon buns and could eat a breakfast of corn flakes, sausages, eggs, bananas, and a stack of pancakes drenched in syrup. For dinner he had a couple of steaks, potatoes and a few apple pies à la mode. So hungry was he, his second wife put a padlock on the fridge. So Brando would get his friends to lob bags of Whoppers from Burger King into his back garden.

Eventually he got fed up acting. He called himself a fraud. A pretender. And a liar. He said he was a glum joke of a man and told anyone who would listen that he would sweep the floor if he was paid enough. And all the time he was gnashing down bucket loads of ice cream and getting bigger and fatter until he got to the stage he couldn't put on his trousers without tearing the arse out of them. Then his lungs decided enough was enough and the doctors told him he couldn't go on without oxygen tubes hanging out of him, and Brando wasn't bothered with any of that, and so off to Palookaville he went.

Oh boy.

Everybody loved him alright. Everybody except himself.

WINDOW SHOPPING

And I was walking the down-town streets. Me and my empty bag. Waiting for my next move to drop out of the sky. Passing the skimpy windows. Looking at the clothes-shop dummies. All the unsold shoes. The ticking watches and antique clocks. The buy-me dresses and the silver spoons.

I paused at the window of Glitzybitz. Nothing but butterfly brooches, caterpillar necklaces and sets of mermaid earrings. In the window of Farrell's shoe shop, a miserable selection of thigh boots, wedge heels, and ballet slippers. A skirt and jacket in Lally's high-fashion shop. A blouse that old wheezebag Lily Brennan would run away from. Flimsy bits of underwear, red lacy stuff, and things that wouldn't fit round a starving stick insect. Ma had enough of them, I knew that. As usual in Beauty by Helen, still nothing but vouchers for faces and eyebrows and back exfoliation and skin brightening; all-over massages and the thing called a Brazilian.

In the Card Shop I stared at a *Congratulations You've Passed!* card I could give to her if she ever passed her driving test. In the window of Everything Is Two Euros, a fridge magnet that said *when the going gets tough the tough eat chocolate*, and an Angel Worry Box so small it made me wonder was there enough room for everything Ma would be shoving inside the thing. Was really tempted by a sign that said *If you can't say it politely say it in French* and a calendar with a picture of a grumpy cat for every month, but I remembered Ma saying one time she didn't like calendars. Then I saw a *Make Up Your Mind* dice. Instead of numbers it had words.

Cook
Have a hot bath
Shop
Go to Spain
Clean
Drink a Cup of Tea

And for a few minutes I looked for a *Make Up Your Mind* dice without the *Cook* option and that offered vodka instead of tea. Couldn't see one, though. Instead, came across a tray of finger rings. Tried on a skull and cross bones. Aha, I thought. I know someone who might like this. At the till I asked for a piece of string as well, in case the ring didn't fit the girl's finger and she preferred to wear it around her neck.

By now I was getting fed up looking, and so I marched into Dunnes Stores Better Value Beats Them All. My hoodie pulled tight. A mean look on my face. My gun-hand ready. A quick look about the place told me one thing: grab something and run.

I was eyeing up a bottle of vodka and a bag of crisps that

said *made with real ingredients* when I felt the strong arm on my shoulder. And when I turned around I saw decked out in his security guard uniform the man with the beetroot face from Flukey's funeral.

Just looking, I said and skipped my way out of there.

I stopped at the window of Logan's Pharmacy, one place that didn't look like it was on the verge of closing down. Stared at the woman in a white coat just inside the door, spraying perfume on her wrist and offering the wrist to one or two customers only too happy to take a whiff, get busy nodding and say *how nice*. I stepped inside the pharmacy and was about to ask white-coat what she was flogging, only to be gazumped by the loud and familiar sound of Big Beatrice Glynn stomping in front of me and wasting no time grabbing a little bottle and giving herself a right good spraying. Hmm, she said, I have to say I'm not sure about this one. I'm not sure at all. And without waiting for a word out of white-coat, she stomped further inside the pharmacy, not stopping until she reached the back counter. White-coat gave her own wrist a little squirt from the same bottle and stretched out her arm to me.

Well, what do you think?

You tell me, I said.

It's got a hint of almond. Maybe vanilla.

Sounds like an ice cream.

Here, she said, pushing the bottle my way. It's called *Illusion*. Give it to someone special. I took the bottle, slipped it in my bag and hurried out of there before she gave me anything else.

FLAWS

I was coming over Station Hill, wondering where Ma stood on vanilla-with-a-hint-of-almond perfume, when I saw them. Bad enough meeting Brains and No-brains and them eager to cut loose on me with an ice cream cone. They were going to get a fair kick out of what was resting innocently in my bag.

Look who it is, said No-brains. You'd swear he hadn't clapped eyes on me in years.

We'll have to stop meeting like this, said the brother.

What's in the bag? No-brains asked.

A bomb, I said. I am going to strap it to myself and walk into the Hungry Worm and blast this town to smithereens. You can come with me if you want. I'll let you hold the detonator.

You think you're a funny man, pipsqueak, don't you? You think you can stand there and make me the butt of your clever jokes.

No-brains went on about some more things he had inside his head that I was thinking. I didn't mind. He could go on for as long as it took him to get around to knocking my head clean off my flimsy shoulders.

Brains wasn't listening to any of it, though. He pushed me to the ground while at the same time grabbing the bag and pulling it off my shoulder. I could see No-brains look-ing closely at it, he even took a backward step when the brother flipped it open.

What the hell is this? Brains said, holding up the bottle of *Illusion*.

Vanilla with a hint of almond, I said. It will help you smell nice.

You poofter! said his brother.

Don't knock it 'til you've tried it, No-brains.

What did you call me?

Go on. Have a spray.

I'm going to have a spray alright.

He flipped the lid off, pointed the bottle at me and sprayed. The misty spray went everywhere, I had to cover my eyes, gagged when the stuff got in my mouth. No-brains kept spraying, enjoying himself now, not stopping until the steady hiss was no more.

You didn't keep any for yourself, I said, after he had tried to get a last couple of jolts out of the empty bottle and then dropped it. He drew out his arm and made to backhand me across the face. Brains let a growl out of him and No-brains lowered his arm again, made do with a hearty spit that he summoned from the arse-end of his throat and then cata-pulted out of his mouth and into my face.

Come on, I heard Brains say. We have some drinking to do.

Kick me hard. Throw a punch in my queasy gut. Nail me to a cross and later jab my insides with a long spear. Didn't mind any of that. Could take it. What I wasn't crazy about was jokers taking something I intended giving to someone else.

I stayed sitting on the ground. Checking myself for any loose kidneys or a hanging-off pancreas. My arms and feet were still attached to the rest of me, didn't even see any gushing blood. Fine men they were. Couldn't even break my skin.

*

I was still on Station Hill, by now leaning over the railings. It had just rained and I was staring at a perfect rainbow arching from one side of town to the other. For a few minutes I could make out each of the different colours. Red. Orange. Yellow. Green. Then, one by one, they began to fade. Then I was looking down at the tracks. Could hear Mellows, the signal man, mumbling as he hobbled along. The way to God-knows-where, I could have sworn I heard him say.

And for some reason I was remembering Ma and me together some time in the past. It was about four o'clock in the morning, neither of us had been sleeping and we ended up in the kitchen, me with a glass of milk and Ma with a glass of vodka. She took her drink into the sitting room, switched on the TV, scanned the channels for a movie she might like, a chat show of some kind, something with music.

She couldn't find anything, though, and she was up

again, heading for the kitchen table. Like the numpty I was fast becoming, I followed her, sat into a chair beside her. Watched her run a finger down the side of her glass. Wondered at the thoughts going through her boozy head.

You know, everybody has a flaw, she said after a few minutes of quiet passed between us. Some little thing working against them, at times without them even knowing what it is.

What's Da's flaw? I asked her.

How the hell should I know, she said, and took a mouthful of vodka.

What's my flaw? I asked her.

How the hell should I know, she said, and took another mouthful of vodka.

What's your flaw? I asked her.

Don't get me started, she said, and refilled her glass.

Screeching car gears took me out of that memory and I looked round me just in time to see Mattie's car come speeding along. I knew it! I knew her gloomy mood wouldn't last. Hey, Ma, I called out, raising my arms. Where are we off to this time? By now, I was flagging down Mattie's car and getting ready to jump in. Only it wasn't slowing down. I knew she must be able to see me, she couldn't miss me because I was practically out on the road in front of her, waving like a let-loose lunatic. If anything, she was speeding up as soon as she noticed me, and round me she swerved and kept going. She didn't even roll down the window and wave out, shout her magic words. Ah, Ma, I said, slumping back against the railings. I put a hand in my pocket, felt for the rusty nail.

COUNTRIES ON MY SHOULDERS

Into August and some teapot on the news was listing out the terrible times in store for us. There was going to be hell to pay, he reckoned. CUTS, CUTS AND MORE CUTS! he boomed. Everyone was going to feel the pain. The old. The young. Those lying on hospital floors waiting for a bed. Everyone. Thanks to the Bank of Wank-me-with-a-Spoon, the whole lot was fast going down the tubes. Ah, there's no need to be like that, chipped in another genius, the rosy head on him going like a nodding toy, and he started on about something called NAMA that was going to solve everything. NAMA. Sounded to me like one of those hideous breakfasts supposed to make you live for a hundred years, something lumpy and green. And I could picture Rosy Face on TV doing his ad for the drivel. *Here you are now. Eat your NAMA and everything's gonna be alright. Hey, you! Pipsqueak! Did you eat your NAMA?* Of course I have, I'd say. And fling the stuff in his happy face.

Meantime, Ma hadn't a word to say about her latest spin in Mattie's car. Fact was, she said hardly a word for the first two weeks of August. Like Flukey in his coffin that time, it was hard to get used to. Into the kitchen she'd appear, in turn opening the doors to the food press, fridge and freezer box, and grab whatever was there. A Mars bar. Shrivelled grapes. Mouldy yoghurt. Another Mars bar. Some orange juice to wash down vodka. Another Mars bar.

One morning she appeared and when she pulled open the freezer door it came off its hinges and clattered to the kitchen floor. She shrugged her shoulders and once she saw that the ice tray was full, she loaded up an empty glass, grabbed the orange juice and vodka bottle and made straight for the doorstep. She made a rollie and lit up. Sipped from her glass. From time to time she grabbed herself and shivered.

When I saw her shivering, I went and dredged the back lane ditch for scraps of timber, hunks of wood, tree branches, bits of logs, anything I could use. I dragged it all inside the house, crammed it into the grate, on top of the pay-up-or-else letters I'd twisted into paper sticks, then flicked a lit match. In no time we had a blazing fire. What are you doing, you maniac? she howled at me, when she showed up in the living room and the gathering flames threatening to take over the place. I'm keeping you warm, I replied. It's the middle of summer, you crazy boy, she roared. But she was still shivering.

Then I was answering the telephone. And telling Cunt-hook and Gob-prick and all the arse bandits that no, Ma wasn't here, she was gone to the moon for the rest of the summer, and sorry, no, she had left no contact number, and sorry again, I have another call coming in, goodbye and good riddance. And when I took that call, I was letting Barry from the Bank-of-Wank know that she was choking on a lump of coal and so couldn't come to the phone right now, indeed it was likely she wouldn't be coming to the phone for a good while into the future and so good luck to you, bank clerk.

And I was opening the front door to a host of teapots who had no qualms about hammering away until someone talked to them. Barrabas Diffley was tiptoeing up to our front door with his letters. Up he came, the sneaky teapot, without a whistle or a boo, and slipped his bad news through our letterbox and made sure he was well out of the way before she had a chance to scalp him with the hurley stick. One or two women called around to haul her off to another Happy Hour but she had no interest. She just made sure her drink was topped up, checked her tobacco pouch and sipped and puffed. She didn't even turn on the radio, that was fine by me. There was no falling-off-a-cliff singing to have to listen to.

A few days into this she started staying in bed. Sometimes not getting up until late in the day, sometimes not at all. Get up, Ma, I said, you need to get some air. Listen to this, Ma, I said, opening out the newspaper. Let's get out of Dodge, I said, trying to summon up some life. I saw a nice car you could drive, I told her. Go away, stay away, was all I could get out of her. No, I do not want to listen to the radio. Touch that curtain and you die.

She skipped her night-time dates with the late movie and yet more repeat episodes of her favourite TV show. Look, I said, if she happened to come marching through the living room. It's Tony Soprano, I said, flicking to a scene involving Tony whacking a lad's nose into the middle of next week.

Look at this, I said, flicking to the news. A madman has set himself on fire inside a fast food restaurant. Look, they are looking for volunteers for a one-way trip to Mars. I might as well have been talking to the back lane trees.

I tried bringing her stuff. Breakfast in bed. Afternoon tea. A late night treat. When I couldn't think of anything else I even considered baking her a cake. I got a hold of the recipe book she'd borrowed from the Hungry Worm ages ago and flicked straight to the cakes section. I read down through a list of stuff our kitchen press had never heard of – double cream, caster sugar, cocoa powder, vanilla pods – and decided to put off that idea for another time. Instead, I thought of dragging the television upstairs. Go away, she yelled at me, shivering. Go away. GO AWAY! GO AWAY!

I had no idea what was going on. It brought out some crazy notions in me. Ma, I'd say, if she appeared in the sitting room, by any chance could you use a new TV? Those LED lads have a great picture.

No chance, she'd say.

What about a new car? A BMW? Or a Volvo? I hear those things go like a dream.

Dream on, she'd say.

We should get ourselves a new tumble dryer.

To replace the old one we don't already have, I suppose.

Tell you what. Let's move house. Let's move to the hill. There are great views.

Look at these shoulders, she said to that, tapping me on the head with the vodka bottle. By now, she was standing over me, waiting for me to look at her shoulders. Now, tell me what you see.

I see shoulders.

Look closer. Closer. Closer. That's my boy. Now, what do you see?

Shoulders.

There are countries on my shoulders, you blind bat. Countries.

Which countries?

LARGE COUNTRIES! The largest countries you can think of.

Russia and Egypt, I said, and the vodka bottle came tapping at me again.

As soon as she was out of there, I grabbed the hurley stick and whacked the television picture back from green to pink. Of course, when she made another vodka run and noticed what I'd done, she took her turn with the hurley and whacked it back to green again.

I didn't know what was going on. I really didn't. And I thought to myself: Women. A pity they weren't more like kettles. That way you could switch them off when they were boiling.

That's how it was for those early August days. She raided the fridge. She took her rollie to her step. She sipped from her glass of vodka and orange juice until it was empty, which it never was. She grabbed herself and shivered, even though the sun was shining bright. She took to her bed.

You need a visitor, I was all set to risk saying one

morning. And again I was quickly thinking of the girl's da and his sorry tears and slamming fists. But the sight of Ma burying herself beneath the duvet was enough to let me know that any mention of visitors and she was ready to slam me with her own fists.

Then one night she showed up downstairs. I had been outside looking at the moon, and once back inside, there she was, in her red and white dress, holding herself and dancing slowly around the kitchen floor. I made a move to turn on the radio, so that at least she could have some music to dance with. But something told me, no, leave it, this is the way she wants it. And so for a few minutes I watched her glide about the floor, slowly turning circles, listening to a song only she could hear.

> *People say I'm the life of the party*
> *'Cause I tell a joke or two*
> *Although I might be laughing loud and hearty*
> *Deep inside I'm blue*

She was still at it when I left the kitchen and went upstairs.

Ma.

I couldn't figure this woman out. One minute she was in great form, dragging Mario up the stairs into her room, cooing away at Paris promises, throwing money my way. Next thing she was smashing up the place, telling me where to go, ridiculing my time with the girl. Now I could hardly get so much as a peep out of her. If she was thinking about anything, it was impossible to say. Her face was a blank page, a folded-up map, an empty place.

It was a see-saw time we were having together, a flip-flop shoe of an existence.

Who knew what was going to happen tomorrow?

THE BIGGER PICTURE

Night.

It brought silence to the town. Emptied streets. Scattered cars into the troubled distances. Brought me out walking. Took me as far as Violin Bridge.

I listened to the creaky sounds coming out of it. Wondered at the cause: the crack going across the road. The ancient stones it was made from. The brittle mortar keeping it together. It could be the black water below, cursed with Flukey's ghost and the ghosts of others down there I didn't know about, others who felt they had to take a running jump, others who were pushed.

I stretched out on the bridge wall, peered over the edge. There was nothing, only the black abyss. A great big nothing. How bad Flukey must have felt to convince himself that all he had left was to hurl himself into a great big nothing. I turned over onto my back and stared up at the black night. What about it, stars? Have you any light to throw on the subject? I tried to find the one that sailors used to guide them. It was up there, I knew it was. But I had no idea which one.

The stars, the stars.

So far away.

Lucky things.

Rolled up my sleeve and looked at a fresh cut I'd made, peeled off the plasters covering other ones, picked at the crusty scabs. Reached in my pocket for the shard of glass I'd kept since Ma's tantrum, traced it along the thick crust that had formed over the very first cut I'd made that time up on Rich Hill. And I was thinking about some of the daft notions I'd had about Flukey, and was wondering what had happened to the Paris trip with Mario and was that still on, and I got to thinking about the girl and what was going on with her da, and then, out of where, I couldn't say, another memory came to me, a long-ago memory. It was late and I was downstairs, watching something on TV, one of those gangster films, and I was by myself and wondering where Ma was and I went wandering about the place looking for her, through the kitchen, then upstairs, and into her bedroom and there she was, curled up in bed, sobbing quietly to herself, and she had something in her hand and I tried to see what it was, it looked like a photograph she had crumpled up, and who was it, I was wondering. Who was it?

I leaned in and tore the scab clean off. The sting was so sharp and thrilling it took away my breath, and for a moment I sat there unable to move. Watched the blood silently drip. Then the waves hit me and I was breathing fast again, excited now and so charged-up I ripped and tore at other scabs. And the more I opened the better I felt. Inside my head was like a spinning top. A whirlpool going around and around and around. Making me happy-dizzy. And all the time the blood surging through me, dying to get out.

The bridge was making its noises. It must have had a lot on its mind. The burdens it must carry. The stories it had heard. That's it, bridge. Let it all out. No good will come of keeping everything locked up inside. What's that, bridge? I'm not listening to my own advice. Well, I have to disagree with you there, I said, ripping another scab clean off. It feels good, doesn't it, bridge? It feels good letting out all the pain, that useless blood inside. Listen. Can you hear that? It's the sound of pain. That's right. I'm letting go of it, bridge, can't be keeping that stuff inside me. Here's my blood. Taste and drink it down, bridge. Better than the scumwater you've been looking after for all this time. What's that? Can I spare it? Of course I can spare it. There's loads more where that came from.

CUTS, CUTS AND MORE CUTS!

That's what it was all about. Like the man on television said.

I gripped the shard of glass, raised it high, watched it glint in the street light, curving like a hook, like a sliver of silver moon. Was about to rip long and wide. But the energy was leaving me now, and I let my arm hang limp, stared at the bleeding scabs. And I dabbed at the blood where it fell, moved my fingers absentmindedly through it, until I had traced the word onto the bridge wall.

DA

*

The quiet night was broken by the boy-racers. Along they came. Roaring across the bridge in their go-fast cars. Engines coughing smoke. Lights flashing on and off. Horns blaring, as though here to alert the sleeping town to the latest disaster. And they kept coming. A convoy of souped-up little cars piling at breakneck speed. I sat down against the wall and watched them all go at their handbrake spin-arounds and skids and reverses, before they all swerved to a standstill in the parking area the other side of the unfinished shopping centre, beneath the gaze of the Tower.

It was some gathering. They parked up in little clusters, side by side, turned off their engines, rolled down windows. Pizza boxes appeared, crates of beer, cans and bottles of the stuff, music thumping out of car stereos, and in no time they had themselves a right little party going. One or two of them swapped cars and others were over to the Tower wall with their flies down and their dongs out, and they were soon spelling pisswords on the Tower wall, leaving streaky stains all over the place and a whiff as ripe as anything you would find inside Ma's kitchen press. And all the time I could hear them chatting away, was almost tempted to join them, ask for a bite of pizza. But I didn't. I just sat where I was, my back to the bridge wall, that useless Tower looking down on this dark-of-night gathering, and I wondered what would become of them all.

And almost as soon as they had arrived, it seemed they were revving up again and tearing up the road to get out of there. Moving on to the next stop for them. And off they charged, leaving the same way they had come in, screeching across the bridge past me, the air around me a sudden stench of exhaust fumes and engine smoke. Left after them a patchwork of skid marks and piss stains and uneaten pizza crusts and empty cans and bottles.

And again it was just me and the bridge.

I was feeling more and more attracted to it. The crack was inching its way. I followed its progress, saw the mazy line pattern, the Tower looming. The black abyss, black and abysmal. The creaky strains determined not to change the tune. And I could still hear the boy-racers, faintly revving into the night, escaping, let loose, free.

And I had us in a go-fast car, Gavin McGoldrick's hi-octane sports car at that, and we were tearing up the streets, cop Lawless in hot pursuit. Here, kid, take the wheel, Brando was saying, and he was reaching for his pistol and rolling down his window and blasting away at the chasing car. And I had us on the open road and still Lawless was giving chase, the fool must have been immune to the bullets from Brando's pistol, he would not be happy until he had the pair of us in the clink and thrown away the key. Oh yes, that would suit him perfectly. With me and Brando out of the way, he could pour a bucket of dust all over his starchy uniform, park his squad car outside our house and wait until Ma showed up. That is until me and Brando broke out of the clink, took care of Lawless once and for all, and then made our way as far as McMorrow's to hide out until the coast was clear.

And there we were, in McMorrow's, up at the counter

together, side by side on the high stools, deep in conversation.

What are you drinking, kid?

I'll have whatever you're having, Brando.

Hey, kid, call me Marlon. OK?

OK, Marlon. I'll have whatever you're having.

OK, then. Shirley, set up two Long Island Iced Teas, please. Easy on the ice. Heavy on the rest. Tell me, kid, what are you going to do with yourself when the time comes?

I haven't decided yet.

Well, would you accept a little advice from an older man?

I'd say so.

And he was into a little speech about his own childhood. How, when he was a boy, he was always up to no good. Stealing silver spoons from hotels. Eating meals in restaurants without paying for them. Lifting trees off bridges at Christmas time. And how his ma would send him down to the corner shop for a loaf of bread and he'd come back with a sack of potatoes, three or four loaves of bread, two pints of milk, a block of cheese, a box of teabags and half a dozen eggs. Man, those were the days, he was saying in his easy-listen-to voice, laughing gently to himself. I hear you, Marlon, I said, laughing just like him, lapping up every word.

Then he was skipping quickly ahead into the future. It's all about the bigger picture, he said and asked me what I thought, had I any plans? At once, I let him know that the town we lived in was a boghole, and that the only plan worth making was one that got us out of here once and for all. He agreed. We need to move on, he said. Spread our wings and fly. He knew the town was a boghole, too. He called it an arsehole. And not just any old arsehole. He said our town could compete with other towns for the title *arsehole of the world*. If there was an Olympics for arseholes of the world, he said our town would win the gold medal. Then he came out with his where-to-next plan. I was fast in with my contribution. There's this girl I know, I said. And she keeps banging on about this place called Ithaca. It takes a man twenty years to find it, but once he gets there he can kiss all his troubles goodbye. I told him some more things the girl had told me, could see him nodding slowly at everything I said, while rubbing his chin with his thumb and finger.

And it was a girl told you all this? he asked me after a quiet moment or two.

That's right.

You keen on her?

Well, I don't know if I'd go that far, I said, thinking it the right thing to say and I could feel him smiling away to himself and I knew I had said the right thing.

You know, he said next, long after we had stopped talking and he had spent time mulling over everything I'd told him, I think you and your girlfriend could be right. This place – what's it called again? Ithaca, I said quickly. Yeah, this Ithaca place, he said, nodding now. A place like that is the last place they'd come looking.

Oh boy. He was really going for my idea. And I was

already spreading out the atlas page and plotting our course. And it made me think: talking about the future was even better than all the stuff about the past. Because it had yet to happen. I could feel excitement travelling through me during our talk, a sense of many things out there, some-where, just waiting to happen to me. And I couldn't wait until I had a past of my own to talk about.

Remember kid, he said, reaching for a peanut, flicking it into the air and then catching it between his teeth. It's all about the bigger picture. There, what do you think of all that?

I think that's good advice, Brando – I mean, Marlon.

And look, here come our drinks. Just in the nick of time. Now then, what will we drink to?

Whatever you say.

OK then, kid. To the answers.

To the answers.

You're supposed to say, To the questions.

To the questions, I said.

Then we raised our glasses and clinked, and down the hatch with the Long Island Iced Teas.

LISTEN TO ME, DA.

I'm waiting. You hear me? Waiting for you to come and get me. Then we can go and live out our days together. Wherever you want. Doing whatever you decide. Maybe we can be the wandering kind. Restless explorers in the big world. Sailors aboard your yacht. Following the sun around the world. Mooring at a different port every day.

Maybe we can be spacemen hopping rockets to the moon. Skipping off the atmosphere. Travelling the galaxies. Spinning. Turning. Catching the yellow dawns of new days. Hanging out with comets. Biding our time through the meteor showers. In time to come they're going to name an asteroid after us. A new planet. We could be drifting up there, somewhere, light years away, taking it all in our stellar stride, our name already among the stars.

Maybe we can be a pair of hold-up men. Every day, risking our necks for a till full of tidy cash. You, with your narrow eyes and stick-em-up face. Me, the fast-car man ready at the wheel to get us out of a tight spot.

Or maybe we can just shoot the breeze together up the back lane. You know. Swap little stories from our lives. Play cards. Tell each other jokes.

Yeah. Think I like the sound of that last one best. What do you say, Da? Can you hear me? Can you, Da?

WE COULD HAVE PARIS

Oh boy.

I was a long way from Flukey now. Even if I was looking down at where he had chosen for his final resting place. And as for Mario Devine. Ma was right again. I was an even bigger-size numpty letting myself think for a second about him. Anybody around here for that matter. Little wonder she had to smash up the place from time to time. Besides, like I said before, Mario talked too much for my liking. Pretended to know things. His hands spent too much time fiddling, either inside his pockets or with Ma's backside. And I didn't like the bull-nut smell of him, didn't know how Ma put up with it every month, even if it did get her off the hook when she had no money to pay the rent.

From here out it was time to think big. Dream only in bright colours. See further down the road. Much further. That's what it was all about. Larger life. The bigger picture.

Like Brando said.

Couldn't get all Mario's Paris talk out of my head, though, no way was that going away. The Moulin Rouge, riverside hotels and the Eiffel Tower. I would have to speak some more to the girl about Paris. With all her talk about where she'd been and where she was going, well, I should remember to get my say in. And I was thinking of the Champagne time we could have of it if we ever got to Paris. We wouldn't be seen mooching about the places Mario Devine was banging on about. Hell, we'd probably not even end up staying that long in Paris. It could be the first stop of many for us. That's all Paris would be. A part of our twenty-year adventure. The bigger picture. I closed my eyes and put us in one of those moonlit river boats that had featured during Mario's sweet talk. Up and down the river we floated. Under bridges. The moon looking down, the leafy trees reaching out to wave hello, the night air soft as pillows.

And fock me! Speak of the devil. When I looked again she was on the bridge.

I was just thinking about you, I said as soon as I saw her.

Why thank you, kind sir. Which part of me were you thinking about? No, wait. Let me guess.

I was thinking about a trip we could take together.

Oh.

I'm thinking Paris, I said.

Paris.

That's right.

That's no big deal.

What do you mean that's no big deal? Paris has the Louvre and the Palace at Versailles and the Bastille where they lopped everyone's head off. I'm going, and soon. I'll be staying in a hotel by the river. Play your cards right and I'll let you tag along.

No thanks.

What! You mean to say you're going to turn down a riverboat beneath the moon in Paris?

You can send me a postcard.

I might. Then again, I might not.

Suit yourself.

She brought her hand to the side of her neck, touched a couple of fingers off the bruise. Darker and darker it was looking. The colour of storm clouds, and yellow-green around the edges.

I didn't know you hung out at the bridge, I said.

I'm always here. It's one of my favourite places to hang out.

Are you always here at this time?

I'd say so. It gets a little tricky in my house at night.

I didn't say anything to that. I climbed up onto the bridge wall. Sat with my legs dangling towards the water. The girl joined me on the wall, except she didn't sit down. She stayed standing, on her tiptoes, stretching out her arms either side of her, then she started pirouetting along the narrow wall.

Have you got anything? she said as she moved.

I have this, I said, scarcely able to speak, in case she took a tumble into the black abyss and I had to go diving after her.

I showed her the Mars bar I'd brought with me. At once she leaned down and took it from me, threw it into the dark pool below. I heard a dull splash as it landed.

Jesus! What did you do that for?

This is sacred water. We have to pay homage, offer gifts.

Since when is a scummy stream sacred?

All great things begin with water.

I was saving that for my ma.

You were going to give your mother a Mars bar?

She loves them.

Don't make me laugh. I might lose my balance.

She danced across the bridge wall. Her arms spread out, her neck arching like a swan's.

Be careful, I said, watching her turn a few cartwheels. Along the bridge wall she went, then back in my direction she wheeled, spun herself into a sitting position, and she was beside me, legs dangling, and I could breathe easy.

That's a good trick, I said.

Of course it is. I can also go invisible, fly, and walk on stormy water.

Yeah, right.

Don't you believe in the extraordinary? In miracles?

Not those kinds of miracles.

Sometimes other worlds intrude on this world. That's all a miracle is. Look, she said next, angling her head and pointing to the heavens. You can see the Pleiades. The Pleiades are the screaming daughters of Atlas. And Atlas bears the world on his shoulders.

Where? I can't see them.

You have to look out of the corner of your eye.

I did what I was told, and yes, she was right. I could make out the flickering cluster of stars.

Sometimes the best things can only be seen out of the

corner of the eye, I heard her say. And then, Let me have your hand.

Here we go again, I thought, and she took my hand, and before I had a chance to pull it away, she had unbuttoned her top and placed my hand on her chest.

Tell me what you feel, she said.

I don't feel a thing, I said, yanking my hand out of there.

Liar, she said. Tell me.

She had grabbed my hand again, and was trying to force it back onto her chest, then she was shoving it between her parted legs.

Quit it, I said.

Come on. Don't be such a spoil sport.

No! I yelled at her, and drew away, nearly losing balance. And when I looked at her again, she was staring wild-eyed at me.

At least let me touch *you*.

Get away.

Ha! You're some tough guy. Afraid of a girl's touch. Off with you to Paris, then. Off with you to your plush palace and the Pastille.

It's *Bas*tille, not *Pas*tille.

And to think I was actually considering taking you to Ithaca with me.

Without another word she dropped softly to the ground and disappeared into the darkness, like one of those ghosts she said were afraid of her. I called out to her, but there was no reply. I sat there for a little while more. Then took myself home.

BATH TIME

When I got back to the house Ma was walking straight past me and heading for the bathroom. A couple of minutes later I heard the water running. She was gathering all the available bubble bath, towels, shampoo, soap, make-up, moisturizer, skin cream. It was all going in the bath along with her.

She was lighting candles and foaming up the tub with bubbles. She plonked herself into the bath and I could hear her humming away to herself in that badly-wired way of hers. Somehow she heard me tiptoeing through the kitchen and lifting bits off the finger-food plates she'd prepared, and she called me into the bathroom.

Hello you, she said, soaping her arms.

Are you getting ready for Mario?

Listen to him. All of a sudden he wants to talk about Mario. As though he hasn't tried hard enough already to ruin that for me. What have you got in mind this time, I wonder?

I haven't got anything in mind.

You better not.

I don't.

OK then. Would you like to make yourself useful?

Yes. Maybe.

Take this and soap my back.

She pitched her bar of soap at me. It leapt about in my hands like a fish out of water, then I managed to grip it. I stood behind her and started rubbing her back.

Ah, come on, she said. You can do better than that.

I rubbed a little harder and she sighed pleasantly and let herself lean back.

Tell me something interesting, she said next, but I couldn't think of a thing to say. Tell me about your friend.

There's nothing much to tell.

Don't be ridiculous. What does she look like? Is she making your blood leap? Has she discovered things about you no one else will ever know?

I didn't give any answers to these questions. I just kept going in circles around her back with the soap.

What's the matter? Cat got your tongue?

No.

Come on then. Is she pure like the snow? An angel, like me? Is she wild? Hmm? Nothing to say about her? Oh, it sounds to me like you're in deep. You better watch out. It gets tricky when your feet can no longer touch the sand. Now, come on. Tell me one thing about her. That's not too much to ask, is it?

She likes travelling, I said, hoping it would shut Ma up.

Travelling. Good! We have something in common. Tell you what. Why don't you invite her around some evening? I'll make us something to eat. Play your cards right and I might even make myself scarce for an hour or two. I'm sure she'll be impressed.

It's OK. We have places to hang out.

Listen to you, she said next, slapping her hands into the bathwater, sending suds and water everywhere. The expert! Well, don't go breaking her heart. My last word on the matter. Now, do me a favour. Pass me my gown.

She was now fast getting ready to step out of the bath.

Her da still wants to come over to see you, I said, grabbing the gown and flinging it at her.

Does he now? she said, tying her belt.

He's been crying for a year. He's going to knock her into the middle of next month if he doesn't get to see you.

Is he indeed? she said, flicking wet hair away from her face.

Well, do you have an answer? He could come the day after tomorrow, after Mario is long gone.

Here's what you can tell your little pip. Tell her I said she should stick to the children's games she's good at, and leave the other stuff to adults.

YOU'RE AN AWFUL WOMAN

Next morning and I was watching Ma in front of the cracked mirror. Shaping her lips. Colouring her cheeks. Pencilling the rims of her eyes, blueing the lids. Attaching a set of warped sea-horses to her ears. Spraying something peachy about her neck. And I thought I could glimpse in her faraway face the little girl she would've been in the not-so-distant past, full of her own ideas and dreams. The open road ahead of her. Like it was whenever she gripped the wheel of Mattie's car.

Well, do I pass? she said, when she noticed me hovering.

I'm heading out, I said, when I was bothered opening my mouth. I'm going down town to rob the bank.

You might as well, she said.

While I'm at it I might start a fire in the Market Square. Good idea.

And I was thinking of taking my axe to a couple of old ladies.

That sounds like a splendid way to pass the day.

I'm going now.

Get me a Mars bar, will you?

The sun was out again, was making swift work of the few excuses for clouds knocking about the sky. I walked the

191

back lane and tried not to think about Ma and what she would soon be up to with Mario, but it was easier said than done, and a picture of Mario showing up with his leery smile and boggy hands, the palpitating head on him as he grabbed Ma, and the horse sounds coming out of him as soon as they were up the stairs and he knew what was in store. *Ah, Jaysus, Jacinta, there's no doubt about it. You're an awful woman.* And once that first image had found a way inside my head, a host of others were not long following hot and hotter on its heels, until, in no time, I had a full-length feature film going on inside that daft noggin of mine, complete with Dolby stereo and surround sound. The pair of them making a fine racket in some riverside Paris hotel, and the grunting and moaning coming out of that bull-nut seller as he sloshed around in his eagerness to get at her. And so I tried to think about other stuff, all the bad news letters and pay-up phone calls Ma had been receiving. Her daft talk about how dangerous she would be if she was a man. And I thought about one or two of the spins we had taken together in Mattie Conlon's car and about cop Lawless waiting for us that last time, and fock me if the feature film didn't cut to her in the storeroom of the Hungry Worm, bending down for some chocolate icing and cop Lawless moving spider-like up behind her and with both hands grabbing a hold of her, and there and then proceeding to have a grand old time of it for himself, and I had to get my head fast out of the storeroom and so I tried thinking about Ma on the phone, and how she had me down as someone with E-coli and renal dysfunction or whatever it was called, in need of a new kidney and pancreas, not that it mattered because any day now I would be dead from the devastating dose swirling around non-stop inside my rugby-ball-shaped numbskulls. And even though she had laughed at my suggestion to have the girl's da pay her a visit and it not my suggestion to begin with, and though I couldn't get away from that image of her and cop Lawless in the storeroom together, still it hit me: today was August 15th. Ma's birthday. The next happy day in her life. And I still hadn't got her anything.

ANGELFACE

I was on my way towards Mel Campbell's shop when I saw her. Sitting up on Mel's wall. Swinging out her legs. Sticking out her non-existent chest. After our last encounter I was in no mood for her. Too late. She had already spotted me.

I'm still waiting for you to impress me.

Why are you so obsessed with being impressed?

A girl needs a hero in her life.

And you've chosen me?

I suppose I'm just a hopeless romantic.

Yeah? Well, last time I checked you were quite happy to sail off without me.

I'm a girl. I'm allowed to change my mind.

Now you sound like someone else I know. What if I don't want to be chosen?

What you want or don't want won't make the slightest bit of difference. Did you ask your *ma* about my father?

Yeah.

And? What did she say?

She said your *father* can call over any time he wants.

Really?

Yep. She'll be expecting him. She'll run a bath and cover herself in suds and wait until he shows up.

Tell her to light candles. That always works.

You *suppose*?

Who yanked your chain?

I think I'll let you figure that one out by yourself.

I was thinking about what you said. And I agree with you. You do look a bit like Marlon Brando. Obviously you're not near as dangerous-looking as him. Not with those cherub cheeks of yours.

What!

That's OK, though. On this occasion I could go for cherub cheeks. In fact, I think I'll call you Angelface.

You're not calling me Angelface.

So tell me, Angelface? When are we getting together? We have to now, you know. Now that I have poured out my heart to you.

Yeah, well, I don't have time to stick around and listen to any more pouring. It's my ma's birthday. I have to get her something.

Like what?

I don't know. Something to cheer her up.

You should get her happy pills. They used to work on my father.

Happy pills?

You know, uppers and downers.

Yeah, I've heard of them.

I might be able to get some.

Really?

Yep. But it's going to cost you.

I don't have any money.

Maybe I was talking about something else.

She had started sticking out her chest again, and jiggling herself, whatever that was supposed to achieve, and, ah Jesus, I was thinking, here we go again, is there nothing else this one ever thinks of.

Speak some French, she said next.

French?

You said you were going to Paris. So . . .

So what?

Speak some French.

I don't know any French.

And for a second there you sounded like such an expert. Don't suppose you have anything in that useless bag apart from photographs of dead actors?

You mean like cigarettes or booze?

I mean like anything.

I've got this.

I took the page from the atlas, unfolded it, and spread it out between us.

Now. Show me the Russian Steppes.

Without needing a second to think about it, she pointed to a far corner of the atlas page.

OK. Now show me where the pharaohs hang out.

Again she pointed, as fast as you like.

Now show me Ithaca.

Ithaca?

Aha! Not so fast now, are you?

Of course, as soon as I had spoken, she was pointing again, this time to the vast sea below Greece and Italy and France.

Ithaca is somewhere between here and there.

To make sure she wasn't trying to put one over on me, I had her point them all out again. I threw in a few others while I was at it. She didn't get one wrong.

Hey, Angelface, she called out after me, after I'd left her sitting there on the wall, and before I'd thought twice about it, I'd already turned around to her grinning head. Catch, she said, and blew me a kiss off the palm of her hand.

WHAT PART OF NO DO YOU NO LONGER UNDERSTAND?

Get the hell out of here, toe-rag! Mel Campbell let rip, when I stepped inside his shop.

There's no need to be like that, Mel, I told him.

Whatever it is you want, I don't have it.

It's not me. It's Ma. She has a yearning for a Mars bar. You know how it is, Mel.

I don't have anything for her either. Now scram.

Now, Mel. We had a good relationship once upon a time. Let's go back to the beginning.

Leave now, please.

Why not, Mel? For old times' sake.

Because I have no problem breaking off ties with customers who haven't paid up in six months. You and your precious ma were barred then. And you're barred now.

Mel, is this your way of saying you want us taking our business someplace else?

No, it's my way of letting you know you're not getting so much as a can of beans from me until you start paying off what you already owe.

How's Mrs Campbell?

She fine, thanks for asking. Now clear off.

I was in here one time and we had a great conversation

about arms. You know, she is such a sympathetic person. I'd say she'd put her own arms around the entire country if she could. I like that in a person, Mel. The place could do with more like her.

Really.

Believe you me, Mel, I wish there were more like her. Then maybe we wouldn't be facing the abyss everybody keeps banging on about.

Tell me something, toe-rag. What part of NO do you no longer understand?

The same part you don't understand. A Mars bar, Mel. Just the one. For old times' sake.

HAPPY PILLS

The girl was in the street. Looking in the window of Pageturners bookshop, I'd no idea why. Pageturners had been closed for a few months and there were hardly any books left to look at. As if she had heard my thoughts, she moved on as far as the window of the Hungry Worm. She had both hands bridged over her eyes, shielding out the light, taking in the cream buns and sticky tarts and lemon meringues and whatever else was fresh out of the oven today. She probably couldn't make up her mind what she wanted.

Are you hungry? I called out.

She didn't react, didn't seem to have heard me.

Is there something you want? I can get you something, I tried again. She looked my way, and for a minute I thought she was going to nod her head, and we could take a table and talk places in the world over a rocky road and a smoothie. Instead she looked around her and hurried off. Her tattered tackies flapping at the ground. Her skinny legs looking like a pair of stilts that had been jammed into her backside.

Wait! I shouted. I have a euro. Make that two euros, we can get something. But she was already on her way down the street, past Patsy Fagan's betting shop, past Farrell's

Shoes and the boarded-up computer place. She paused at the blinking green cross of Logan's Pharmacy. Then she stepped inside. I followed.

Hey! I hissed at her. Did you not hear me?

She was moving further ahead of me, drifting among the aisles of pain-killing tablets, the soaps and perfume.

Hey!

Still no reaction.

And she was walking past all the creams and lotions and hair gels. Past stuff for painting your nails and stuff for removing it again. Past toothpaste and shaving foam and aftershave. Tubes of vitamins. Past all the make-up kits. And the cardboard cut-outs showing off the results. The perfect faces. The whiter-than-white teeth. What did she want in here?

I didn't have a chance to ask her. Big Beatrice Glynn was bounding through the aisles, on her way to that back counter she was so fond of. Gabbing into her phone as she moved. *Yes, yes, I hear you. I just have to pick up my pills. Then I'm on my way.* She was still gabbing away into her phone when she reached the counter and Logan the chemist handed over a paper bag which Big Beatrice scooped away from him and landed inside the huge handbag swinging from her shoulder. As soon as she about-turned and was out of there, the girl grabbed my arm and hauled me after her.

Out on the street, Big Beatrice had stopped to chat to Nora McGuinness. She hadn't closed her bag properly and the girl yanked me off the footpath and in behind a parked car.

Are you ready to impress me? she whispered.

Huh?

See that big whale's bag? I need what she just put in it. I'll be lookout, while you go fetch. OK?

What is it we're after?

The question was no sooner out of my mouth than it hit me.

Happy Pills. Big Beatrice's Happy Pills.

Beatrice was still talking to Nora and her handbag was swaying and I was angling my outstretched arm towards it when out of Slevin the butcher's marched Virgin Gemma carrying a chicken, headless and raw, and of course she had to stop and join whatever amazing topic of conversation Big Beatrice and Nora had lit upon.

Go on, I heard the girl urge, and was about to reach my arm out again when out of the same butcher's hobbled Scary Mona Quinn. She had a chicken too and she joined the others, raised her prize and roared: *Everybody for himself said the elephant as he danced among the chickens.* And the four of them erupted where they stood.

Then Big Beatrice's mobile started ringing again and she rested her handbag on the bonnet of the car to go rooting for the noisy thing, and when she answered she turned round, leaving the bag on the car.

Now! the girl hissed.

Inched my way round the car, reached my arm inside the open handbag, felt a package, lifted it out and showed it to the girl. Donuts! She rolled her eyes, I slipped the donuts in my bag and tried again. Seconds later I had fished out something flaky. A croissant! Again, the girl rolled her eyes, and I thought: this is not going according to plan. I made another lunge and this time the girl was nodding when she saw what I came away with. GO, GO, GO! I heard the girl call out. And I straightened myself up, turned on my heels and legged it out of there.

Without turning round I kept going. Slow down, will you! I heard a voice shout out, no way was I doing that. I pulled my hoodie tight and moved as fast as I could, not stopping until I was sure I had given my pursuer the slip.

Was deep inside Cutthroat Alley. Figured I'd be safe there. Away from prying eyes and any posses on the look-out for pill thieves. Tore apart the paper bag and took a look at what I'd taken. A few boxes, labelled with long, daft-looking names. I opened one, removed the strip of foil, saw the blue lozenge-shaped pills. Six, twelve, eighteen, twenty-four of them. What else? A haul of little yellow discs in the next box.

Oh boy.

I had a full set of uppers and downers. Enough to keep Ma going until the next happy day in her life.

A few minutes later I moved quietly out of the alley. Looked around and wondered where was the girl.

No sign of her.

I crossed the street and ducked inside McMorrow's.

SUICIDE

Harry and Fergal were practically touching heads. At her low table by the wall, the pale-faced woman was smoking her unlit cigarette. The card game was still in progress. Shirley was staring at the high-up TV.

The one and only, she said when she turned to me.

How are the mood swings, Shirley? I said, already on a stool at the bar and keeping my bag close.

Never better. Right now, I'm thinking of opening your head with my dodgy bacon slicer.

I can think of worse things.

Shirley grabbed a bottle, uncapped it, waved it in front of me, along with a bag of nuts.

Fanta and a packet of peanuts. That comes to . . . one euro.

Tell me something, Shirley. Did we ever get that tab up and going?

Let me take a moment from my hectic schedule to investigate. No, we didn't.

Well, in that case, this might be a good time.

She set down the bottle in front of me. She hadn't quite formed a smile, but she wasn't a million miles from one either.

By the way, how's that trick carpet treating you?

It's gone in for a service, Shirley. I'm afraid you're stuck with me for another while.

That's too bad. I was really hoping to watch you fly that thing out of here.

I'm trying my best, Shirley, I said to that, just as the card players let a whoop out of themselves.

I took my drink over to the card table. Watched the men at their game. Tried to get a handle on what was going on.

The one with the brim hat seemed to be doing most of the winning. He had a small puddle of coins gathered at his corner of the table. Plus one or two notes. The one with the toothpick seemed to like dealing. The one with the scar running down the side of his face looked as though he was going to kill someone. The last one was smiling at every card set down. Didn't seem to care if he was winning or losing. So long as he was involved in the game, that was good enough for him.

Can I play? I asked after a couple of more hands, even though I still had no idea what was going on.

Got any money? Brim Hat asked without looking up.

Yep.

Take a seat.

The one with the non-stop smile made a little room and I slid in beside him. I was opposite Brim Hat. He was giving me the full stare.

So. You think you are a card player? He had taken the deck of cards and was shuffling them with one hand.

Got to start some time.

The others sniggered. Then the one with the toothpick piped up.

Take him on, Chancer. Just you and him.

A little game of Suicide will soften his cough, Chancer.

Without acknowledging any of the comments, he dealt me a card. Then himself. Then he left the deck on the table.

What are we playing?

We're playing Suicide. Like the fellows suggested. Take the card and clamp it to your noggin.

Without looking to see what it was, Chancer had already taken his card and slapped it against his forehead. I copied him, even sat back comfortably in my chair the way Chancer had.

The others looked from one of us to the other and let out long shrill whistles.

Highest card wins, Chancer said. Place your bet.

I looked at the card on Chancer's forehead. I looked at the others. I looked into Chancer's eyes. They were hard and unblinking, I didn't want to see what lurked behind them.

I bet a euro, I said, and a collective laughter erupted. Some knee-slapping. General yahoos.

A euro, Chancer repeated.

Yep. A euro.

OK. Let's see the colour of your money.

I dredged my pocket for the euro, tossed it onto the table between us. Out of the corner of my eye I noticed Shirley looking in my direction, shaking her head, smiling slowly to herself.

Fair enough, Chancer said. I'll see your euro. And out of nowhere, it seemed, he flipped a coin onto the table too.

What's he got boys? Chancer asked the rest of them, all the time staring my way.

A king, they all chimed in, scarcely able to restrain themselves.

A king, said Chancer with a heavy sigh, rubbing the tip of his chin. That's a good card.

So I win, I said, reaching out an arm to gather in the coins.

SO YOU DIE! Chancer said, with a rapid fire movement grabbing my busy arm and at the same time spilling his card onto the table. Aces are high in this game, kid.

And the rest of them were having an awful time suppressing their chuckles, high-fiving their man, warning all-comers not to mess with the Chancer Fay, the sharpest card man in town.

You win some, you lose some, kid, one of them said, ready with a gentle slap on the back for me.

I left them to it and climbed back into my stool. Threw what was left of the peanuts in me. Finished the ends of the Fanta. Harry and Fergal offered me another.

No thanks, men. I've had enough.

I slid off the stool again, gave Shirley a salute and headed for the door. Don't be a stranger, one of the card players called after me, I didn't know which one.

TO THE TOWER

Late now. I was still out and about. Trying to look unsuspicious after my trip to the pharmacy. The streetlights weren't working tonight. It gave the place an eerie feel, how it might be if it had been deserted by everyone once and for all. It was quiet too. There was no one about, a few parked cars. Neon flashing outside Dante's empty chipper. Either side of me, the buildings looked as though they wanted to come together, squeeze me in like the tree branches on that country lane Ma and me had taken that time in Mattie's car. They looked darker than normal, taller and emptier.

It was so clear. A sliver of moon and dazzle of stars, clearer than ever in the unpolluted dark, sending out their tiny specks of light from all that distance away. I could've walked for ages on a night like this. I could've crossed Violin Bridge, turned the last corner and walked all the way out of town. Kept going. Let my feet do all the work. See where I was when dawn arrived.

Climbed up onto the bridge wall, took off my hoodie. Closed my eyes, felt the night air cool on my skin. Opened my eyes again and there she was, up on the wall beside me. Rubbed my eyes to make sure I wasn't seeing things. Yes, there she was. On her toes, moving over and back, dancing again, framed in the shallow moonlight. Now she paused, teetered on the edge, balanced like a ladybird upon a wisp of grass. I held my breath. A single movement, one sound out of me, would send her over the edge.

What are you doing? I gasped.

I'm going to jump, she said, looking straight ahead.

No, you're not.

Yes, I am. You never have anything to say to me. You don't like my knockers or any other part of me. You won't put your thing in me. You won't even touch me.

I couldn't think of anything to say to that, and anyway, figured she'd have something to say right back. With nothing better to do I inched my way until I was standing right next to her, looking down.

What are *you* doing? she said.

If you jump, I will too, I said.

Don't be daft.

You're one to talk.

We didn't say anything for a few minutes. We just stood there, side by side in the dark, peering down into the black abyss. At some point I was thinking, those lads at Flukey's funeral were right. It wasn't such a long way down, and then there mightn't be so much water. I wondered what she was thinking. I looked over. She was rigid, fixed to the spot, hardly moving, as though all along she had been part of the bridge and nobody had taken any notice until now.

It's not as far a drop as I thought, I said.

That's what I was thinking.

Well then. Let's get down.

Let's. We can always find someplace else.

Like where?

Like where do you think? It's practically staring down on us.

Five minutes later, thanks to another wonky window, we were inside the unfinished shopping centre. Her, making a fast dash for the Tower. Me, fumbling my way behind her, wondering what we were going to do when we reached the top, and at the same time trying my best not to come up with any answers.

She was bounding ahead of me, her feet fast on the stairs winding their way up, up, up. A door faced us when the stairs ran out. I almost prayed it was locked. It wasn't and she was through it like a knife through butter. I was after her and then we were standing high and I did not want to look down.

Get over here, she said, already near the edge. Well? Are you going to stay there after coming all this way?

I moved uneasily towards her. Was stepping slow, feeling light-headed, did not want to face the view below. She reached out an arm and I took it. She was hovering right at the edge and one more step would paralyse me. She held my hand in hers, and the feel of her fingers, skin, flesh, put me at ease and I edged my way until I was standing beside her.

Whoa! I said, and she gripped my hand, held it firm.

Now, this is more like it, she said. Look down.

Like an idiot, I did what I was told, and at once I was dizzy, reeling where I stood, the heart inside me clapping against my chest, my two legs wobbling like a drunk from the back lane. I clasped her hand even tighter.

Guess what, she said.

What?

We're holding hands.

Right now, that suits me just fine, I said.

Here, she said, and let go of me, sat down, let her legs dangle over the edge and tapped the space beside her. For a minute I couldn't figure out what to do. I reached for her hand, she took it and I lowered myself down beside her. Awkwardly, I stretched out my legs, tried my best not to look down.

It's hard to get used to, I said.

That's what's good about it.

You're not going to . . .

To what?

You know.

Jump? Did you think I was going to? Ha! You *are* a fruitcake. I think I'll sit up here for a while, though. Anyway, I've told you before.

Told me what?

I have a life to live. Places to see. People to meet.

Well then, what are we doing up here?

I think I'll let you come up with an answer to that yourself. As for me, I like the quiet.

The boy-racers soon put an end to that. Along they came. Tearing up the road in their spluttery cars. She didn't seem to mind. By now she was lying face down, her chin resting in her crossed arms, taking in the car-rally spectacle way below. I did the same and we stayed like that until long after the boy-racers had racked up dozens of fast swerves and handbrake turns and were now parked-up way below us, with pizzas and beer and pisswords along the Tower wall and all the time the music thumping out of the car stereos and the town lights still not working and still more cars arriving and more pizza and beer and pisswords, and we stayed right where we were until long after I knew she was right. That, despite all the noise below, it was peaceful up here. That I could have stayed here, lying right beside her, for as long as she wanted.

Hey! she said, I almost forgot.

What? I said, not wanting to turn to her in case she started on about knockers and putting my thing in her.

The Happy Pills. You got them?

Jesus! Yeah. I'd forgotten all about them, I said, fetching a box or two out of my bag. Here. A box of blues and a box of yellows.

Wow! You have enough to keep your mother going until doomsday. Tell her to take the blues with her morning toast. The yellows after another repeat episode of *The Sopranos*.

Is that what your da does?

They stopped working on my father. But don't worry. The way he is these days, I don't think anything will. Give them to your mother. They might do her some good.

Do you want one?

No thanks. They don't work on me either.

Fair enough, I said, and put the boxes in my bag and stretched fully out again.

You know what we should do? she said into darkness. We should go down there and steal one of their cars. Look at them all. They'll hardly miss one less.

Can you drive?

No. Can you?

No.

Well then, what are we waiting for? Come on.

Minutes later, we had tiptoed as far as a tiny banger of a thing, eased the doors open and slid inside. Me in the passenger seat, on lookout duty. Her in the driver seat, behind the wheel, the key in the ignition as if waiting for us all our lives. A second later she was revving like there was no tomorrow.

Release the handbrake, I hissed at her.

OK. Here we go, she squealed and we chug-chug-chugged out onto the road.

You have to change gears, I said.

OK, she said, and yanked the gear stick this way and that.

Now press the accelerator, I told her, and the car growled and coughed out smoke and that was enough to attract the boy-racers pissing up the Tower wall and they were tucking in their dongs and zipping along their strides and sprinting up the road after us, one or two of them wrestling for their own car keys, one or two tripping over themselves to give the best chase.

DRIVE! I yelled. DRIVE, DRIVE, DRIVE! And she

pressed down for all she was worth, and took the sharp bend rapidly approaching and all the time we were picking up speed and she was squealing and I was watching the road ahead and checking behind us for pursuers and there was no doubt about it, we were getting away.

You drive better than my ma, I told her.

Of course I do, she squealed, I was born to drive, and she revved some more and the car accelerated and I was already convinced we could have driven all the way out of town and continued all night and been as far away as we wanted to be if we hadn't met cop Lawless coming the other way in his squad car. He knew something wasn't right and he swung his squad around and we now had a proper pursuer.

We pulled off the main road, onto a road with nothing going for it other than potholes, none of which the girl wanted to avoid. Lawless followed us. He's catching, I told her, and she accelerated into another pothole, one that made the car skid. Watch out, I yelled, and next thing we were leaving the road, bumping over gravel, onto a grassy bank and then the car dipped headfirst into a ditch.

We scrambled out the driver door, crawled up the other side of the ditch. I could hear Lawless hollering at us, you could tell he had no idea who it was or what exactly had happened, and once we had climbed the ditch and squeezed through a gap in a wire fence and into a field, we wasted little time putting ourselves a long way out of his reach. We kept running until we were out of breath, until we collapsed in the soft grass. We lay on our backs, side by side, waiting for our galloping hearts to calm down, for our scorched lungs to recover, and when at last they did, we looked at each other and laughed like a pair of let-loose lunatics.

FOUR MINUTES PAST FOUR IN
THE MORNING

Ma was gone.

Three or four hours I must have spent mooching about the place, convinced that any moment now I was going to hear her crazy singing, her key scratching at the front door and she would come waltzing in, complete with her merry news of a mighty night on the town. But none of that was happening. And the longer I waited, the less likely it seemed that it was going to happen. To make doubly sure she hadn't been here all along, I went through the place again.

She wasn't in the kitchen. Not on the sofa. Not upstairs in her room.

The TV was switched off. The radio wasn't blaring. There wasn't an ooh, aah, the merest whimper to be heard.

I drew back the sitting-room curtain and looked out onto the road.

The rust bucket was gone.

Wait. That didn't mean a thing. Gavin McGoldrick had been taking care of it since Ma filled the tank with the wrong kind of petrol.

I looked at the kitchen clock. Ten to eight. It couldn't be that time. Of course it wasn't. It was the middle of the night.

Then I remembered the clock hadn't been working since the start of summer.

I turned on the TV. The late night news was on. Some lad with a bushy moustache going on about, what else, the shite-and-all mess the country was now in. Factories closing down. Youngsters packing their bags. Old people crawling hospital floors looking for a doctor, for crying out loud. And all the time a look on moustache face that meant one, and only one, thing: we should all take a running jump.

I sat there on the sofa.

I stood up and paced circles around the sitting room.

One more time I pounded upstairs and through her bedroom door, made sure she was not in the bathroom, hidden inside the basket of dirty clothes.

I looked out the window of my room. Hurried back downstairs.

The time is four minutes past four in the morning, the newsman was announcing to anybody who cared. I cared. It was four minutes past four in the morning, not a doctor in sight and Ma had disappeared.

I walked into the kitchen.

On the table I saw a page from the atlas. Lipstick marks on a near-empty glass.

It took a moment, then it hit me: Mario had come good on his promise. He had whisked Ma all the way to Paris. On her birthday.

Oh boy. I would need to think about this.

I walked back into the sitting room, sat down on the sofa again, took a last glance at the serious head on the newsman and turned off the TV. Then I reached in my bag, took a look at the boxes of Happy Pills. And I thought: might as well.

MORNING PILLS

They must have legged it when I was playing Suicide in McMorrow's. Otherwise how could Ma have managed it? Not with Barty Brophy the out-of-pocket handyman showing up on our doorstep at first light, and lovesick cop Lawless parading away the daytime hours up and down our road, and Mattie Conlon looking for her to pay for all the apple tarts and sticky buns she'd been taking from the store-room of his café even if they were out of date. Not with the TV licence man on the prowl and the witchy voice from the credit union on the line and Barry the bank clerk with his polite letters asking her to call in for a chat.

For a chat.

I could imagine how that chat would have gone. *Hello, Jacinta, is it alright if I call you Jacinta? Why of course it is, Barry, and is it alright if I call you Barry. Call me whatever you like, Jacinta. Why, thank you, Barry, in that case I'll call you gobshite of the century. Fair enough, Jacinta, but know that I have been called worse. A lot worse. Now, Jacinta, I've hauled you in here today because, as you may be aware, you have a long outstanding loan and you've fallen a little behind on your repayments. More than a little. I've run some checks and I know you owe the credit union twenty thousand plus interest, which is steadily accumulating by the way, and we were wondering had you any comments to make before we throw the book at you once and for all.* She'd have a comment for you, Barry, be in no doubt about that. Drop dead, loser. In your dreams, money man. Pull the other one, it plays 'Wank Me With A Spoon'.

Even so. It's a wonder she made it out of town. It's a wonder cop Lawless hadn't been parked up, watching her every move. It's a wonder me and the girl hadn't spotted them. Maybe Mario knew a way. One of those quiet roads Ma liked. All trees and bushes and tufts of grass. Sheltered from the greedy eyes out to get her last penny.

Well, off with her. I hope she enjoys Paris. Let Mario take her to that riverside hotel and show her the Louvre and the guillotine and all the skulls chopped off by the thing. Let him show her the flower market and pour her wine and feed her all the bread she can stomach. One thing she doesn't have, and that's Happy Pills. All the bread in Paris won't make up for that. I was looking at them now, boxes of the things, spread out on the kitchen table. Well, Ma, all I can say is that it'll be a shame for all these pills to go to waste. Especially after the hard work put in getting them in the first place. Now what was it the girl said? Take the blues with morning toast. OK, then. Let's see what we've got by way of food around here. Porridge. Ha! Good luck to that. A bowl of leaves and withered tomatoes. I don't think so. Wait. An extra-large plate of mince stew. I wouldn't give that to the rat that's been gnawing at my ear. Aha! What have we here? A slice of cake. Looks good to me. I jammed the pill into the spongy wedge and wolfed the lot down.

Hey! The blues go well with sponge cake. This just might be the first of many a happy eating experience.

Well, then. Here's to Paris, Ma. For me, it'll have to be another slice or three of sponge cake and blue pills. I just hope you have time to make the most of the place before word gets out about you. I'm prepared to stay quiet myself, they'll have their work cut out for them if they want to prise your whereabouts out of me. But this is a small town. Someone is bound to have seen or heard something. Lily the Nose won't be long getting on the case. Harry Brewster's eyes and Fergal Flood's ears. Rommel and Himmler, the mongrel dogs.

Now then, what next? Ah yes. It's nine o'clock in the morning and that can only mean one thing.

The ringing telephone needs answering.

Hello there, you have reached the bowels of the black abyss. Leave a name and number and I will have my assistant call you straight back with our very best offers as soon as she is finished baking me a very delicious sponge cake.

Hello. Who is this? The muck savage from the ESB. What's that? You have a question to ask about an unpaid bill. Well, let me ask you a question. Why don't you turn off the lights once and for all? Answer me that, will you. If you answer me, I'll answer you. That sounds fair, doesn't it?

Hi there. You're looking for the bill payer? There's no such thing as a bill payer in this house. Goodbye.

And you are? Chalice Mitchell. That is a fantastic name you have there, Chalice Mitchell. And where in the world are you from with a name like that? Eureka, Oregon? And tell me, Chalice, what dragged you all the way from Eureka, Oregon to our boghole town? That would be telling, wouldn't it? And what can I do for you today? You sold us some oil. Last winter. First of all, may I call you Chalice? I can? Thank you. Second of all, go suck an ice cube, Chalice.

I have a medical condition, I said to the rowdy voice on from the bin company. What's that? Well, would you like the long version or the short version? The short? Very wise.

But he had no interest in my health, not even when I started in about my sordid pancreas and rancid goolies. If his bin bill wasn't paid, he was sending his heavies around. I look forward to the new faces, I told him, and hung up.

And who's this? Cunthook the fridge repair man? Bollox the boiler fixer? Wait. Are you the cranky old bat from the credit union wondering about the twenty thousand and steadily accumulating interest? You are! Well, I have two words of advice for you, lady. Shove it up your cooch!

Phew. I was tired after all that gabbing.

I plonked myself down on the sofa. What time was it now, I wondered? Look at that. Half past ten in the morning according to the talking head on TV. My, my. Around here, time doesn't even fly when you're having fun. By now my head was spinning, my heart was thumping like a train. *Thudum-dedum. Thudum-dedum.* Must be all that cake I'd eaten. That's OK. I knew what to do. I popped another pill and hit the back lane.

IT COULD BE WORSE

– this was Patrick Cox's story. He was out in the lane, chatting away to Rommel and Himmler, and he hardly noticed me approach.

What could be worse, Patrick?

Ah, young Jason, he said as soon as he saw me. Look at you. You're like a lad on cloud nine.

That's right, Patrick, I'm on clouds nine, ten, eleven and twelve, I said right back to him and he had a good chuckle for himself.

I was just sharing a thought or two with my best friends, he went on. Then he started pointing at one of the ditch trees.

You know, Patrick began, I once saw a five-euro note fluttering on that tree. I was going to pluck it, treat myself and Rommel and Himmler to a kebab. Then I had second thoughts, and said to myself, you know, Patrick, leave it there. Leave it, and if ever again someone has the nerve to say that money doesn't grow on trees, you can take him by the hand, lead him to this very tree, point to the five-euro note flapping away and say look, look at that. Around here, money *does* grow on trees. Around here, anything can happen.

I had no idea what he was on about. Didn't get a chance

to find out because now he was mumbling something else, something about cop Lawless asking about me. No chance to hear more about that either, because by now Harry and Fergal had joined our little gathering by the tree. Afraid that she might be missing out on a matter of great importance, Lily the Nose wasn't long waddling as far as us either. Her arrival soon had Rommel and Himmler growling and gnashing their hungry teeth.

Call off those hell hounds! Lily screeched. Call them off or I won't share my news. Patrick coaxed his dogs away from her and at once she was into some sorry saga about the Slug and how he'd been given thirty days to get out of the house he had been living in for about the past five hundred years and how he had hauled himself down town and chained himself to the courthouse railings.

It's a sign of the times, Harry said, and the others were nodding away and agreeing with him, including Rommel and Himmler, who now looked as if they would like to sink their teeth into whoever was telling the Slug he belonged on the streets.

It's not like it used to be, said Patrick, as he tussled with his dogs.

Do you remember, Harry said next, as soon as Patrick's dogs had simmered down. Do you remember they used to make a sandwich in Dublin that cost one hundred and fourteen euros?

Umbrellas in Tipperary used to be two hundred and forty-five euros, said Fergal.

Aye, and that was on a dry day, said Harry.

A fountain pen in Cork would set you back four hundred, said Fergal.

Well, I'm not going to Cork for a fountain pen, said Harry. I wouldn't go there for a barrelful of fountain pens.

You'd go there for a barrelful of mucky porter.

That's different.

Would you go to the Leitrim hills?

For a fountain pen or porter?

Porter.

I would.

There used to be gold in the Leitrim hills. That's what I heard.

You heard arseways, and not for the first time. It's in Cavan the gold was.

Yous are all hearing arseways, said Patrick Cox. The gold was in Monaghan.

Monaghan!

Yep. Monaghan.

Well fuck it anyway, that place is full of headbangers.

They were still at it as I skipped away. Couldn't be listening to them. Sandwiches and umbrellas and fountain pens and mucky porter. Gold in Monaghan. Fock me! What would they think of next? Strings of pearls along the streets of our boghole town. Rubies on top of the Tower. Diamonds in the back lane. I looked to the Swamp. Oh, good. The girl was out on the rock. It was still early in the day and already I was badly in need of some normal conversation. I popped another pill, skipped the ditch and slid through the trees.

SWEET TALKING

What do you mean she's gone?

I mean she's gone. And get this. I know where to.

Oh yes?

Paris.

I see.

She's with Mario Devine.

The bull-nut seller?

That's right.

In Paris?

Yep.

She should have gone to ancient Greece. What are we going to do?

What do you mean?

I mean how is my father going to get to see your ma if she's swanning about in Paris? Time is running out, you know.

Well, she's gone and I can't do anything about it. But look on the bright side. I have the place all to myself.

How is that looking on the bright side?

Because I am going to throw a party. I'll invite you if you play your cards right.

Can I stay the night? I need to get away from my father. He's crazier than ever.

You want to stay in my house?

That's right. Just for a few nights. A week at most.

A week!

Maybe two.

Two?

It'll be fun. Hey! We can jump into bed together. You can put your thing in me all night.

Nobody's putting anything into anybody.

When I end up in your bed you won't be able to resist me.

You are not getting in my bed.

We'll see.

No we won't see.

I hope you're not one of these boys who are happy to do it to themselves. It causes blindness, you know. And warts. Then you get cancer. And you'll go bald.

Jesus, you're sounding like my ma again.

That's why you wear a hoodie, isn't it? Admit it, you're going bald because you do it to yourself until your hand is ready to fall off.

Hey!

How many times a day? Fifteen? Thirty-five?

Come off it.

Be careful, you might hurt yourself.

Is your da still taking everything out on you?

He is. And his aim is improving. With your mother in Paris I don't know what he's liable to do.

Maybe you can stay.

That's better. Before we jump into bed you can make me

something nice to eat. And don't forget to sweet talk me while we're in the bath together.

We won't be in any bath together.

I'll come around tomorrow. Or the day after. You know, for once you may be right. Your mother being away *is* a good thing.

DODO THE CLOWN AND A HORSE
CALLED TORMENTOR

So this lad goes to the doctor. Says he's depressed. Says life is harsh and cruel. Says he feels all alone in a threatening world. Doctor says, treatment is simple. The great clown Dodo is in town tonight. Go see him. That should pick you up. Man bursts into tears. Says, But doctor . . . I am Dodo.

Is that another joke, Slug?

Ah, Christ!

But how is it a joke? The clown is sad and depressed.

You really need to change your attitude. Has anyone ever said that to you?

Who did this to you, Slug? I asked him next, looking at the chain he'd wrapped around himself at the courthouse railing. You had to hand it to Lily the Nose, her news was always spot on.

What do you mean, Who did this? I did it myself, you nitwit.

I get it. You're making a protest. Have you got a list of demands?

Don't be so childish. I am here to make a point on behalf of this couldn't-care-less town.

I didn't say anything to that. And the Slug manoeuvred himself so that he could sit with his back to the courthouse railings. The wart-and-speckled hands on him. The caved-in face. He didn't really look like a protestor. More like a condemned man waiting his turn for the guillotine.

Hey, Slug. It's going to be cold out here. Can I get you anything? A blanket. Or a hot drink.

No thanks.

But you don't look very comfortable. I could bring you a pillow. And a sleeping bag. No self-respecting protestor goes without a sleeping bag these days. You should know these things, Slug.

Ah, don't be completely daft. I'm going home to my bed as soon as the sun drops.

I was just trying to help, Slug.

Right so, pipsqueak. Get me a sugar donut.

A sugar donut? You're going to be out here all day and all you want is a sugar donut?

That's right. I need to keep up my energy levels. And here's a euro. That's not for the donut. I want you to put a bet on a horse for me.

What horse?

Tell you what. I'll let you choose. Pick the winning horse and I'll even split the pot with you.

I'll even split the pot with you. I liked the sound of that. Would be nice to have some cash taking up room in my pocket. Would come in handy when it came to splashing out on my party.

Past Bill Corrigan's pet shop. Past Happening Woman and Slevin the butcher. Past Freeman the auctioneer with the crooked smile and Doc Mullaney's surgery. Past Shady Daly's second-hand clothes shop. Past Puck Mahon's men's fashions, his CLOSING DOWN IN TWO WEEKS sign still in the window, as it had been every day for the past six months. Past Everything Is Two Euros. Dante's chipper. The Hungry Worm. Past the post office and the credit union. Very quickly past Logan's Pharmacy. Past Masterson the jeweller, after checking the time on one of the watches in his window. Felt for the Slug's euro in my pocket. Checked the time again. Crossed the road. Fished the Slug's euro coin out of my pocket and marched through the doorway of Patsy Fagan's betting shop.

On the screens the midgets were fast with their whips and the horses were galloping. Over the fences they leapt, the cream of the town's gamblers urging on their favourites. Go on, Blue Murder. Come on, Gethsemane. Up you get, Dreamy Lady. Gripped the euro coin. Grabbed a betting slip and pencil, looked at the list for the next race.

Lucky Star.

Half Pint.

Kilfenora Beauty.

Tormentor.

Black Beer.

Savage Times.

Cantankerous Old Lady.

Freida's Delight.

A Donkey Called Dude.

Cinnamon Tart.

The Wife Doesn't Know.

Little Miss Macho.

Was all set to bet on A Donkey Called Dude, but he was withdrawn from the race. Cantankerous Old Lady was a beautiful-looking horse, but kept kicking up her hind legs and the jockey was getting really fed up. Lucky Star was the favourite and was tempted by that. Decisions. Decisions.

Tormentor. A hundred to one.

I preferred the sound of that.

There was a gaggle of betting men in front of me. Waving their slips. Patting each other on the shoulder for good luck. Most of them already certain they were chasing a lost cause.

One euro on Tormentor, I told Patsy when I got to the counter.

To place or win?

Well, seeing as Tormentor is going to gallop home a country mile ahead of the rest of them, I suppose you better put me down for a win.

If you say so.

You can pay me half now if you want, Patsy. Save you having to count it all out later.

You're a funny man, Jason. Tell you what, though, seeing as you made me laugh I won't charge you any tax.

I squeezed my way through the crowd, stood below one of the high-up screens. In the crowd I saw Brains and No-brains, following the same race I'd bet on. The white flag came down. AND THEY'RE OFF! the commentator roared, and the room erupted, you'd have thought this was the last time horses were going to run.

Come on, Lucky Star.

Go on, Half Pint, you good thing.

That's it, Kilfenora Beauty.

Nobody mentioned Tormentor. Good. Didn't want to ruin its chances.

The horses were moving now and the whips were out and the commentator was listing out the names that crash-landed after the jumps. Cinnamon Tart. Black Beer. Freida's Delight. They were down and out, and the losers around me were throwing up their arms and tearing up their slips. And the commentator was starting to get into it now. Kilfenora Beauty is a length ahead. She's looking good. Like her mother before her. Lucky Star is fading and the others may as well have stayed at home in their stables. But wait! Hold on to your whips, Tormentor was making a late run. Up through the field she galloped. Past Little Miss Macho and Cantankerous Old Lady. Past The Wife Doesn't Know and Cinnamon Tart, who was still galloping like a mad thing even though she had dumped her jockey jumps ago. Savage Times was left for dust and at this stage Lucky Star may as well have been travelling through outer space. And they were coming round the final bend and it was a two-horse race. Tormentor and Kilfenora Beauty. They were neck and neck. Kilfenora Beauty edged ahead. Then Tormentor. Then Kilfenora Beauty. Then Tormentor. Then they were past the post and it was impossible to say who crossed first. A photo-finish was declared and we'd have to wait until Mr Eyesight made his decision.

KILFENORA BEAUTY! the shout went out, and No-brains was leaping out of his stool, waving his betting slip, roaring out the name of his horse.

Who did you have? a lad with sagging shoulders asked me.

Tormentor.

Loser, Brains said, sticking his face right into me and he went up to collect his winnings.

But wait. Nobody was getting their winnings just yet. A steward's enquiry was the call. And the screen was showing a re-run of the race and towards the end things got really interesting, especially when the camera zoomed in and showed the midget on Kilfenora Beauty leaning over with his whip and taking a swipe at the midget on Tormentor. And I'd say you could've heard as far away as Paris the collective howl that went up in the betting shop. And, just like that, Tormentor was the winner. And one or two of them in there were patting me on the back and nudging me up to the cash desk to collect my windfall, not that I needed nudging.

No-brains was still gyrating around the place, still thinking he was a winner. A few coins spilled out of his pocket, rolled everywhere. He bent down to pick them up and was crawling on hands and knees after them when Brains caught up with him and landed his black boot up his brother's backside.

Easy come, easy go, some of the others jeered as the pair of them hurried out of there.

I'll be back, Patsy, I said when I was leaving myself, with a pocketful of cash. I know the name of next week's winning horse too.

SHOPPING LIST

Sky-happy with my windfall, it was time to celebrate. I made a list of what I'd need on the back of the betting slip, wobbled light-headed and dizzy all the way from town as far as Mel Campbell's shop. He looked up from his crossword, already shaking his head when he saw me.

Look who it is, he said weakly, when I stood swaying at the counter in front of him.

The one and only, I said.

And yet that's still one too many.

You always give me a hard time, Mel.

Do I now? he said, drumming his fingers on the counter.

I suppose it's because you bring out the worst in me.

And you're starting to bring out a permanent headache in me.

Relax, Mel, I said. Your headache won't get any worse. Not today, anyway. Did I tell you I'm throwing a party? Well, consider yourself invited. Mrs Campbell, too. Now, I have a list of things I need.

I reached in my pocket and pulled out the betting slip, set it down on Mel's counter. Watched him snatch it and start to read.

I hope you have everything, Mel.

You do, do you?

If not, I can always go somewhere else. Tell me, have you double cream, Mel? And custard. I need loads of custard.

What!

Baking soda. Jelly. Caster sugar. I need a fair amount of currants. Better give me all the currants you have. And throw in some candles. One of my guests has a fondness for candles.

What!

Oh, and the Slug wants a donut. Make it two. Did you hear about the Slug? He's down town chained to the courthouse railings.

Any excuse for that layabout.

He's making sacrifices you and I wouldn't dream of.

No fear of it being the ultimate sacrifice, I suppose?

The world doesn't see its best people, Mel. That's what the Slug told me. I think it's men like you he has in mind when he says that.

You think too much. Have a think about that before you step inside my shop again.

Tell you what, Mel. Make it three donuts and you can have one yourself. By the way. Did I tell you? The Ma is gone to Paris.

He narrowed his eyes. I could see him trying to figure out my agenda, what was I going to spring next. It was bugging him that he couldn't figure it out, could practically see the pain in his eyes as I started pulling from his shelves, and then piling onto his counter, everything I needed.

What's she up to in Paris? he growled.

Well.

Well, what?

Well.

Well, what!

Well now, Mel, I don't know if I should answer that.

Are you trying to mess with my head, boy?

No.

I think you are.

I'm just making conversation, Mel.

He grunted at me and I gazed at the shelves, saw a couple of more things my party could do with. Paper hats. Balloons.

Then I spotted the crowning glory.

A bottle of Champagne.

Mel was watching me all the way and shaking his head when I pointed to it.

If you oblige me, Mel, I'll see that your name goes on the VIP list. You and Mrs Campbell will get the red carpet treatment. You'll think you are a prince.

Oh, so now I'm a prince.

Mel, in my pocket I have something that will put a smile on your face.

You don't say.

I do say, Mel. I can safely say this is one deal where you come out on top.

You must think I'm some kind of feckin' eejit.

That's one of the last things I think, Mel. No chance of the bubbly, then?

Ehhh . . . .No, Mel said, shaking his head, and I pulled

out the bundle of money notes and dropped the lot on his counter.

Keep the change, I said.

He was still shaking his head as I stepped out of there with my sack of supplies, still giving me a look and twisting his brains trying to figure out what bad-mind trickery I had conjured this time.

DINNER FOR TWO

A couple of blues and a pair of spat-out yellows later and I was bopping wide-eyed and kite-high, ready for my dinner party. The kitchen full of food. The table set. Candles and music, and over-the-rainbow happy I was. All that was left for me to do was hold the door for my guests, greet them all personally as they arrived.

But hang on. There was only one guest at the half-open doorway. A tall man in a high hat. Snazzy shoes. Cigarette dangling from his mouth. Now who could that mystery stranger possibly be? Wait a minute! WAIT A MINUTE! I knew who it was. I sprang for the door and pulled it fully open. Yes. I was right.

Da.

He looked good. Better than I expected. Relaxed. Enigmatic. Poised. Already he was stepping inside, removing his high hat, tipping ash off his cigarette.

Hey, Da! Look at this. It's some spread, isn't it? Took me ages to get it ready. Well. Don't just stand there. Take a seat. Make yourself at home. And *bon appétit* as they say in Paris.

Hey, Da! How's the soup? What's that? It needs a little more salt? Well, why didn't you say so? Here, try some bread with it. Yeah. It's good bread, alright. French, don't you know.

Hey, Da! How do you like your steak? What's that? All over the plate? Ha! That's a great answer, Da. I'm going to use it next time I'm in the Hungry Worm.

Hey, Da! Let me top up your glass, there. It's good stuff, isn't it? A bit fizzy, though. Gets up your nose, if you know what I mean.

Now don't tell me you didn't leave room for dessert? You did? That's what I like to hear. Well, here is a little something I prepared earlier. Got the recipe from a French cook book. What's that, Da? You detect a running theme to this dinner party? A French theme? Well. I suppose I have to admit that I do have a soft spot for French things. The Eiffel Tower. The river bridges. The guillotine. Stuff like that. Tell me something, Da, have you ever been there?

You know what I was thinking, Da? I was thinking – after I've done the dishes – we could hit the back lane. You know. Hang out for a little bit. I could introduce you to some of my friends. There's this lad who talks to the trees. And there's this other pair who think they have all the answers. And there's another lad who tries to tell me jokes, only they're not very funny. It's the way he tells them, I suppose. And there's this other one – what's that, Da? You don't have time. You have somewhere else to be. Where's that then, Da? Can I come? Can I? What's that, Da? Not a good idea. OK. Maybe next time, then.

And just like that – snap – he was gone again.

*

I sincerely hope this is a party for just you and me, the girl said when I opened up. She was standing there in a black leather mini-skirt and matching boots. Red tights and eye-liner. A new hairdo for crying out loud. And so much make-up I could no longer see the bruise on her neck. She even had her lips painted.

What colour is that? I asked her, looking sideways at her mouth.

Blueberry, she said, pouting her lips and blowing a soft breeze in my face as she padded past me and on into the house.

She must have gone to Beauty by Helen. Or Nora McGuinness. The one-man glam squad, Ma called Nora. And Nora must have wasted little time getting busy with her glamour kit, going to work on the girl's hair. Part of it was brown and frizzled. Part of it was streaky red. Part of it was black like her skirt and boots. With all the chopping and colour-changing, it was like being with three or four versions of the one person.

Well, what do you think? she said when she saw me looking.

Not bad, I said, before I could stop myself.

I'm so glad you approve. Now then, loverboy, where's the bedroom?

I had to pinch myself. One minute, I was downtown grabbing presents for Ma's birthday and she goes and does a runner. Next minute, the girl had invited herself over and was wanting to jump into my bed until her da calmed down. Well. If Ma thought it was OK to swan off for a Champagne time in a riverside hotel, well hey, I could organize my own little bit of Paris.

What the hell is all this? the girl asked when she stepped into the kitchen and saw my baking supplies spread all over the table.

No point having a party without eating something, I said, holding up a packet of custard. Do you know how to make cake?

Next thing, the two of us were busy in the kitchen. In no time, the girl was convinced she was a French chef and was making a list of everything she was going to whip up – sherry trifle, sponge cakes, hot-cross buns, strawberry jams, apple tarts, rhubarb crumbles – while I grabbed the French recipe book and set up the ingredients. I opened out every press and drawer in the kitchen, grabbed whatever was there and spread the lot across the table.

OK then, the girl said, holding high a mixing bowl. Before we jump into bed we are going to create a little bit of Paris right here in this slum of a kitchen.

What are we going to make first? I asked. Cake, she quickly decided. It's Pastille Day, she announced, holding up the cutting knife like a sword. The anniversary of the French Revolution. Let them eat cake, Marie Antoinette said. Then they lopped off her head. Whack! Just like that. And she scalped open the carton of double cream. Next she grabbed a mixing bowl and threw in handfuls of custard, sugar, flour, currants. Dunked in several splashes of sherry, double cream, whatever she could find. On this day they burned Joan of Arc, she said, ripping the smiley woman out of the cook book and taping the page to the kitchen door. They tied her to a stake and said she was a witch. Five sizzling minutes later she was toast. This cake will be in Joan's memory. And she raised up the bowl of slop. The next bowls were for a princess gunned down in cold blood and an innocent woman locked away in a prison cell for something she didn't do. Then, as I knew would happen, the heroes from ancient Greece got a look in. Achilles gutted Hector with his sword. This is Hector's cake, the girl yelled, and pulled out of the oven something that smelt like burning rubber. Helen of Troy had a face that launched a thousand ships. This is Helen's cake, she howled, holding up something a starving baba would've crawled quickly away from. Are you following the instructions? I said and she threw a fist of custard at me. There were so many occasions to mark she ran out of sherry. Then she used Ma's vodka.

Her favourite French occasion was the anniversary of Édith Piaf's death. Édith Piaf is the most popular dead person in France, she said. Everyone visits her grave. She is called the little sparrow. I have no regrets, she announced, removing Édith's cake from the oven. I could be descended from the French, she said, and who knows, maybe you are too. We could have very sophisticated blood. Don't ever forget that. And she licked the fingers she had just poked into the lump of char that passed for Édith's cake.

The special occasions were coming faster than the last of the last days the drunks in the lane were always laughing about. And they no longer had anything to do with France or ancient Greece. I dedicate this sponge cake to the Swamp, she said, holding up her latest effort. Go forth and save lives, she said, blessing a tray of hot-cross buns with the cutting knife. It is the first Thursday of the week, she announced. This is my delicious Thursday cake.

We need something else, she said next and she twirled around the kitchen floor, turned on the stereo. Then she started to sing. She was singing and choosing the ingredients for the next cake, spinning around while tossing them any old way into the mixing bowls. Unlike with Ma, every note didn't sound as if it was coming from someone who had just fallen off a cliff. *Pour some sugar on me*, went her husky voice as she spun around with her cutting knife. *Boy, you better make her raspberry swirl*, she swooned when she spotted me trying to tiptoe out the door. *Lick me like a lollipop*, she sang, bunching her blueberry lips the way I'd seen Ma do it.

How many cakes have we baked? I asked at some point, thinking we'd made enough and that I could do with a rest.

Not enough, she replied, shoving her next effort into the oven. And she got straight back into her song.

The more she baked the bigger the mess. The kitchen table was littered with spilled cartons of sugar and over-turned jars of baking powder. Blobs of custard flew onto the walls and ceiling. Gouts of jam stained her clothes. She slid around the buttery floor with her oven trays. Humming away to the next song. It was a miracle she didn't go belly-up. I won't fall, she said as though she was reading my mind. I know my centre of gravity. She didn't even wear the apron I took out for her. It got so bad, I put on the apron myself and tidied up.

Look at you, she howled, when the kitchen was as good as new again. You're the best tidy-upper in the world. What would your mother do without you?

But she wasn't fooling me. Not for one minute. I knew she was going to pounce. She was going to grab me and drag me up the stairs and into Ma's bedroom and there would be no budging until I'd done what she'd been asking me to do all summer.

There's some good stuff on TV tonight, I told her, thinking it would distract her for a little while.

I know what you're up to, she replied. Don't worry. I'm biding my time. We can watch some TV. But you won't be able to resist forever. You'll see. You better just hope it's not too late by then. And she made a swoop, plunged her knife and cut us both huge hunks of chocolate sludge.

At long last we ran out of ingredients. She wanted to make a fast trip to the Hungry Worm to collect a new batch. Or send me. Even make another trip to the one-woman glam squad when she realized all the baking had melted the make-up she'd put on, played havoc with her hairstyle.

Instead, she took a step back to admire everything she'd done. Wiped her hands in the apron I was still wearing. Took a rag to remove custard and streaks of cream from her leather skirt.

And now it's time, she said after a quiet moment or two. Boy, you may run my bath.

A bath? You want a bath? I had to get her to repeat for me and she did. Fair enough. I could waste some time fiddling with the taps and the candles and messing with the bubbles. By the time she had managed to scrub herself clean there wouldn't be time for anything else.

Soon the water was steaming and I put a few lit candles about the room. I waved my hand through the water, tested the temperature, closed the taps.

It's ready, I hollered, looking up from where I was kneeling, but she was already there, standing right in front of me, not a stitch on her, the steam from the hot water drifting up and around her like a shroud.

She stepped into the water and let herself stretch fully out.

Well. What are you waiting for?

Huh?

Get in. The water is great.

The bath is for you.

Wrong. The bath is for us. Now come on. Get your kit off.

I don't want to, I said.

Why not? Are you an alien underneath that useless hoodie?

No.

Well, then.

She splashed some water at me. Blew suds through the steamy air. I still hadn't budged.

The water isn't going to stay warm all night.

That's OK. You can have it all.

What is wrong with you? Wait. Let me guess. You don't have a belly button. Your nipples are missing. I know. You have a rare condition that has petrified your skin. Come on. Show me. I want to see.

I stood there without doing a thing. She was staring hard at me now, with each passing second becoming more and more suspicious.

I hope I don't have to get out of this bath and remove that hoodie myself.

You don't have to do anything! I yelled, and stormed downstairs, grabbed the happy pills from the kitchen table, raced back up to my bedroom, and banged the door closed after me.

NIGHTSOUNDS

I was hearing things. Water dripping from the faulty tap. The useless ticking of that bockety wall clock. The ghosts of battered-into-pulp rats back from the dead for one last scurry. I drew back the curtain and peered out the window, into the darkness, into the silent night of trees and parked cars. Ma was on the prowl. Shuffling about the place. Mumbling to herself. I could hear her shivering too. Her wandering voice started to spook me. I opened the window. It was completely black outside. Somewhere out there I heard a clinking in the darkness. That's all. I had no idea what it could be, couldn't tell where it was coming from. *Clink, clink, clink.* That's all I could hear.

Wait a minute.

It wasn't Ma. Couldn't be. She was in Paris with the bull-nut seller.

How long had she been gone? A day? Two days? A week? Why hadn't she been in touch? When was she coming back? Had no answers to these questions. And I stared out the window thinking about what the girl had said. About how Ma being away was a good thing. But now I wasn't so sure.

Gradually, other sounds came. An owl's *who who whooo.* A drunk's late-night melody. The night train pulling out of the station. Its wheels rattling slowly over the tracks, *thudum-dedum thudum-dedum*, fading in and out as the engine tried to pick up speed. I heard the boy-racers. A siren. Barking dogs. My friend, the rat.

I wondered what she was up to in Paris. What was the bull-nut seller treating her to? River walks and cobble-stones. Lamp-lit squares and red wine and all the French bread she could stuff herself with. Again I wished she would get in touch. Or maybe I could get some kind of message to her. I could almost see the happy look on her face. *Don't worry about me, kid. I'm having a blast.*

Inside my room, I flicked pages of that ragged atlas in the half-light and thought: the world is huge. She could be anywhere. I grabbed myself and shivered.

Then I was sleeping. Only something kept waking me up. A sort of whispering in my ear. Jesus! It was the rat from the yard. I could hear his nibbly voice in my ear. You little toe-rag. You scumfuck prick of a boy. You tried to kill me. Well, just you wait. Just you wait and let's see what happens to you.

Fock me!

Talking rats.

Then I was moving. Floating almost, through the night, through its silence and dark secrets. Except tonight it wasn't so silent. I heard more hooting and the night train still creaking its way through. I ducked into the ditch trees, and when I looked up again, I was staring right into a pair of witchy eyes. But it was only the owl and I batted it out of my way. Then I heard the girl's voice. Coming from the Swamp. I moved through the reeds and then I saw her. Sitting by a gathering fire. Breathing in the flames. Gurgling mouthfuls of beer. Inviting me beside her.

What are you going to be when you grow up? she roared across the flames.

A parachutist, I shouted back, I want to fly through the air.

And what else?

A gold-digger, I whispered, staring into her mermaid eyes, I'm going to buy you a diamond ring.

And what else?

A knight in shining armour. I am going rescue you from the dreaded Cyclops.

I knew you would be my hero, she said in her grown-up way, and she looked into the heavens and she glowed.

We leaped through burning hoops and crowed and hollered. Chanted strange names and collapsed in each other's arms. We worked ourselves into a pandemonium that scared the night itself away, and when I brought myself to look again, she had the face of the rat and I had to shield my disbelieving eyes. She reached over, took my hand, and shoved it between her legs.

Then I was sitting up in my bed, breathless, and the sweat dripping off me, wondering how I was going to escape. I whipped the blanket and pills away, took a fast look around, and was all set to make a dash for the other room when I saw the girl lying there beside me, quietly sleeping. And something about her lying there started to relax me – something comforting and safe – and so instead of bolting, I lay back down in the bed and wrapped my arms around the sleeping form beside me.

HAS ANYONE GOT A PHONE
I COULD BORROW?

First thing next morning I tried calling Ma's mobile. But our phone was no longer working. Aha! At long last the phone lads had had enough and pulled the plug. I checked in on the girl. She was sleeping like someone in a morgue. I left her be.

I took a walk as far as Virgin Gemma's house. Gemma would have a phone I could use and she liked to do a good deed. She opened her door, the sharp points in her face looking sharper than usual even though she didn't look too disappointed to see me.

Hello, Vir . . . I mean Gemma. I need to speak with Ma.

I haven't see her, Jason.

She's in Paris. Can I use your phone? I have some important news for her.

Of course you can.

A talking woman came on telling me Ma's phone was powered off. I thanked Gemma, told her I'd see her in McMorrow's for Happy Hour and left it at that.

I called around to Nora McGuinness. I didn't like the colour of her beauty spot today and was tempted to step away from her door, but Nora reached out an arm and hauled me inside her front room and I tried calling Ma again. Nothing.

I called around to Carmel Brophy, wife of Barty. She was a strange shape of a woman and wearing far too much lipstick.

Hello, Carmel, I need to speak with Ma.

I wish she was here, Jason, I really do. But she isn't.

She's in Paris. I need to call her. They've pulled the plug on our phone. I need to get an important message through to her.

I'll try her later, Jason, Carmel said when I couldn't get through. But I'll tell you something for free, if I get a hold of her she'll wish she stayed in Paris when she had the chance. Uh-oh, I thought. She knows all about Ma shoving her fleshy bits in Barty's face after that fiasco with our blocked radiator. And I knew what Carmel might have in mind as far as Ma was concerned.

OK, Carmel, I said, doing my best to look innocent. It seemed to work too. She started wiggling some of her own flesh at me, just not as effectively as I'd seen Ma do it. Then she bunched up her lipstick mouth and blew her idea of a kiss my way. I ducked just in time.

Fionnuala Quirke lived next door. I tried her next.

My, my, Jason. You're turning into quite a boy, aren't you, Fionnuala said before I had a chance to speak a word. Your ma's not here but you're welcome to come in. I've got two wonderful blueberry muffins with your name written all over them.

No thanks, Fionnuala. I've had some blueberry this week.

I'll make you a passion fruit smoothie.

No thanks, Fionnuala.

How about a lemon meringue?

Save one for me, Fionnuala.

Come by again, Jason. Come by any time.

I was at the gate of Big Beatrice Glynn's house before I realized I hadn't even asked Fionnuala for the use of her phone. And I was just about to open Big Beatrice's gate when I remembered it was her pills I had in my bag. As soon as I turned away, along came the McManus brothers.

Have either of you got a phone I could borrow? I asked them.

What? No-brains growled.

I need a phone. You know. Little gadget that allows you talk to people.

Are you giving me lip, midget? he asked.

Just answering your question, No-brains.

What was that you called me?

You have to admit it, Mark. You're a bit of feckin' head-banger. More than a bit.

I was already half way down the lane before he realized what I'd called him. By the time he started to give chase I was well out of sight, buried in the reed grass beside the Swamp. A borrowed telephone would have to wait.

Down town I paused at the window of Oliver Sheehan's electrical shop. All the televisions were tuned into the same channel. Bits of that missing jumbo jet being pulled out of the Atlantic. Pictures of distraught relatives. Then I saw the date rolling across the bottom of the screen. August 17th. Or was it a 19? Couldn't make it fully out, my eyesight was blurry, and now the letters and numbers were dancing across the television screen like music notes come to life. And what if it was August 19th?

That meant it was four days since I'd last seen her.

Fock me!

*

It was getting towards that point when day starts to become night. I had walked as far as Station Hill, was looking down at the tracks, at Mellows the signal man mooching about near his cabin, at the empty tracks disappearing into the gathering dark. I was all set to carve a message into my lower arm with the nail I was uselessly searching my pockets for. I looked in my bag and fished out the next box of pills. Pressed a pill – a blue one – out of its foil, held it to my mouth and bit into it. It was chalky and bitter and I popped the rest of it in my mouth and quickly swallowed it before I changed my mind. Then I tried one from the yellow box. It tasted better.

That night I looked out through Ma's bedroom window. The rowdy bushes. The useless weeds. The lifeless trees. Shadow branches. Skeletal arms reaching for the dark. And the moon. Low over the Swamp, making it look like something out of a postcard collection, which was how it always looked to me anyway. I opened the window. Let in the calm air. The black night. I thought I heard my name in a scream. Faraway and faint. But there.

I must have stayed at the window all night. Lost inside some night-time spell of blue seas and hot sun and the water glistening, and dipping the oars of my boat and pulling hard, all the time steering a course for that island that takes twenty years to find. A pounding at the front door brought an end to all of that. It was loud and persistent and this time I had no intention of answering it.

IN DEMAND

It was Mattie Conlon. What did that scone-selling fruitcake want? His French cookbook? Some uneaten buns? Wait. Gavin McGoldrick was with him. What was up with him? Had he a patched-up rust bucket that needed paying for? Mattie rapped the knocker loudly, while Gavin peered in through the sitting-room window. I didn't like the look or the sound of this and kept myself upstairs. They weren't put off so easily, though, and Mattie let the door have it for another few minutes, a wonder the knocker didn't break off in his hand, so severe was he with the thing. Finally fed up with all of that, he joined Gavin at the front window and the pair of them looked long and hard. Then damn it if the madmen didn't walk around the back and start gawking in the kitchen window. I was all set to open an upstairs window, pour a pan of boiling jelly down on top of them, watch them melt before my eyes. Then I could hear them stomping away, all huff and tut, and you could just tell that they weren't going to give up so easily. No sir. As soon as they could, they would be back. Well, let them. Next time I could set the girl on them – if she ever woke up.

Meantime the letterbox was in use again. Bills, demands, pay-up letters shoved through. I could hear Barrabas Diffley and the cheery whistling he was at, as though he was bringing news of winning lotto numbers, instead of all manner of threats from just about everybody it was possible to owe money to. I was going to open the door on him and give him the same message I'd given the witch from the Credit Union. Then I reckoned someone might be lurking, and had second thoughts. I thought of taping up the letter-box like the Slug had done with his place, but I couldn't find any tape, and no way was I setting foot outside. At least not until after dark and the coast was clear and at that stage shops would be closed, and right now it all seemed like too much effort.

From time to time I plugged the telephone cord back in, who knows, we might have been reconnected. Ma might've called and left a message as to what she was up to in Paris. At some point I was sure she would try to get word to me. *Hey, Jason, and bonjour from this swell place. Everything they said is true. It's a super swell place, superbe, as they say over here, so superbe that I have decided enough is enough, I am not coming home. That's right. You didn't mishear me. I am going stay right here in this place and stuff that bog-hole town once and for all. I know, I know. Lots of people over there are going to miss me. The manager of the Credit Union. The rubbish collectors and the ESB. The telephone rental people. And a whole lot more. Well. They are going to have to find a way to survive without me, aren't they? And don't you dare say a word about where I am. Until then, I'll be staying out of radio contact. I'll be lying low, biding my time, waiting for the best moment to get in touch.*

Oh yes. I could almost hear her speak the words. *It's time to check out of this hotel, kid.*

Sit tight, Jason. She'll get word to you very soon. But every time I plugged in the phone and waited for it to ring and for the messages she wanted to get through to me, all I got was a lot more of absolutely nothing. It was better than a plague of cunthooks and arsebandits getting angrier by the second and wondering why they hadn't been paid and what did Ma think she was playing at, and them threatening all sorts of warfare if I or somebody didn't produce some fast cash. Still though. How long had it been now? More than a week? Get in touch, Ma. Please.

Then cop Lawless called around. He parked his squad car and tipped his garda hat at waddling Lily the Nose and he stepped up to the door. He didn't knock as loudly or for as long as Mattie Conlon, but he knew I wasn't far away. I even thought about opening the door to him. After all, maybe I could put him to some use. Then I had another thought. It was me he was after. Big Beatrice had noticed her missing pills and remembered me being in Logan's Pharmacy. Not to mention the boy-racer car the girl and me had taken for a spin. Wait a minute. It wasn't just me. He was after the girl too! Her da had spotted her missing. Knew where she was. And here was Lawless showing up to take her home and haul me in front of that bastard judge Deeley for kidnapping.

By now I was on the upstairs landing, standing on the high-stool Ma had waltzed home from McMorrow's ages

ago, and with the hurley stick, was nudging free the trap-
door up into the attic. It gave easily and a moment later I
had squeezed my way through the narrow opening, was
plonked on a timber beam in the dusty dark, surrounded by
cardboard boxes. The place was covered in dust, cobwebs,
crawling things. It was tough to breathe. Water plinked.
Something scurried, scratched, squealed.

Then I heard the letterbox flapping. And a gruff voice
coming through it.

Jason. Are you there, Jason?

Was about to let a holler at him to get lost, then I heard
another voice, not-so-gruff this time and coming from
somewhere very close to me.

The girl. It was the girl!

Up here, I hissed, and heard Lawless again as I reached
an arm down through the open trap-door while she climbed
up.

Jason! Are you in there? Is your ma about?

As soon as the girl was through the attic, I bundled her
into the dark space beside me.

What the hell, she said.

It's Lawless. He knows you're here. I need you to stay
quiet while I head him off.

Oh, I get it. You're trying to be my hero. This is exciting.
OK. I'll stay here. You go down and gut him with your
sword.

Nobody's gutting anybody.

Go to it, Achilles. Take him down.

By the time I climbed down out of there and got as far

as the sitting-room window, Lawless had cleared off. He'd be back, though. I knew he would. I would have to think hard about this. Come up with a plan. Otherwise we'd be stuck up in that clammy attic never again to see the light of day.

Watched one or two episodes of the gangster show Ma liked. Figured I would need to toughen up. Acquire some new language. There were some good lines in them. Tony Soprano had a line I liked. You fuck up once, you lose two teeth. And the hoodlums had some really good faces. Later, I stood in front of the bathroom mirror. Traced my finger along the diagonal crack. Snarled my way through some tough talking. *Freeze. Screw you, mug. Have a nice life, sucker.* Took a good look at myself, too, then frowned when I remembered the things Ma's friends had said in McMorrow's during Happy Hour. Cherub cheeks and melting eyes. And what was it the girl had called me? That's it. Angelface.

I would have to have a think about that. Angelface wasn't going to cut it any more. No way was it.

BIRTH CERT

Then I started to forget what Ma looked like. Jesus! Whatever about looking for someone I had never met, what would people say to me when I couldn't even describe the woman I had been living with for the last twelve years? The girl would have a great time with that. Then I thought: Jesus! The girl. I've left her in the attic. Tony Soprano wouldn't be long taking out my teeth if anything happened to her. Fast as I could, I scrambled back up into the dusty space.

Are you there? I called out, pushing boxes aside. There was no answer. I dragged more boxes out of the way, and in my hurry, one or two of them tipped over, sending letters, envelopes, newspapers, out through the open trapdoor. Are you there? I tried again. Still nothing.

You fuck up once, you lose two teeth.

Oh boy.

Where was she?

I shoved another box towards the shaft of light coming through the trapdoor. The box was full of knick-knacks and a red photo album with the words *Our Family* written in wavy gold lettering. Grabbed the album and flicked it open. Turned the page. And another. Not many of them had photographs. One or two of me. A couple of Ma. A few of her with other women I didn't recognize. Prised them loose, looked at the back to see if anything was written there. Nothing.

Wait a minute. I was supposed to be looking for the girl. I tossed away the photo album and slid down out of there.

Papers lay scattered about on the landing. Postcards. Letters. Newspaper cuttings. And look. Birth certs. I picked up the first one and saw that it was Ma's. Then I was clutching the second one and it was my own. Aha, I thought. At long last an answer I've been looking for. I grabbed it and scanned the entries. Date of Birth. Yes. Place of birth. Yes. Mother. Yes. Father. No. The box for father had been left blank. There it was. Da was a blank. An empty space. Not even worth a black mark in a square box.

THE LOVED AND LOST

Dizzy now. Head spinning. Around and around and around. I staggered downstairs, bumping off the walls, the banister. Slid down the last few stairs and landed on my backside. Dragged myself to my feet and wobbled into the kitchen. Reached inside Ma's secret press and grabbed the wine bottle – the full one, the one she'd been keeping for the next happy day in her life. A wonder she hadn't grabbed the bottle when herself and Mario were taking off. Probably didn't need it where she now was. She was having plenty of happy days since her fast dash with Mario. What were they up to right now? Still dancing, I bet. In another one of those lamp-lit squares Mario had been banging on about. Going around and around and around. The light of the moon. The old cobblestones. And later, after they'd worked up an appetite, down by the river with all the bread and cheese and grapes. And all the bottles of wine she needed.

Reeling all over the place. Blurry, and wondering exactly what size of a numpty I was. Colossal. Enormous. Or merely gargantuan. Bad enough me not getting a hold of one parent. Now I'd somehow managed it so that I'd lost the other one. I had to laugh. Ha! Ha! Ha! Ha! Ha! Ha! I lurched for the back-yard door, and swaying from side to side where I stood, popped two blues and a yellow. Ha! Ha!

Ha! Ha! Ha! Ha! Ha! Ha! Ha! Ha! Ha! Ha! Wading through the wild garden, and the crooked head on Mrs Redihan when I bit into another yellow. Ha! Ha! Ha! Ha! I just couldn't stop laughing.

Tramping up the back lane. Top of the day to you, Harry and Fergal. Have you met anyone better than yourself, Patrick? Hello, Lily, and did you hear the news? You didn't, well, you're missing out on one of the best stories to hit this place in ages. And what story would that be, Jason? For me to know and you to find out, Lily the Nose. A note of caution, though: you fuck up once, you lose two teeth.

Down the dark town I spotted the Slug. Hey, Slug! Is it not past your bedtime? I yelled as I joined him by the courthouse railings and let a hearty laugh out of me. He glared at me and wanted to know what was so funny. So I slurred through my trip into the attic and my little discovery there, and I mentioned Ma taking off to Paris under cover of dark while I was left to look after the fort, and Lawless and the rest of them trying to beat a way through the doors. Five days she's been gone, Slug. Five days! What do you think of that? But he wasn't reacting the laughing way I had. No. He was scratching his chin and shaking his head slowly at me. He knew I was a gargantuan-sized numpty. He knew I had no idea what I was at. As if to let me know this is exactly what he was thinking, the Slug then let out a long shrill whistle. Then I waved him closer to me, which was a little tricky, what with him still in chains on the courthouse railings. So I leaned into him to ask again why he wasn't at home in bed. But I couldn't get a single word to come out of my mouth, sounded like gobbledegook, and I was laughing again and the Slug was looking awfully serious, and the more serious he became the more I laughed. I couldn't stop. Jesus, Slug, I slurred, waving crazy with the wine bottle. What is the world coming to? Then I hunkered down and bid him join me in a low huddle. Slug, I said, someone is trying to pull the wool over my eyes. Take me for a fool. But the Slug still wasn't laughing. For all I knew he could have been in on it. He must have been able to see into my thoughts, because before the next words were out of my mouth, he had started into a mild chuckle. At last! That set me off even more and next thing I was asking him for one of his jokes. Come on, Slug, I yammered on. Give me one. For old times' sake. He'd had enough of me, though, and he batted an arm at me and turned away. I knew how he felt. I gave him a great big slap on the back and continued on my way.

Then I was hanging out by the bridge, queasy and looking down at the crazy river and getting queasier by the minute. The river had a mind of its own, couldn't even flow in a straight line. It zigzagged round jutting-out rocks, castaway prams, shopping trolleys, rushed away from me and out of our boghole town. Where are you off to, then? I hollered, watching it all the way, as my stomach lurched, once, twice, then spewed up a splendid spongy mess of what I'd been putting inside me for the past few days, and all the time the waves of dizziness coursing through me.

Walking the back lane again. Staggering past the ditch trees and the dandelion weeds. Waving at the nettles. Looking skywards. Well, well, well. Would you look at that? We had our own moon here. Lighting up the way in front of me. Hey, Ma, I said, reaching for another pill. Guess who has the moon in their pocket? And look. I wasn't alone tonight. The drunks were out, circling their collections of cans. I should pay my respects. Offer them a drink of wine. Pay them back for all the times they'd offered me a slug from their cans.

Look at them. Hailing me as I approached. Like I was a long-lost hero returned from the wars, a sailor back from a sea voyage that was never going to end, a favourite son everyone had long-ago given-up on. They were delighted to see me and I was happy to be among them. They even had a little fire going.

I approached them and offered my wine bottle. The gargoyle accepted gratefully and he wrapped an arm around me, gently guided me to the flames. Squint-eye put a can in my hand and I took it and drank deep.

My da is an empty space, I told them, and they laughed and took some drink.

My ma has flown the coop, I told them, and they laughed some more and took another drink.

You know who we are, kid, another one said, someone I hadn't seen before. We're the loved and lost.

We stood around the collection of beer cans and stared down at our feet. For a time nobody spoke, and I looked into these haggard faces, now lit up by the light of the moon, now scrunched up in darkness, now lost in whatever regions they needed to find to keep themselves from whatever it was that awaited them. Yes indeed, I announced in my best newscaster voice. We're the loved and lost. In the last of the last days. And if I had been the giant I thought I was, I would have gathered them in my arms and somehow tried to let them know that everything would turn out alright in the end. I dropped onto the flimsy flames my crumpled-up birth cert.

ANSWER ME THIS, ANNIE

The very person, I said first thing next morning and I walked straight up to the scryer and asked her what my da was at.

Come on now, Annie, I said. This time I want an answer out of you. Give me something. Tell you what. I'll provide some answers and you just confirm with a nod of your head or one of those shudders you're so good at. OK? Here goes.

Da is alive and well and living on a yacht.

No reaction to that, eh? Well, I was just testing you there. Sure, how could he be living on a yacht? That's good, Annie. You're on the level, as Tony Soprano says. Your teeth are safe. OK. Try this one.

Da is a freedom fighter doing his best for a lost cause.

Nothing doing there either, is that it, Annie? I see. You're probably right. What about these.

Da is a miner digging his way through all the Monaghan gold.

Da is buckled into the space shuttle about to take off for the one-way mission to Mars.

I gave her a few more. But each time she had no answer for me. Truth was, she didn't seem all that interested in anything coming out of me. Just grabbed herself and swayed. But that didn't mean anything. Did it?

I might have to get the word out about her. Let people know they were kidding themselves thinking this one held the answers they were looking for. I let her know as much, too. Annie, I said, we're through. And just so as you know, anybody wants to know, I'm going to tell them exactly how it is when it comes to getting information out of you. OK?

Still no reaction.

Still didn't care.

She had probably forgotten things I would never know.

CHICKEN AND THYME

I was sitting at the kitchen table. Surrounded by four- or five-day-old sherry trifles and hot-cross buns and bowls of multi-coloured jelly. Raisins scattered about the place. Baking soda and double cream. Blobs of custard. And flies. They were back in force. Clouds of the things. Hopping on and off the goodies in the kitchen.

I was looking at some of the photographs I'd missed, some that had spilled out of the attic. There was one of me, aged three. Sitting on a patch of grass. Sulking about something. Another one of me, aged about six. Standing in the back yard in shorts and a peaky cap. Still sulking. One of Ma. Sitting on the sofa in the sitting room. Looking up with a glass in her hand. She wasn't sulking. She just looked surprised.

Then someone else was talking.

What are you up to? the voice asked me. Jesus! The girl. I'd forgotten about her again. Twice in two days.

Nothing, I said, clearing away the photos.

I'm hungry.

Help yourself, I said, waving at the table of goodies.

I need something savoury.

You want some crisps?

Sensations. Chicken and thyme flavour.

I can't leave to get you crisps. It's no longer a good idea. Don't be so childish.

What if I'm spotted?

You'd go if it was your mother wanting a Mars bar.

Yeah, that's only because she can slice me lengthways with her eyes.

If you don't go, I'm going to do something to myself.

Like what?

I found a sturdy rope in that attic dungeon you imprisoned me inside.

What are you going to do with that?

That depends. Now, are you going for my Sensations?

Promise me you won't do anything while I'm gone.

Just make sure you get me chicken and thyme.

*

When I was sure nobody was looking, I ducked out of the house and skipped up the back lane as far as Mel Campbell's. Mel had never heard of Sensations. And so I had to make a fast trip down town as far as Dunnes Stores Better Value Beats Them All. I snuck down the crisps aisle, spotted the Sensations, shelves of the things. And all the flavours in the world. Caramelized onion. Thai sweet chilli. Balsamic vinegar, for crying out loud. But not a chicken and thyme in sight. I got the hell out of there. I tried the Hungry Worm. McMorrow's pub. The ancient paper shop beside the cathedral. I even took a walk as far as the by-pass and marched into Aldi. Aha! Dunnes Stores Better Value Beats Them All no longer beats them all. They had chicken and thyme Sensations, going for a song they were. They even had cheap Champagne, and ha! I was thinking, everywhere you look in this town we have Champagne, and ha! again, no need to go to Paris to have a Champagne time of it after all. And I thought: someone is going to get a kick out of this. I grabbed the Champagne, stuck it in my bag alongside the Sensations. Quick as a slap, I was out of there.

Outside I was fumbling with the Sensations, trying to close my bag over the rustling crisps, and who did I practically walk into only Mario Devine. I thought I was seeing things. Blinked my eyes in case I was. No doubt about it, though. It *was* Mario.

Hey! I called out, but he didn't answer.

Hey, Lug! I tried again, you're supposed to be in Paris. He didn't hear me. Either that or he wasn't used to being called Lug.

Hey! I roared. But he was already walking away from me and heading towards his car, getting in, and driving away.

And to think I'd actually thought he was related to me.

Well, what about that? What was Mario playing at? Had he led Ma up the garden path with all that Champagne talk? Had he fooled her into thinking she was on her way to a quaint riverside hotel?

Wait a minute. WAIT A MINUTE! If Mario was here, that meant Ma was in Paris on her own. And so what was she up to? Wait again. I think I have it. She was never intending to go to Paris with the bull-nut seller. It was Da.

She was rendezvousing with Da. Yes. That had to be it. Oh boy. That's what had her so keen on all that Paris talk. She had been planning this all along. And now she was lying low with Da. Biding her time until things simmered down. That's why I hadn't heard a thing. And as soon as she knew it was safe, she was going to send word for me to join them. Yes. That was it. What a brilliant plan. And hey, if she could come up with a plan like that, guess what? So could I. Get the hell out of town and rendezvous with the pair of them in Paris. Think of it. We could meet up under the famous arch or along the banks of the river. We could meet up on the viewing deck of the Eiffel Tower. Or at one of the plush palaces. My heart was racing now. I would have to have a good think about this. Get some advice from the girl. One thing I was now certain of: I was out of here.

Oh boy. It was all coming together now inside my head. Get to *Gay Paree* and hook up with the pair of them. After that, the world was ours. We could go anywhere.

Think of it. The three us making a fast dash for the nearest way out of Paris. And already I had us on the open road, in one of those snazzy French cars, the kind with no covers and lots of *va-va-voom*. We fooled them, I was saying as we coasted along. We fooled them all. From here out, it's just the three of us.

My heart was fairly going now. I had to take another pill to calm myself down. Except I didn't calm down. And I kept putting myself into future scenes. Me and Ma and Da, screaming up a storm together. Ma waking up to a breakfast of croissants and coffee, Da with the map laid out on the bonnet of the car, plotting our next move. And all the time the French cops on the lookout for us, and one of their inspectors – a lad with a tidy moustache and precise lips – getting in touch with cop Lawless to determine how dangerous we were, and Ma having a good laugh at some joke Da had just cracked, and then we had plotted our next move and before anyone had a chance to get within an *ooh-la-la, there they are*, we were on the open road again. Vanished. Out of sight.

CHAMPAGNE TIME

I bolted back to the house. Guess what! I yelled as soon as I was in the door. Flip! She was gone. Probably fed up waiting for me to show up with chicken and thyme Sensations. Made sure I still had them and the Champagne tucked safely inside my bag, and took off again. Bolted up the back lane. Glanced into the Swamp. No sign of her there. Kept going. Checked the bridge. Not there either. Kept going.

Running down town. Hoodie tight around me. Goodies shaking away inside my bag. Thinking up my plan. Outside the Hungry Worm I paused to take a breath, and yes, there she was. At a window table by herself, tucking into a plate of chips.

The very person, I said when I sat in opposite her. I have big news.

Where are my Sensations?

Never mind them. Now listen to me. I've just seen Mario. The bull-nut seller. He's not in Paris.

So?

So Ma isn't with him in Paris. She's with Da. And get this.

Wait. Let me guess the next bit. They're waiting for you and so as soon as you're ready, you're off to join them.

I was thinking you could come with me.

No thanks.

But your crazy da? You could get away from him, once and for all.

I can take care of myself.

But it's Paris. Think of the riverside café.

Don't want to.

And the lamp-lit squares.

I prefer dark-lit squares.

Think of all the bridges and the guillotine.

No thanks.

Think of . . .

NO, NO, NO!

Why not?

I don't want to go to Paris.

Suit yourself.

She lobbed a chip into her mouth and gestured to me with her middle finger. I slumped back into my seat, watched her pick at her chips.

Are you splashing out? I said, when she grabbed a bottle of ketchup and started drowning her chips with the stuff.

Well, I got fed up waiting for a certain person to show up with my Sensations.

I looked at the soggy chips on the plate in front of her, the sea of red sauce she was dipping them into. She was talking again.

The world around me then was kind of grim. I had to learn to pretend in order to block the grimness.

What?

It's just something I saw.

Let me guess. On the internet.

Not everything comes from the internet.

Paris is going to be good, I said. I'm going to get a haircut and pick up some new clothes, maybe a new pair of shoes. I might even have to change my name. You know, in case Lawless has his cronies on the lookout for me.

Pipsqueak is a good name for you.

What about Nasty? Nasty Lowry?

Oh, yes. That sends shivers down my spine.

Or Notorious. Notorious Lowry has a good ring to it.

Tell me, Notorious, did you manage to get my Sensations?

I have this, I said, reaching into my bag and pulling out the bottle of Champagne. At once her eyes lit up.

At last, she said. Something I can use. Here, let me.

She grabbed it from me and started pulling off the silver foil and twisting off the wire holding the cork in place. Next thing the cork popped, and a geyser erupted and sprayed everywhere. She grabbed two paper cups and managed to direct the gushing Champagne into each of them. She slid one of the cups towards me and raised her own. Then someone was hovering over our table. And when I looked up, it was Mattie Conlon.

You can't drink Champagne in here, he said.

Spin on that, moron, the girl said, showing him the same finger she had produced for me.

I'll be back, he said, turning on his heels. And then you'll be sorry.

He walked to the till, grabbed his phone and started to call someone.

Quick. Do you know any good toasts? the girl asked.

To the answers, I said, raising my own cup, but she didn't know the response. You're supposed to say, To the questions.

See you in the next world, she said instead, then gulped down every drop in her cup, stood out of her seat and marched to the door of the café. Her skinny legs jammed into her backside. Her tattered tackies flapping at the ground. She pulled open the door, looked over her shoulder briefly, at what I couldn't tell, then she walked out into the street and disappeared.

SCARFACE

Early morning. Just me and the chirping birds and a cloud of flies flitting about the place. I'd gotten a good night's sleep, cleaned myself up. In the bathroom now, standing in front of the cracked mirror holding a sturdy scissors liberated from Ma's room.

Hello there, young lad, and what can I do for you on this bright August morning? the mirror said to me.

I'd like a haircut, I said back.

Well, I didn't think you were going to ask for a fishing rod, mirror said, chuckling away at me, and gestured for me to step right up.

Well, don't just stand there, mirror said. Tell me what you want. A short, back and sides? A trim and wash, perhaps? A hot towel shave? Wait. I have it. You want a buzzcut. Am I right? Thought so. Well, Jason, I don't have my shaver with me today. It'll have to be the scissors. OK? Though I have to say, if it was me I wouldn't touch a wisp of those curls.

Stepped closer to the mirror. Whipped the hoodie fully off me. My t-shirt too. Grimaced the way I'd seen Tony Soprano do it. And screamed for all I was worth.

GONE! I WANT IT ALL GONE!

Then I raised the scissors and attacked my hair.

Snip, snip, snip, I went, and watched it tumble to the floor. Snip, snip, snip. Cut, cut, cut. Bye, bye. *Slán leat*. And as they say in France, *au revoir*. Hair today, gone tomorrow. That's the way things were these days.

Kept going until the scissors couldn't get a hold of any more. Then I grabbed the blade. Nick, nick, nick. Cut, cut, cut. Took a good look in the mirror. The blotchy head on me. The flecks of blood. And an expression that said one and only thing: *Another satisfied customer*.

My shaved head looked good. Went well with my Tony Soprano snarl. My dagger look. Something was still missing, though. Something to disguise me further, make me look even meaner. A mark. A mark on my face. Yes! A scar. Now where was I going to get one of those? I could always ask Brains and No-brains McManus. But they'd already given me their best shots.

The mirror was talking to me again.

Do it yourself, you numpty. You've had loads of practice.

Why yes! That's a great idea. Thank you, mirror. Thank you so much.

You're welcome, Jason. And let me say: it's been a pleasure.

No, mirror. The pleasure is all *mine*.

Now then. What kind of a scar would I like? And, more importantly, how will I make it?

Took a look at my collection. Laid them out, one by one, in front of me.

Steak knife. Razor blade. Shard of glass. Rusty nail.

What to use? What to use?

Decisions. Decisions.

Took a hold of each of them and looked them over carefully. Raised them separately to my face and made a practice run.

I really couldn't choose. Set them down in front of me again and ran my eager eyes over them. Gripped them separately again in my itching-to-go hands.

My, my.

They all looked good to enough to eat.

Closed my eyes and hovered my hand over my choices.

Touched the shard of glass.

Good choice, Jason. Good choice, indeed.

OK. Close your eyes now. Here goes. It won't hurt a bit. That's it. Get it in there. Push. Press. Drag it down. Like I said. It doesn't hurt a bit. Hell, I might as well do it properly. Go the length of my face, all the way down my cherub cheek, like that lad, what's his name? That's right. Pull it down, all the way. And listen. Can you hear her, Jason? Listen to what she's saying. *Keep going. Don't stop. We're almost there.*

There. Done. You can look now. Wow! That's one long scar you have the makings of there, Jason. Why, thank you, Jason. I'm so glad you approve.

Took a good look at myself, dabbed away the blood with a facecloth, traced my finger along the mark I'd just made.

Not bad. Not bad at all.

Wiped away the rest of the blood. Took another look.

Yep. Should be good enough to make them think twice before giving me any lip. And if it wasn't, well, I'd just have to give myself another one.

What was it Lily the Nose had said to me? You look like your mother, Jason. Ha! Ha! Not any more, did I. Not any more.

I just hoped the girl would recognize me when we met up to say goodbye.

PARIS IS A BLONDE AND DOGS
ARE CITIZENS

*Well, Ma, hold on to your Champs-Elysées. I'm on my
way. And before you start reaching for a fork or hurley stick
or the nearest guillotine, don't worry. I haven't said a thing
to anyone about where you are. Of course, with you being
out of sight for so long, it's been kind of tricky. Suppose I
never realized until you were gone how much in demand
you really are.*

*So, tell me, Ma, how is Paris? And exactly how long has
it been? Two weeks? Three? I've lost count. And to think I
thought it was all talk. The bull-nut seller must be made of
moolah. Only it's not the bull-nut seller you're with over
there, is it, Ma? That's right. I've worked out who it is and
here I am to let you know I have a surprise for you. And I
think you will like it. Are you ready? I'm on my way to join
you and Da in Paris. And yes, before you say to yourself,
what are you talking about, you crazy boy? I will say it
again. I'm on my way. I'm coming to join you and Da in
Paris. I was thinking we could rendezvous at the café on the
left bank. That's the place to hang out, isn't it? I was looking
up a few things about Paris and that's one of the tips I was
given. Here's another one: Don't answer any questions.*

Instead, shrug shoulders and raise eyebrows. That's a pretty good tip too, I think.

The girl has been staying here. Just for a few days until things calm down with her da. I asked her did she want to come to Paris with me, but she has her own travel plans. I'll probably catch a train up to the big city. Then hop on the ferry and catch another train to Paris. If you like, you can meet me at the ferry port. Cherbourg, it's called. But I understand if you can't. Now let me see if I have any more news from this end.

No I haven't.

If the café on the left bank doesn't suit, get word to me about where we should rendezvous. That's the word over there, isn't it? I've been learning a few. As soon as you can let me know where, send a postcard. It would be nice to see something coming through the letterbox that isn't a pay-up-now-or-else-it's-a-dirty-dungeon-for-the-rest-of-your-life. I wonder do these people realize how ridiculous they sound. I should get you to send over a guillotine. Then off with their heads.

Oh, and I should warn you: at a first glance, you may not recognize me. I've had to change a couple of things about my appearance. Can't have anybody recognizing me now, can I? Wait till you see me. I'm sure you'll be impressed. OK. Here comes Barrabas. I can hear his happy whistling. I might open the door to him holding your hurley. But at this stage I don't think it will make any difference. He just does not know how to give up. Here's another tip for you: Paris is a blonde and dogs are citizens. Bet you didn't know that. So don't let them rag you about your bleached hair, ok?

A Bientôt.

J

LIFESAVER

Packed what I would need. Sunglasses. French phrases ripped out of the cooking book. Map of Paris ripped out of the atlas. Some trifle and sponge cake left over from all that baking. The last of the pills. Even threw in that note I scrawled out for Ma – in case those tips came in handy. Pulled the sitting-room curtains closed. Took a peek out the kitchen window. The coast was clear.

My plan was right up there with the best of them: simple. Head for the station. Catch the train to the big city. Hop a ferry and make my way to Paris. Nothing could be easier. The only thing bugging me was that I hadn't thought of it a week ago. Not to worry. Better late than never.

Well men, I said to Harry and Fergal. The time has finally come. I'm on my way. Out of here. Once and for all.

Good man, Jason, they said. Don't look back.

No fear of that, I said, and kept going.

Good luck, I said to Patrick Cox and his mongrel dogs. I'll send word when I meet someone better than myself.

I'll be seeing you, I said to Lily the Nose, and a warm feeling travelled through me when it occurred to me that nothing could be further from the truth.

I waved at Old Tom Redihan and the Bangladesh man, and the council men making their way into the Swamp. I waved at one or two early drunks. So long, suckers. Have a nice life.

Now all I had to do was say goodbye to the girl.

I skipped over the ditch, brushed through the trees and made my way to the Swamp. She wasn't on the rock near the hidden pools. I stood at the cracked edges, going up and down on my toes, staring at the surface water, at the busy midges. The council men were wading through the scum. I tracked their movement for a minute or two, but they weren't really going anywhere, and when I looked out into the Swamp again, I saw her in the water.

This time she wasn't kicking or spluttering. She was floating towards the centre, letting herself disappear below the surface without so much as a whimper. No, NO, NO! I yelled. Then I was rushing into the scummy water and beating my way towards her. And I could hear the council men screaming at me to get back, and then some others were shouting out, what's he at, and who is it, and it's OK, I wanted to tell them, I know who it is, I can get to her, even though she was already sinking, all I had to do was reach her. Reach her and pull her out of there, just like I'd done that time before. And instead of goodbye, we could leg it together. But that dizziness had come over me again, my arms were so heavy it felt as though I was moving through treacle instead of water. And all I was thinking about was the two of us catching the train up to the big city and then the night-crossing on the ferry and then another train to Paris and I didn't want us to miss any of that. And suddenly I could no longer see her. Where are you? I yelled, trying to keep my mouth clear of the scumwater. Hey, come on! Don't leave me now. We've got places to see. Paris. Egypt in the time of the pharaohs. Ancient Greece, for crying out loud. And I was thrashing about in the water for a glimpse of her. Come on! You're going to be someone. You're going to be a celebrity. And I'm going to play my cards right and be your minder. Remember? This is no time to be disappearing inside a dirty old swamp. Hey, I know! We can leave some graffiti on the Russian Steppes. I've thought of some great lines, you'll be really impressed. But it was no good. It was murky and bottomless and I couldn't make out a thing. I gurgled some swamp water, more waves of dizziness arrived, and the last thing I remember was moving clouds blinking the sun on and off, and that image of her disappearing below the surface water. Then a man's voice saying, Relax, lad, we've got you.

THINGS COULD BE EVEN WORSE

I could be a Nobody, like Harry Brewster or Fergal Flood, every day walking up and down the back lane. I could be Patrick Cox or one of his mongrel dogs, waiting for the next kebab. I could be a forgotten drunk, forever lying at the bottom of the Swamp. I could be Annie the scryer, all the time staring at the ditchwater.

I could be stuck in an office like Barry the bank clerk, pushing paper from one tray to another. I could be a council man digging up a stubborn road, clearing out a bottomless swamp, trying to knock down a wall and build it back up again better than before. I could be a prisoner on death row, waiting for some smiling wise-guy to come and tell me my time is up. I could be a space-waster, a dead-leg, a worse than useless thing. I could be nothing.

I could be Old Tom Redihan, every day forgetting the way home. I could be Mellows the signal man, every day walking up and down the same set of tracks. I could be a sailor, singing a song about a chug-chug boat. I could be Ma – Jesus, do not go there.

I could be the Slug Doyle, forever looking for the witch that stole his heart. I could be on board the plane that fell out of the sky, the ship that got lost in the fog. I could be a rat living among ditchwater trees. I could be a mug, a sucker, a louse, or a sap. I could be a broken cup, a flat tyre, a noisy wiper clinging to a no-go car. I could be the clinking in the darkness that scares the wind out of me.

I could be the rubbish man, forever trying to tidy up the dirty lane. I could be a mild-mannered jeweller, about to be held up by no-mercy gangsters. I could be a cobbler with no shoes to mend, a bicycle repair man without a ticking spoke to straighten. I could be a hungry man with no home to go to. An old lady being told she has two minutes to get out of hers.

I could be the owl that goes *who-who-whooo*. I could be the tommy gun, *rat-tat-tat tat-tat*. I could be a ladybird that has to crawl all over the place, a buzzing bee soaking up the sunlight. I could be a crow gnashing down a juicy worm. I could be a worm.

BURY ME ON TOP OF MARILYN MONROE

A little bit of time has now passed. A day. A week. A month. I don't know. Doc Mullaney is keeping an eye on me. In and out of my line of vision he appears. With his bag of tricks and healthy head. His medicine voice going on and on about the lucky escape I've had, and the fast way they were able to empty my stomach, whatever it was they were so keen to get out of me. And lots of talk about resting up and proper food and keeping me out of school for a while. Suits me.

And Ma was back.

There she is, hovering over me. The pale face on her, the worried mouth. From time to time, her hand brushing through her hair and then covering her mouth. Turning away from me as though she was in the presence of an alien or one of those dreaded Gorgons. As though one look from me would turn her to stone, head to toe. And what's that she has in her other hand? A page from a copybook. With writing. Writing that looks a lot like mine.

And what's that I can hear? Another voice. A voice I recognize. An uppity-sounding voice. Where is it coming from? Has someone robbed my mind? Am I now in the land of crazy dreams? And who owns these arms I can see attached to me, whose is the voice I can hear? What's going on? And it's her, I was saying, it's her it's her it's her it's her. And look! The salty sea and the blue sky and the long oars pulling us through the immense waters. And look! Land ahoy! Yes, indeed. An island. An island of leafy trees and sunlit paths. And row, row, row the boat. We're almost there. After all this time we've almost reached our destination. And the waves gently lapping and the water so clear and fish darting here and there among the oars. And the saltwater spraying high and stinging my face and arms. And I was kicking and shaking, and where is the girl? Where is she where is she where is she? We have a voyage to make together, an adventure to complete.

And all the time Ma's voice was coming at me, desperate and anxious.

What are you talking about?

What girl?

There is no girl.

Do you hear me, you crazy boy?

There is no girl.

How was Paris? I mumbled when I briefly opened my eyes and saw that she was looking at me, the horrified expression on her face going from me to whoever else was in the room.

And there was more talking. More whispering.

His arms, his arms.

And his face. His beautiful face.

Why would he do such a thing?

Who is the girl he keeps asking for?

The whispering faded out and I was sleeping blissful again, sleeping the sleep of the dead, and it was peaceful and the feeling not so unpleasant and I could have stayed that way, but knew I wouldn't.

Da.

Is that you? Is that your voice I hear? It's me. Jason. Your son. Tell me something, Da. Anything. First thing that comes into your head. What's the weather like where you are? I hope it's not too hot for you. Is the sea blue? And your boat making waves? Come on, Da. Talk to me. Talk to me, for fuck's sake.

Ma.

I could hear her again. Spinning one of her stories. She hadn't been to Paris at all. She'd taken the sports car from Gavin McGoldrick's garage and driven it like a bat out of hell until the thing had run out of petrol. But the petrol had lasted for ages and Ma was a long way out of town. Wherever she had ended up, there was no garage in the middle of nowhere giving out free petrol, nobody to listen to her poor-me story, and she had eventually made her way to the big city and rested up there for a few days.

Come on, Ma.

There was more to it than that.

There had to be.

Tell me, Ma. I'm all ears.

And, yes, there was more to it. Tell me about the big city and deciding to hole up there for a few days. Why not? It's not every day you get to travel so far. Tell me about the prince charming only too happy to come to your assistance when you told him how you'd travelled all this way to find a doctor for your one son, your only child, and instead had been stopped at gunpoint by a couple of thugs wearing ski masks. How they had taken your purse, your bag, your change of clothes, the keys to the apartment you were booked into for the weekend.

Your phone was gone, all your contact numbers, you were in shock to tell the truth, and you had been given the loan of a car and they had taken that too.

And tell me about how surprise, surprise, things had worked out pretty well for you, so well that you had decided to spend a few extra nights in the big city.

And you had tried to call me and leave a message, but of course they'd already pulled the plug on our phone. I understand, Ma. I really do.

I was waiting for this story out of her, and thinking about the laugh I'd get out of the girl when I told her about Ma's big city adventure. Except Ma wasn't telling it like that. She was talking instead about Mario and his call to let her know that the Paris trip, along with everything else they had going together, was off, off, off.

My head.

It felt heavy. As if a train was thundering through it. Or one of those articulated lorries Ma liked to wave out at. And my eyes. I tried to open them. But the lids were so heavy. I tried again. Could see bare walls. A door. Someone standing there. Then I felt I was underwater, in thick, sluggish, dirty water. I was sinking. Had to get out of there. Swim for the grassy banks. But my arms. I could hardly move my arms. They were heavy too. So heavy. And what was that? A chair. Right beside me. Wait. I was lying down. Lying down in a bed. And now my stomach. Oh boy. It was lurching like a high sea and now I was throwing up. A liquid-gold sap came out of me. It didn't want to stop. Wait a minute. It wasn't gold. It was yellow. Blue and yellow.

Fock me!

Then I remembered all the pills I'd taken, and the lurching didn't want to go away. And I opened my eyes a little more, and saw Ma on the chair, and cop Lawless standing, and beside him Doc Mullaney, the lot of them hovering over me, and one more time I was asking them where is the girl where is the girl where is the girl where is the girl. And then everything was a purple haze.

*

A little more time has passed. Ma is just about getting used to my new image. When she thinks I'm sleeping, she comes in my room and sits on the bed. She doesn't say anything but I know she's there, can sense her presence. Sometimes, I can feel her touch the side of my face.

And I can still see her wince when she catches sight of me. When I appear in the kitchen at breakfast time. Or when I step into the Hungry Worm.

She's showing up for work these days. Putting in long

hours. Getting big tips. She keeps telling me we're going somewhere together, as soon as she's enough saved. For my birthday, she says. My twelfth birthday. And she seems to have patched up her differences with Mattie again – we'll see how long that lasts. Changing his car seems to have helped. Tell me something, Ma, I asked her the other day, when we were all one big happy café family, what was it with Mattie's car? What did Mattie's car have that all the others didn't? She finished the Mars bar she had been chewing, looked me, and said, It was yellow.

*

Early in the morning and I'm buried among the long reedy grasses. I stayed there all day, until the sun started to go down. Then it cooled and the fading sun turned everything into gold. The cathedral spire, the freight boxes at the railway station, the tracks, the back lane, the trees and reedy grasses. Even the Swamp, rising higher all the time, looked like a bath of liquid gold. The council men had stopped by for their daily look. They stood near the KEEP OUT sign, straightened up the thing, shook their lazy heads.

At some point could feel something in my pocket pressing against my thigh. Put my hand in to check what it was. It was the finger ring. The skull and crossbones finger ring I'd bought for her. Damn! I'd forgotten all about it. I fetched it out of my pocket, along with the piece of string. Looped the string through the ring. Tied it around my neck. Sat there for a little bit, letting the ring bump gently against my chest in the light-blowing breeze.

Anyone using this seat? a familiar voice sounded. Without waiting for a reply, the Slug sat down into the reedy grass beside me.

Guess what Stan Laurel said to his friends before he died? *If any of you cry at my funeral I'll never speak to you again.* Tell your first girlfriend that. She'll get a kick out of it.

Yeah, it's funny.

You bet your life it's funny. Nearly as funny as Groucho. Who's Groucho?

Groucho Marx was the funniest man in the world, the Slug said, looking off into the distance. You know, when Groucho died, a letter was found in his coat pocket requesting that he be buried on top of Marilyn Monroe. Don't tell your first girlfriend that. If you do, don't mention my name.

Marilyn Monroe. I've heard of her, Slug.

You'll hear more some day. Put her on your list of things to look forward to. Put her at the top of the list.

He started to say something else to me then, but his voice faltered. Instead, he pressed my shoulder and went on his way. I stayed sitting where I was.

The drunks had gathered at the low end of the lane. They'd set down their supply and were standing around it. Pulling open their cans, sharing their bottle of hard stuff around, warming their dirty fingers on their little fire. From time to time, they cackled at each other. Soon the stories began. And the singing.

Songs about women waking up in the morning and realizing they've had enough. Songs about men who were trying their best but could give no more. Hearts were broken, there were rivers called Misery and hotels called Heartbreak, and songs wishing the singers to lonely places like New Orleans and the black and blue hills of Dakota. God is away on business, everything is going to hell, there is nothing back in Jersey except a broken down jalopy and they all need to borrow a couple of dollars from a lad called Frank to go waltzing with a dame called Matilda.

The same worn-out voices, the broken tunes. They slurred their words and belched through the notes. Verses were left out and lines got mixed up. More than one of them didn't keep up. The daily punch-up started before they reached the end.

One glance at the drunks was enough for Lily the Nose, at long last completing the end of her daily nose-about.

Life has finished with that lot, she said. They know it too, know that there's no point waiting.

Waiting for what? I asked her.

For things that will never come. And do you know where that puts them? One step ahead of the rest of us.

C'mere, tough guy, one of them growled at me when I was on the move. Come back here and let us buy you a drink or two.

Come back here, tough guy, we've got a spot here for you, I heard another one shout after me as I made my way up the lane. I half-paused at the words, but kept going.

Further up the lane I could still hear them. Singing their

clapped-out hearts out. Heckling each other and anything else that got their attention. Howling at the distant moon.

Near the back fence of our house I saw Old Tom Redihan gently turn Annie round and point her towards her own house.

We're sinking, she rasped.

I know, dear, he replied. I know.

LETTER TO DA

Well Da,

whoever you are, and wherever you are, and whatever you're up to, I have two words of advice for you: stay there and keep doing it. That's five words, but who's counting? I'm not. Ma has been saying that whoever you are, the bottom of the Swamp isn't good enough for you, but now I know she doesn't fully mean it. Like me, she hasn't a clue who you are or what you are up to or where you're doing it. So, I suppose putting you at the bottom of a pond of scummy water is her way of saying stop asking questions I don't have answers to. And so I'm going to leave it at that – for now, anyway. I just hope that for your sake you are not a wealthy man. Otherwise we may be hot on your heels next time the whistling postman appears with his letters. And who knows? Maybe a valuable clue will show up when I least expect it. I might put this note in a bottle and sail it down the dirty drain of a river, let it travel where it wants to. And if it finds you on that yacht you're living on, stick your own note in the bottle and sail it right back.

Until then, partner, keep your eye on the Bigger Picture and watch out for the leaping fish.

Your son

Jason

THE MOON IN MY POCKET

I was coming down the lane, had already passed Harry and Fergal on their way down town to fix the country in McMorrow's, had passed Patrick Fox and Rommel and Himmler, had marched quickly by Lily the Nose before she had a chance to start.

I was thinking about the girl, picturing the freckles either side of her nose, reaching out with my hand to touch the bruise on her neck, when I saw them. Stepping my way. No-brains flexing his arms and cracking his finger joints and looking very happy to see me.

Well, well, he said as he blocked my path.

When you least expect it, said the brother.

We hear you've been making a name for yourself.

What name would that be? I said, and waited to be tumbled to the ground.

For a moment, they just stood there. No-brains with the fists clenched, the little toy pistols and knives dangling out of his *I am a killer* hat. Brains beside him, the sneer all over his face, the kick-hard boots ready for action.

Come on then, I said. Get it over with.

And still they didn't stir. They just stood there, glaring at me. Watching me closely. Their idea of allowing a condemned man his last wish.

Lads, I haven't got all day. Enough of this shilly-shallying about. Come on. Get stuck in. I pointed to my head, mimicked taking a box at myself, but there was still no reaction.

This isn't good enough, lads, I said. Look, I'll make it easy for you. I planted my feet, spread my arms, and with a nod of my head invited them on to me. Still nothing.

Watch this, I said, and tore the hoodie off myself. Look at me, I said. I'm all yours. Now! Do your worst. Still nothing. They just stood there. They even looked at each other and started shaking their heads. This was a let-down like no other. Then, and without saying another word, they turned round and started to walk away.

I watched them. They'll be back, I said to myself. They're going to turn round, walk back and shove me headfirst into the ditchwater. They're going to produce a knife and go to work on me like never before. They're going to open my head once and for all. But they didn't do any of that. They kept walking down the lane away from me. No-brains didn't even turn round like he usually did with one of his next-time-I'm-going-to-slit-your-throat gestures. And I kept watching them, stayed rooted to the ground until after they had faded into little versions of themselves and then vanished altogether.

I ran my hand over my head. The hair was starting to grow back. I held out my arms in front of me and looked at the network of marks. The forming scabs. Then I ran a finger down the side of my face. Not a lot I could do about that. Still. It was a good reminder. A good place to stop.

I reached down for my hoodie, flapped dirt off it, slipped it back on and started down the lane.

*

I looked to the Swamp, to the rock near the hidden pools. She wasn't there. I took a walk as far as Mel Campbell's shop. She wasn't on the wall either. I walked the down -town streets and couldn't find her. She wasn't in the Hungry Worm or Dante's chipper. Anybody I asked looked at me as though I was talking about a ghost. What girl? they said. The girl from the Swamp, I said. The girl with the bruise on her neck and the freckles either side of her nose. What's her name? Shirley asked me when I went into McMorrow's, and all I could do was raise my arms and shrug.

Fock me! I didn't even know her name.

I dragged myself up Rich Hill, as far as Fat Grehan's place. Stood looking at the unfinished wall. The graffiti was gone. Washed away. Made my way as far as Mario's place. His buzzer gate was open and I looked to the bottom of his wall, to that hard-to-spot place where the girl had told me to scratch my signature alongside her own. I could see that mine was still there. But what had happened to hers?

I went back to Fat Grehan's driveway. By now I was tired, and plonked myself on the glittery rocks and stared down at the town below.

And I was gazing down at the cathedral, and at the school I wouldn't have to rush to, at the Tower and that still-standing bridge. What girl? Ma had asked me when I was laid up, recovering from all those pills. Who are you talking about? she'd said, the pleading tone in her voice as she gripped me and held me close. And then I was remembering all that time with the girl and all our conversations and all the places we'd talked about and, Jesus, what was I supposed to do if they didn't know who I was talking about? What did they think?

That I was making the whole thing up?

Think big. See further down the road. Dream only in bright colours. That's what it's all about. Larger life. The Bigger Picture.

And I knew that some day I would get out of this town. That I would get to all the places she had mentioned during our time together. I would go to Egypt in the time of the pharaohs and Ancient Greece and the Colosseum in Rome, and hell, I could even tramp through the Russian Steppes. And after all of that I would get hold of a boat and sail around those Mediterranean islands she'd always been talking about, could stop off at that place she'd been on the lookout for.

Ithaca.

And suddenly I was stepping out of myself and walking down the hill and the faster I walked the clearer my thoughts became. And I was skipping through the streets, and there was a beat in my heart. And I was already way ahead of myself, putting myself on the train, kicking back in my seat, chatting with the other passengers, making friends with the conductor. I could see my destination, the new faces, the proper streets I would soon be walking. Hanging out in bright bars, eating a decent meal in restaurants, sandwiches of my own choosing. I was taking in the sights of my new stomping ground, crossing bridges, making conversation with the clear waters below. I was admiring buildings, asking questions about the architecture. I was eyeing up the new pad I would live in, a high-up place with big-view windows, views of everything that was going on. I might have a little balcony and I could sit out in the warm evenings. I would have the world to look at.

I might even look for a job. Be good to have some cash in my pocket, be good to have some money to spend, no doubt I'd be needing it where I was headed. I'd buy a bicycle or two, start saving for a car. Wait. I could get one of those little motorbikes and race through the narrow streets.

And there I was, revving up for a spin, making room for my passenger. Let's go, I yelled, without fully stopping, and she jumped on behind me and clasped her arms around my waist so she wouldn't fall off. Where are we off to this time? I could hear her ask in her uppity voice, her breath in my ear as we sped away, weaving our way through the streets, looking for the fast way out of there, looking for the open road. I could feel the breeze streaming through us, see people in the street waving at us. We waved back, blew kisses off the palms of our hands and we were on the open road and the sun had disappeared and, look, I called out, pointing to the dark sky ahead of us. Look! And the moon had appeared and look, Ma, look what's in my pocket and I revved for all I was worth and we were hurtling for that shining light as though our lives depended on it . . .

ACKNOWLEDGEMENTS

Aoife Casby, Paul Lynch, Charlotte Greig, Donal Ryan, Kevin Barry, Belinda McKeon. Thanks for taking the time to read and your generous engagement.

All at Mulcahy Associates, especially Ivan Mulcahy for your faith, energy, and all-round good advice.

Paul Baggaley, Ansa Khan Khattak, and everyone at Picador. For your enthusiasm and inspired involvement.

My early publishers, Tony O'Dwyer and Gerardine Burke at Wordsonthestreet; Alan Hayes at Arlen House. Thanks for putting me on the road.

My keepers past and present, Gerry Hanberry, James Martyn Joyce, Geraldine Mills, Hedy Gibbons Lynott, Siobhan Shine, Hugo Kelly, Fionnuala Hanlon.

A very early teacher, Patrick McCabe, for kindling a flame.

James Ryan, Pat McMahon, Michael Gorman, James Harrold, Vinny Browne, Des Kenny, Mike McCormack, Adrian Frazier, Conor Montague, Lisa Frank, John Walsh, Tom 'Villanelle' Lavelle, Fergus Kennedy, Lisa Taylor, Chris Bremble, Cvetka Bevc, Edward Madrid Gómez, Sinéad Gleeson, Dave Lordan. Writing friends everywhere from Banff to Ballinasloe. Thank you all for friendship, support and encouragement.

The Arts Council of Ireland. The Banff Centre for Arts and Creativity. The artists' community in Yaddo. La Fundación Valparaíso in Spain. The Heinrich Böll Cottage on Achill Island. The Tyrone Guthrie Centre at Annaghmakerrig. For their part in my writing adventure.

My sisters, Ruth, Louise and Aisling, for all the 'starter-for-ten' moments. Martha Joyce, for the pharmacy clarifications.

And that literary charm, Eleanor Hooker, for inviting me to Dromineer in October, 2013.